The AXE & GRINDSTONE

PAUL PHIPPS-WILLIAMS

Cover art by dave@hmdesigners.com
Cover design by BAD PRESS iNK

ISBN: 978-1-9160845-0-6

published by www.badpress.ink

To Champ and Big G
From Fortnights, to today, to tomorrow.

Alternate

They're coming!'

The little boy runs down the cobbled lanes of the small town at the edge of the harbour. He keeps brushing his wet blond hair from his eyes but it's far too long and keeps getting in the way.

He's never run this fast before.

He never used to have to, in the olden days.

When he was four, or five.

He keeps shouting as he runs past the general store. People open their doors and slam them shut as they hear his cries. The unwelcome sound of locks and bolts follow the boy, and they echo across the near-silent streets.

'They're coming! Tell everyone!' He has to stop, just for a second, or he'll fall. He did that once last week. He grazed his knee. It hurt.

He stops to catch his breath and hugs the post which lights the small street. Not far now. It's slightly downhill – that'll make it easier.

There's a crash behind him and he spins round, transfixed by the sight. He's got to keep moving, but he just stands there staring at the impossible. Another crash shocks him to his senses and he starts to run again, faster than before, towards the end of the street. He shouts and shouts again as he gets closer. Someone, somewhere, starts screaming – but only for a second, as if they suddenly realised it was the worst thing they could do. The boy turns back again to check what happened. It's an unnatural thing, hearing a scream stop suddenly dead. As he does so he trips, his knees hit the cobbles first and tears well up in his eyes.

Big boy, James. You're a big boy. Nana'd say. Be a big boy. Pick yourself up now. Don't cry. Don't scream. You know he'll get you if you scream. It'll all be fine.

1

His knees are stinging; but he's a big boy so gets up again. He doesn't cry and doesn't scream. There isn't the time. He stumbles round the corner of the lane and there it is.

The little pub at the end of the lane sits, squat and narrow, waiting for him. A dim yellow glow peers out of the windows and lands on the wet cobbles outside. The light reminds him of home, and smoke rises from the small chimney atop the slanted terracotta roof. So close.

The boy runs for five, maybe ten more seconds, until he finally reaches the door, turns the iron handle and bursts in.

'They're coming! They're nearly here! I was told to warn...'

He falls onto the floor in the middle of the startled company inside and shuts up. The boy looks around. In his short but eventful life he'd never seen anything of the sort. He'd read the story books, of course – well, those with the short words – but the scene before him was just like the pictures.

Everyone is... different, and strange; magical but terrifying at the same time.

All chatter stops, and the monsters – for James thinks they are monsters – turn to look at him as one. The man behind the bar, who was cleaning a glass, puts it down.

'What did you say, young man?'

James struggles to catch his breath as he kneels on his grazed knees, afraid to speak in front of everyone. He points at the door and whispers, 'They're coming.'

The man puts his towel down on the bar. He looks at his friend to his left, a strange man with strange orange skin, and nods sadly.

'OK, everybody. You heard the lad. That's Time. Everybody out, please.'

There's a beat, while the Landlord's words sink in. Then, as if a power switch has been suddenly turned after a dark night, there's movement. Everywhere. All at once. Everyone around the boy slams their glasses back and down onto the tables. As they hurry out of the door, they turn and nod at the Landlord who acknowledges each one in turn as they leave. He says something to a monster made of rock still sitting calmly at the bar; the tallest thing James has ever seen. The monster shakes his head and jabs a fat stone-like finger into the bar. The Landlord points at the boy, and the monster's shoulders slump. He turns and walks over to James, picking him up under his arm in one smooth action and taking no notice of the boy's frightened kicking. As with the others, when the rock reaches the door he turns to the Landlord.

'You take care,' the rock-man says.

The Landlord nods, as he nodded to the others. As he's carried out, back down the little cobbled lane, James stops struggling, takes one more look behind him, and sees the Landlord looking out after them. But all too soon they leave him behind.

Without knowing why, James starts to cry.

The Landlord watches the last of his customers flee down the little lane, turns his head the other way and sees what James told him was coming. He slowly closes the door and walks back inside to face his two remaining friends. He reaches under the bar and takes out a small leather jacket, which he passes to his barman. He says one word.

'Go.'

The hairs on the orange skinned barman's arms rise up in defence.

'No, yer not facin' them lot on yer own.' The Landlord throws the jacket at his friend, who catches it with one hand.

'Go,' the Landlord says again. 'We talked about this – what we'd do. Don't fight me. You need to see tomorrow, to show the new guy the ropes. Remember what it was like for me and be that man again. Teach him what he'll need to survive where I couldn't. Go.' The barman looks at him, torn, wondering whether to argue. Finally, he turns to the door.

'All right – but don't you think this is it. I'll look after the new lad or lass... whatever or whoever she finds. For you. But only as you asked so nicely and that. Guess I still owe you one.' He turns to the woman standing in the shadows in a doorway behind the bar, making it clear he means what he says. 'Whoever it is, they'd better be tough.' He nods to the Landlord, his nod is returned, and he too leaves.

The Landlord crosses to the woman in the shadows. From

outside comes a faint roaring noise, like a storm heard through the mouth of a tunnel. There isn't much time.

'We knew this was likely,' he says.

She edges forward, keeping to the dark. 'Not this soon. We're not prepared enough.'

'That's a shame,' he mutters, almost to himself. He walks over to the front door and places a large iron key in the lock. He turns it, bolting the door shut.

Safe.

'Go on,' he waves at the woman. 'You too. You know your role in the wider scheme of things. Keep the chain running. Find someone else to keep the link between the Oak and the Dogwood. It's not my job any more. You've got three weeks to find someone, or the Scratching can't be stopped.'

'A new man with a new licence to this place won't stop it. You know that. It'll buy us a week, at most.'

The Landlord shrugs. 'It's a week. Who knows what you can do in a week? The Council trusts your judgement. They know you'll pick someone strong. Now go on. Don't make me bar you like I used to.'

The woman steps back, and edges into the small, dark, corridor leading out to the cellar behind the bar. 'Until the next time,' she says.

'There'll be no next time, Natasha.'

And then he's alone.

He walks to a table, which seems grown from the walls of the building itself, and calmly sits down. But as the roaring outside grows in volume his breath starts to get shorter and shorter. His fingers start to tap on the wood, drumming and drumming to distract from the noise outside – until it suddenly stops and all is quiet once more.

'Come on, Nat,' he whispers to himself. 'Someone strong. Someone better than I was.'

The silence is haunting and oppressive.

And short lived.

The door crashes open, the Landlord jumps but stays seated,

fingers incessantly drumming, faster and faster. He thought he'd be calm; he'd practised being calm. But as he sees The Man With The Crab-Like Feet stride confidently and purposefully towards him, eyes like tar and fingers like needles, the calm flees as he knew it would.

And as The Man With The Crab-Like Feet starts to grip his chest he screams, and at once hates and curses himself for screaming.

For Screaming starts the Scratching.
And Scratching starts the Night.
For Scratching starts the Scratching,
Starts the Binding Brothers' Light.

The Axe & Grindstone

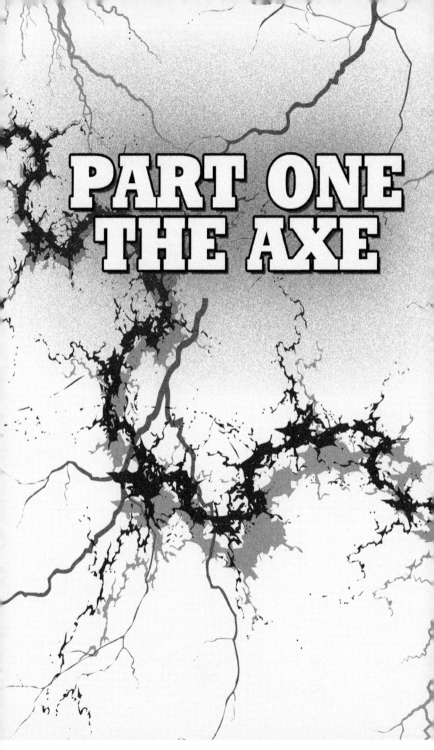

PART ONE
THE AXE

Chapter One
The Barman of Porter Street

He's going to make them scream again, I know he is.

He likes doing it – he says it's his thing, and who am I to argue? There are some battles I know I'll never win.

I can see him pumping his hands in the air, and he looks over to me and smiles. I wonder if I can get out in time.

'Let me hear you scream!' he roars through the microphone.

And the entire bar goes wild.

Dammit.

Welcome to Fortnights, Staunton. We're a classy sort of place that'll serve you fish and chips in the evening, watch you throw it up again later, and secretly chuckle at you when you eventually slip over. At the moment, it's a throbbing, jumping, sweaty collection of people all bouncing up and down to the inevitable same tune they screamed to last week.

This is my world. These are my locals, and I love most of them to bits.

I make it to the bar just as the DJ makes the crowd scream again and look proudly at my three staff running themselves silly. I glance over towards the far end where a spotty lad in a black T-shirt and black jeans stands near an unmanned Till One forlornly waving a fiver in my general direction. I can see him mouth it now.

'When you're ready mate...'

If I don't make eye-contact, he'll figure it out eventually.

I cross over to Till Two where Jon hands me back my keys. Jon's one of these blond-haired teenagers who's too thin but too muscled for his own good. He's studying sports science at the local university and, as such, is one of our most popular barmen. I could look like him if I wanted to. I just choose to eat more crisps and drink more heavily, that's all.

The Axe & Grindstone

Becky hurtles past behind us, almost throwing a large gin and tonic into the hands of a woman with more tattoos than sense. She points at the man in his forties who she's now taken pity on, and decided to serve.

'YES!' she bellows. He's taken aback, and pauses a second too long. That's it – he's lost it...

'YES!' she bellows to the student the other side of her till, who just points to three pumps on the bar like a pro, and she begins to pour. The forty-something looks down at his sensible shoes, sighs, looks at the clock and shuffles away.

'We're busy tonight!' shouts Jon, as he serves a lad who's blatantly under-age. He's on a stag do and not his fault he was born three months too late to be served anywhere else.

'Pay day isn't it?' I key my code into Jon's till. 'Last one before Christmas – half of this lot have been drinking since lunchtime! How's the new girl doing?' I look over to a young lass who's staring at the screen of Till Three, as she has done for the last two minutes.

'Better than she was! Leave her to me, Mark,' he says, with that look in his eye. 'Baptism of fire, tonight!'

'Knew I could count on you, mate. Just don't scare her too much!'

'I'll leave that to Becky!'

'Yes mate!' I shout at the lad in front of me, itching to go again.

'Five Overproof Rum and an Aftershock!'

I spin round, and with one hand quickly spread five shot glasses in a row. I spin again – the bottle's in my hand – one, two, three, four, five. Lid on bottle, slam down. To the back of the bar and the test tubes of red liquor. I grab one, invert up then down and pass to the lad in the mottled pink T-shirt. 'Gym-Bob' – definitely with the stag do. I reach for my key fob, scan two barcodes, then show Gym-Bob the total. He hands me the cash, I punch in the amount and slam the drawer shut.

'Who's next?' I bellow at the crowd, having totally made my mind up a moment ago. New Girl is still staring at her screen. 'Top Button, third from the left!' I shout at her. She presses it, then smiles and goes looking for tonic. I point at a girl who shouldn't be dressed like that. 'Yes!'

'Vodka Red Bull!' she slurs at me.

'Double up?'

'Double up!' She gives me the thumbs up, and she gets two shots for only a pound more. Best value in Staunton, is Fortnights.

People to the left and right wave money in my face to get my attention.

And that's when the first pint glass is thrown across the bar.

Gym-Bob's shoulder misses mine by about an inch as the doorman – Steve – wrestles him to the ground. The other side of the bar, Jon's taking New Girl into the back room as two blokes slam themselves into the fruit machine by the stairs. The taller of the two, a thick set squaddie type, grabs the other guy, throws his forehead back and butts him between the eyes. The bloke smashes him into an old table and turns back towards his girlfriend.

'Fucking COME ON!' he screams to anyone nearby. People move out of his way and he turns to beckon the respect he thinks he's owed. With his back to the man on the floor, he doesn't see the bar stool come down, crashing on his head with a crack – and like that he's down himself. But the shouts go on, and to my left there's three – no four – other guys throwing punches. Jesus, it's a full-on riot!

Steve pulls Gym-Bob to his feet and nods at me.

Door code.

1066.

I run over to unlock as Steve pushes the guy through the doors and throws him out of the fire escape, nose first. I know the policy, if there's a fight, stay out of it.

If there's a fight, let the people you pay to stop it, well, stop it.

This is my bar, this is my home, and I pay people to protect it for me.

Another glass gets thrown, and suddenly my corner doesn't feel as nice as it did a moment ago. The bar – get back to the bar. I'm – Jesus, that was close!

I leg it the ten feet, and crouch over Becky.

'Get into the back room!' I shout.

'But I'm having fun! Look!' She blasts a trampy looking girl full in the face with a jet of soda. 'She's been pissing me off all night!'

'Becky!' I hiss. 'You'll make it worse!'

'Bollocks, will I!' She laughs as she does it again.

'Becky!' She looks at me crouched by her feet next to a broken cupboard, as another glass smashes nearby. With a sigh, she places the soda nozzle back in its holder.

'Fine.' She rolls her eyes, turns on her heels and walks – upright – to the door to the back room. I crouch down behind her, as the cold fluorescents turn on, and the police storm in *en masse*.

Outside, there's peace, but dear God, it's cold. Pity the people who have to actually go outside to get home. I could go and smoke this fag in the office, I guess, or up in the flat, but people keep telling me I need some sort of fresh air once in a while, so hey. Let's rough it.

I take a draw of the cigarette and the smoke mixes with the mist of my breath against the night. It's dark, and even through the lights of Porter Street I can look up and see the stars above. It's a clear night – there'll be a frost in the morning. I step out, and the familiar crunch of the gravel follows me into the tiny car park at the back of the pub.

'You alright, girl? Going to be a cold one.' My beautiful blue 1987 Austin Mini Metro is standing proudly, as she always has, just underneath the window of the office waiting for the day I'll actually drive her somewhere. Between you and me, it may be a long time coming. When a man has a flat above the shop, a Tesco Express round the corner and three pizza places that deliver, there's little else worth travelling for.

I pat the car goodnight and stub the fag out on the edge of the kerb. One last look at the stars before I go.

My breath floats up, and it's almost like I'm still smoking. It wafts and disperses into the night and – it's strange – but for a moment I think I see a few strands of a faint purple smoke, floating silently down the street.

Bit odd.

Black smoke I've seen, but purple? Must be nearly Christmas.

Whatever. It's gone. It's been a long night.

But still...

I pause, and I shiver. I'm sure that's the cold. It must be the cold.

Porter Street at kick-out time is full of laughter, shouts and cat-calls. We close at two, but Spicers a few doors down is open 'til three. The shouts and the screaming are normal for this time of night.

That girl I can hear down the road, screaming, is normal.

'Mark!' calls Jon from inside. 'We're just about done.'

It's a well-deserved pint, this, even if the head's a little large. That's not like me at all. Out of all the staff we've ever had, I normally pride myself on being able to pour the perfect pint. Not tonight, though.

Hmm.

'Hurry up, Mark. You've been ages!' Becky's standing over at the large sofa by the window with a pint of her own in her hand. Jon and New Girl are sitting together, supping their own drinks. 'We need your toast before we go.'

'Yeah,' I shout over. 'Yeah, sure.' I go and sit down on the sofa opposite and raise my glass. 'To the night.'

'To the night!' shout Jon and Becky, with New Girl following a split second after.

I toast them again and take a drink. The best drink of a night is the one you've earned at the end of it.

'I've been meaning to talk to you, Mark,' adds Becky, after a large slug. She looks down at the rest of her pint. I've never known her to break eye contact before. What's going on? 'I've been offered a job at Fortnights in Hollowhead, and I'm going to take it.' I put my glass down on the table.

'You're leaving?' I ask, stupidly. She takes another drink and looks up.

'Can't stay here all my life. Got to move up and at 'em at some point.'

'Why?' I ask. I can't understand. She can't do this. Not Becky...

'Because it's normal, Mark. How long have you been here now?'

'Eleven years.'

'You realise that's not right, don't you?'

'It's right for me.'

This is happening again. They all do it, in the end. All get offered something bigger, and better. Sometimes it seems my entire social circle is made up of people who have worked for me, and then move on just when I come to rely on them. Jon raises his glass.

'Good for you, Becks,' he says with a smile. 'Nice one. Step up?'

'Yeah, management trainee. I'll be Mark, one day.'

This is turning into a shocker of a night.

'But Mark with a bit of ambition...' Jon adds.

Hang on.

'Oi!' I point. 'Leave it out, mate! You're supposed to be on my side.' He laughs.

'I'm sorry, but she's right. Eleven years, and you're still stuck here.'

'I like it here.'

'I know!' he drinks again. 'You've got a cushty flat upstairs and everything in your lap. You never wanted your own place?'

'No,' I reply quickly. 'Too much hassle. I'm happy here. You can keep your career progression, thanks. Being a landlord is too much hassle. You have to be the boss. I don't think that's me.'

'Yeah, don't we know it?' Jon takes a swig of his pint, and smiles. 'Anyway – another toast. To Becky and her plans to take over the world.'

We all stand, clink glasses and I give her a hug. I don't know what I'll do without her, to be honest.

Dammit. Another one gone.

There's a noise from behind us, and I down my drink in one. I think I'll need another.

'You drinking my profits again?'

'I think that's a night,' I mutter. 'I'll see you all soon.' They nod as they see Richard, my boss. He stands by the door, all six foot three of him, with his scarf hanging limply from his shoulders and his arms crossed. He looks tired – well, I guess it is almost three in the morning.

'Goodnight folks,' he says. 'Sorry your first night was so eventful,' he says to New Girl. He opens the door for them as they say their good nights. One by one, as they pass along the front of the bar and disappear from sight, their expressions say it all.

There are no words. There's nothing to say, nothing to justify. Richard just looks at me as he locks the door and surveys the trashed scene before him.

And for the very first time since I started working here, all those years ago, I really, really want to be somewhere else.

Chapter Two
The Talk of the Town

Gross misconduct. It sounds weird when you think of it. I keep rolling the words around in my mouth. Gross misconduct. Underage drinking. It was me or the bar. I'm fairly sure I have to get out of this bed sometime.

I was going to be a Ghostbuster on New Year's Eve, you know. I'd bought some overalls from B&Q and everything. I was definitely going to win the fancy-dress compo in the bar. I guess that's not going to happen anymore.

Bollocks.

I'm still not sure quite what I'm going to do, even now, two weeks later. There's nothing here in Staunton and I don't know anywhere else. I've never really had this problem before. It's this sort of issue which made it easier just to stay in one job and let the other people worry about career progression. I told you anywhere but your comfort zone isn't a good place to be.

I'm fairly sure I can stay in this bed for a little while longer, after all.

The laptop's on the floor where I've left it and, as I pick it back up, it gives a tinny little tune and the face of my sister fills the screen. Do I want to accept her call?

Go on then. Beats talking to myself.

'Hello Clare,' I sigh, as she pops up. She's had a new haircut. Doesn't look all that bad, for once. 'New haircut?'

'Yes!' she beams. 'Do you like it?' She touches the bottom of her bob with her palm, as they do in the adverts.

'It's very you,' I reply with a smile on my face. 'Hang on a minute.' I try and extend the small Formica table with one hand, lifting the sides up and pushing them flat. I have this down to an artform. 'Hang on...'

'Dear God, Mark, your bedsit's a mess!'

I haven't got decent camera angles down to an art form, it seems.

'It's not a bedsit, it's a flat.'

'Mark, I can see your sink and I've been there, remember? Chloe nearly broke one of your toys.'

'They're not toys, they're limited editions.'

'Not to a three-year-old.'

'She should know better!'

There's a sigh. 'Any chance of Richard letting you back?' I strike up another cigarette and watch Clare's eyes roll.

'Not really,' I say, taking a deep breath. 'He says he has to prove to the council he's taken action to stop that sort of thing happening again.'

'You are a bit of an eejit, mate.'

'So I've been told.' I take another look around the flat, as Clare inspects her nails.

'Saw the Staunton Suicides on the news again last night,' she says.

'We're getting to be quite popular, all things considered.'

'The officer they interviewed on the news was pretty hot. I may move back there.'

'You're married!'

'Barely.'

'How's that going, anyway?' Clare starts to bite her nails. She does that when she's nervous and has done ever since she was a kid.

'I guess it's better than it was. Going away for Christmas should help. But I feel guilty about that now.' She changes nails. 'Are you going to be all right? I would have invited you over, you know that.'

'I'll be fine,' I reply. 'It'll be fun. Most of the gang will be going back to parents. I can compare their Christmas dinners on Facebook. That's what you do now.'

There's a distant sound of scrambling and shouting, as doors slam, and Clare's computer wobbles suddenly.

'Don't touch the...!' I hear my sister shout as the screen shifts and she makes a dive for it to the gorgeous sound of my nieces giggling in the background.

'Uncle Mark! Uncle Mark!' shouts Chloe, the eldest, as her face swims into view. It's only partly obscured today by her long, scruffy blonde hair. 'We're going on holiday!'

'I know!' I beam, 'Mummy told me. Are you looking forward to it?' She nods and is pushed out of the way by her younger sister, who climbs ungainly onto the chair.

'We're going holiday!' adds Ella. I laugh.

'So I hear! What are you going to do on holiday?' They both start talking at once.

'Paintings.'

'Beaches.'

'Sandycastles.'

'Ponies!'

'Seaside!'

'Yes, Seaside!'

I lean in to the screen and just take them in for a minute. They keep on yabbering on, trying to outdo each other with the things they're looking forward to. Ella keeps on saying ponies – she may be getting her hopes up there. And, as bad as things may seem, Clare's done her job as she knew she would. I love them all so much, they brighten up my day, every single time I see them. I may not be the barman of Porter Street any more, but I'll always be Uncle Mark. And as jobs go, I think it's the most important one in the world.

'They say it's a new suicide pact – like the one in Wales a few years back,' says Jon, as he offers me a beer. It's turned into a bit of a cloudy day and the fresh air's doing me good.

'I don't buy that. It's all too public,' I reply, as we chink bottles. The table outside The Seven Sisters rocks on the pavement. Wouldn't have happened in my pub. 'If you're going to commit suicide, you'd do it at home, surely. With a note and some Celine Dion or something.'

'Not if you want to make a point, Mark. If I ever topped myself, I'd want the world to know.'

'If you ever topped yourself, half the university would go into mourning.'

Jon points his bottle at me. 'That is true,' he says, 'you do have a point there.'

'Besides,' I say, taking a swig and putting it down slightly too hard on the table. 'Why drag it out so long? I've read enough to know how to do it properly. All these in the news – from what they're saying, some of them dragged it out for hours.'

'Has anyone told you you're a little screwed in the head, mate?'

I draw in the smoke. 'You're not going to put that in a reference, are you?'

He shakes his head. 'No one's asked me for one yet, but I'll consider it when they do. Still no luck on the job and a flat front?'

'No,' I sigh. 'You still haven't got a spare sofa?'

'Sorry. They kick us out at the end of each term anyway. Richard's doing his nut at the pub since you left. Half of us go back for Christmas in a couple of weeks. I think he's starting to realise you did the work of three people when you were there.'

That sounds about right. I answer with a plain 'Hmm' and we sit there for a couple of minutes, people watching and drinking beer. Jon doesn't smoke, of course, being a sports science student. Every new week he'd give me a reason to keep the body pure. Then he got used to working for me. Now he drinks beer like a proper student.

Mark Adams – making students act the way they ought to.

That's a legacy for you.

'How many people are turning up to Becky's leaving do later then?' I eventually ask, as I stub out the fag in the little foil tray the wind's trying to steal. Jon looks at his watch.

'Six or seven? Not quite sure. She's got a few people coming who don't work at Fortnights, so I dunno.' He clocks my mock confusion. 'Yes, Mark. Turns out people do know folk who don't work with them night and day.'

'You're full of the shit, today, Jon,' I tease.

'Aren't I just? Anyway, she's late, which makes it your round.'

Dammit.

'You wouldn't ask an unemployed, almost homeless man for beer, would you?'

'You better believe it! You wouldn't ask a penniless student whose ex-boss made him clean toilets for beer, would you?'

'Touché.'

'I thought so.'

'Same again?'

'Please.'

The Seven Sisters is an alright sort of bar, if you like a bit of spit and sawdust. We generally only come here to warm up for the night ahead, just as we're doing now. Seeing the girls earlier did me the world of good.

I wasn't going to go out tonight. I wasn't going to set foot in any of the bars who knew me and knew what happened. Sometimes it's easier to keep your dignity by staying inside until everyone's forgotten you. For someone who puts on a show every night at work; for someone who goes out of his way to make himself approachable, and friendly, and at your service, I don't half want to lock myself away from the world at times.

An ambulance races by. They tend to do that these days.

'What can I get you, Mark?' the barmaid asks. Everyone knows me round here, which isn't the best when you're trying to be shy.

I hear a fire engine blaze its siren in the background. And then another.

'Mark?' she asks. 'Same again?'

'What? Oh. Sorry.' I nod and look out the window. She puts the bottles on the bar and I offer up my card, which she taps on the machine and hands back. 'Thanks.' I take the bottles without looking and just pause for a moment.

It's fine.

I'm sure it's fine.

I'd know if things weren't fine, right?

This bar has always smelled faintly of burnt toffee.

The Axe & Grindstone

I walk back outside, hand Jon his beer and clink bottles again.

'Cheers, Mark.'

'Cheers. See the ambulance just now?'

He nods. 'Steamed past into Fern Road. We'll have the Sky Copter in the air soon, just you wait.'

'You think it's another one?'

'Possibly.'

I catch his eye, and he knows I agree. There's something in the air, something I can't explain and can't quite put my finger on. It's the feeling you've left the gas on, or you know someone's looking at you from a distance.

The feeling that something's not quite as it should be.

I get my phone from my pocket. 'I'll give her a ring. See where she is.'

A few months back, I smashed the screen. Stupid really, was trying to change a barrel a little too quickly. I really ought to have got it fixed, but you know how things are like. I tap in vaguely the right place, and Becky's picture comes up like an angry mosaic who's had a bit too much to drink. And it rings, and it rings.

'Hi, this is Becky. Make sense after the beep, and I might get back to you.'

I hang up.

'She's not answering,' I tell Jon. 'Drink up.' I neck the rest of my drink – which may not have been the greatest idea this early in the night. Jon rolls his eyes and throws the rest of his beer down his throat.

'Fine,' he says, 'but if she's not got her slap on, she'll lynch you. She won't thank you for knocking on her door.'

'Yeah, I know,' I say, as we push the chairs back. 'I'm willing to risk it. I told you they call me Brave Adams.'

'They call you a great many things, Mark. Brave ain't one of them.'

We walk back down Porter Street as the last of the shops pull down their shutters for the night. Budget Christmas lights twinkle sadly from lamp posts. I glance into Fortnights as we go past – looks like Richard's decorated our Christmas tree. It's weird living above a place you're not allowed to enter any more, let alone have a say in how things are done.

Becky lives above a chip shop about ten minutes' walk from town. I try her number again and once more it goes straight to voicemail. It's a bit strange, truth be told, because she's never more than an arm's reach away from it. Her flat's behind a small packing warehouse at the corner of Fern Road and Arthur Street, and as it comes into view, I slow down.

'Jon,' I stop. 'Look over there.'

'Mark...' starts Jon, but I'm ahead of him and am running already. I don't want to think, but the picture's in my head before I can shake it away. I have to get there.

Jon's beside me but his legs are longer so he gets to the corner first, and I can see the look on his face before I see the flames for myself. The slowest second later, and I'm by his side.

The fire's spread from the flat, to the shop, and to each of the properties next door, and I can feel the heat from here.

I can smell the heat from here. I can taste the heat in the back of my throat, and it's acrid and sickening.

Jon puts his hand on my shoulder, and I'm glad for the weight of it as it grounds me and stops me from stepping back, and back, and back. I can feel the bile rising, and without thinking I put my hand to my mouth. I look up at my friend, who's done the same and without another word he turns his face away from me so I can't see the tears I know are there.

It also means he can't see the ones stinging the sides of my eyes.

I can't hear the sirens, I can't hear the cries. I can't hear the officers miming to me to get back for my own safety and that of their crew. I can hear nothing but the roar of the fire, and the faint, faint sound of screaming from inside which slowly, and softly, dies down to silence.

Jon and I sit on the kerb for an hour, as the fire is brought under control and eventually extinguished. Neither of us talks. Neither of us acknowledges the other, because to do so would be to accept that what is happening is real. A woman asks us what we know and brings us tea which goes cold on the pavement. Things like this don't happen to people like us.

I take out my phone, press to unlock, and press twice to redial. This time there's no ringtone, no incessant double drone before Becky's voice barks back at me, just as she used to do at the pub every night.

'Hi, this is Becky. Make sense after the beep, and I might get back to you.'

But there's no sense to any of this, and because I don't have the words to say what I feel, I switch off the phone without saying goodbye.

Chapter Three
The Face of the Past

Dammit, I'm late and it's raining. My eyes are stinging like crazy.

My hair gel has started seeping down my face and for the life of me, I can't stop blinking.

This is seriously not a good look.

I press on, and as I run, all I can hear is my heartbeat protesting the exercise. I run, then stop, then walk, then run until eventually I turn a corner and there it is. St Saviours, in all its 18th century glory. When I came here as a child, I thought the place was a castle where Jesus lived with his twelve Knights of the Long Table. To me, it was the large stone fortress where miracles and magic were stored like the stones of Castle Grayskull. You read the book, you spoke the words, you believed, and all the protection you ever dreamt of was yours.

That was a long time ago.

I stop in a bus shelter across the road to compose myself and calm down a little. I don't have much time but I can't go in straight away. It seems running a mile on a diet of pasties was not a good idea, after all. I'll give it a minute. Maybe two.

My phone beeps. I reach into my sodden pocket and look at the screen.

No. It can't be. He's having me on. He'd better be bloody having me on.

Oh my word. I sit down on the sloping red seat and read it again. Instead of waiting two minutes, maybe no one will notice if I don't turn up at all.

Bollocks.

Natasha's here, and I'm at a total loss as to what to do next. I can't go in, obviously, because she'll see me and we can't have that. On the other hand, I really need to get inside, because it's Becky's funeral and I have to say goodbye. I can sneak in at the back and just avoid her. If I'm lucky, Nat won't even know I'm here.

My stomach starts to freestyle. I'm not going to let her have that effect on me again. Not after the last time. Not after that night.

I stare at my phone. The message isn't going anywhere.

OK. Another deep breath.

I stand and cross the road just as Becky's cortège begins to arrive, and the rain embraces the mood of all those within it.

The church smells warm and full of life, even though people speak in hushed tones and careful glances. The vestibule flowers are the brightest things I've seen all day and next to them I suddenly realise how shabby and dishevelled I look. Everyone here's made an effort. Everyone here's grown up enough to know what's right and what's expected. I run my hand through my hair in the hope it'll make me look half decent.

I don't think it's working, somehow.

'Mark. Thank you for coming.' Joan, the vicar of St Saviours, offers her hand with a sympathetic smile. This hand used to guide me safe across the road, as I looked left and right after school. It used to put my paintings on my mother's fridge, and make me lemonade on days when the world seemed too much. As I take it, she pulls me in for a gentle kiss on the cheek. 'It's lovely to see you,' she says. I nod awkwardly, suddenly without words, for seeing her always reminds me that I choose not to see her more often. 'We'll have a catch up after the service.' She smiles again, because no one else around her can. I put those laughter lines on her face, but also the grey in her hair. I nod once more, the child

26

I was when she first looked after me, and walk into the chapel.

'Death is not the end,' she says.

'Find strength in forgiveness and community,' she says. 'I see death, but I also see compassion, and peace; forgiveness, and love.'

I look around and her words hang in the air, as the coffin is lowered and we say our goodbyes. There's a lot of endings at the moment, and this is just one of them. But, looking around at all the proper mourners, with their proper ties, it's the one which puts all others into perspective. My problems aren't important. I'm not important, not in the grand scheme of things.

I think it's time to grow up a little.

I pause just outside the church hall, where everyone's drinking tea out of those old same blue china cups and saucers. Growing up has to start somewhere. Why not here, and why not now...

Jon catches my eye and, as he beckons me in, she turns to face me.

Natasha Bennett is standing there, upright and tall, in a black jacket and a tight black skirt. Her white blouse is legal drama crisp and my throat is dry at the contrast to the Nat I used to know. The air by my feet seems heavier than usual. She's cut her hair so she looks older than the three years would suggest, but I still find myself struggling to breathe as I walk up to her and nod an unfazed hello.

'Hey Nat, how are you doing?'

I hope that sounded confident.

She smiles, her lips pressing themselves together, and I hold my breath at the sight.

'I'm OK, Mark. It's good to see you again.'

'Really?' I grin so unsubtly I see Jon roll his eyes, so immediately retreat back into my shell as my cheeks start to burn.

'Really,' she answers. Her eyes gleam at me, like they used to do, but there's a weariness within them now. Something different.

She's changed.

I'm staring. I know I'm staring. It's time for the shoes again, so I look back down. She takes a sip of tea. I can feel Jon looking at us both as the awkward moment passes a little too long.

'I'm going for a piss,' he says, patting me on the shoulders. 'Won't be long.' As he shuffles away, neither of us says anything, taking it turns to politely sip tea. I can't stand this anymore.

'I'm fairly sure you can't say piss in church,' I mumble, to break the silence.

'He doesn't seem to have changed,' she says, leaving a line of lipstick on the outside of her cup. She takes another sip and places it on the paper tablecloth, the edge of which doesn't quite reach the corner. 'I heard about Becky on Twitter. Thought I'd come to say goodbye.'

'It's a nice thing to do, saying goodbye.'

She frowns. 'Mark...'

'Sorry, I didn't mean that.'

Her eyes scan the room, and I hold my cup tighter. I try to ignore the pause and look up, but it hurts. It's a hurt I thought I'd got over, with the vodka and the shots and everything, but it turns out that doesn't work long term.

'How have you been?' she finally asks. 'Jon told me about...'

'I'm fine,' I answer back. 'Perfectly fine, thanks.' She squints at me.

'You don't look fine. You look like you've been dragged through a bush backwards in a storm.'

'Well you look...'

'Have you been sleeping?'

'Of course I have.'

'Tell me the truth.'

'No. Not much.'

She puts one hand on her hip and raises one perfect eyebrow. I can get this back – I'm fairly sure I can get this back.

'How have you been doing the past three years?' I try with an awkward smile. 'Look like you've gone up in the world. Bigger and better things?'

She drops her hand. 'Bigger things, not necessarily better

things.' Now she drops her eyes, and I want to step forward and make sure she's OK, but I don't. 'It's been good,' she says, looking at me again. 'Seen a lot, learnt a lot.'

'You're looking good. Looking the part.'

She allows herself another smile. 'Thank you.' She steps forward and gives me a kiss on the cheek. 'I guess I owe you that. Let's go and sit down, catch up,' she says as she reaches for her bag. I'm not going to argue, so grab a couple of chairs.

I spot Jon in the doorway, who waves his thumb up and down. I nod and give him a subtle thumb up.

'Jon says he'll meet us outside,' I tell her.

'Cool.' She takes off her jacket. 'So tell me what happened to Becky. What do you know? What's been happening around here?'

'Is this the right place for that?'

'If the past few weeks have taught me anything, Mark, is that I haven't the time to mess around anymore.' I look at her. She's definitely different to the last time I saw her. Harder. Worldlier wise. But I don't think I care.

'One more statistic for the suicide figures, I guess. They say she chained her arm to the hob in her kitchen, then turned it on.' I shiver again, but Nat looks deep in thought. 'You OK?'

She nods. 'And she wasn't down or anything, no history of depression? None of the stuff the police always ask? And definitely no one else involved?'

'Nope.' I finish the tea and look around as people start to make a move. 'She was excited at her new job. Couldn't wait. Was taking the piss out of me 'cause I'd stayed in the same place for so long.'

'I'm fairly sure you can't say piss in church.'

'Whatever.' I stand up, and Nat pulls on her jacket. The two of us walk out – I want to hold her hand – and I give Joan a hug and another promise to call her. It's stopped raining, so at least one prayer I've made today seems to have worked. Nat sits on the first of five stone steps and looks at me, as if trying to work out something in her mind; a calculation she knows the answer to, but isn't sure if it's right.

'You knew something was wrong,' she says, after a while.

'Sort of,' I answer after a second, taking a cigarette from my pocket. I offer her one and she shakes her head. I breathe in the smoke, holding it inside. This one's well deserved. 'Only because I knew Becky, though.'

'Any other times?'

'What do you mean?'

'Any other times you've felt that way?'

I pause a little too long, but don't want to come across as crazy, so just concentrate on making sure the fag doesn't go out. 'Apparently another girl topped herself on my last night at Fortnights, but...'

'And you knew?'

'I...' Do I tell her? She catches my eye, and she can tell I'm thinking before I speak. 'That was a mad night,' I bluster. 'I didn't know. I was out having a fag and it felt like someone walked over my grave. Funny looking smoke. But it was nothing, and anyway...'

She groans and buries her head in her hands.

'Oh, Mark...'

'What?' Instinctively, like it's the most natural thing in the world, I put my hand around her shoulders and pull myself close. I didn't think about it, but here I am, and she's not complaining and not pulling away. It feels like it used to.

'It's you, isn't it?' she asks.

'What do you mean, it's me? Of course it's me! Who else would it be?'

She lifts her head back and shakes her hair with her fingers.

'You don't understand...' she starts. You can say that again.

'...But I'm such an idiot.'

'No you're not,' I reply, 'don't be silly. I mean, you've made some questionable life decisions, but...' Her look stops me there. I won't push it.

'OK. Let's do this. It's not like I have much choice in the matter.' She turns to look at me, and takes me by my free hand. I stub my freshly lit cigarette out on the step so she can have that hand as well. It feels like she's about to propose or something.

'You've just lost your job, right?' she asks.

'Well...'

'Mark, let me rephrase this. You've just lost your job. Right?' I nod, a little bit ashamed. 'How long have you got left in the flat?'

'Five days.'

'And then?'

'Then I sleep in my car.'

She blows out her cheeks and lets out a long breath that's only matched by the one I'm holding.

'Come and work for me.'

I'm sorry?

I take my hands back, and immediately go to light another cigarette.

'Say that again?'

'I said come and work for me.'

'That's what I thought you said.'

Can this be happening? Is this real? Is Natasha Bennett asking me, the bloke who once employed her and the bloke she once... to go and work for her?

'I work for... people... who own a number of pubs,' she explains, stressing each word as if she's practised them over and over again. 'One of them is in Devon. I need a landlord. Quickly. You get a flat – a proper flat, Mark, not a bedsit – and your name above the door. Do you want it?'

I'm stunned. I sit for a second. Of all the days and of all the people. I bring the cigarette to my lips and find my hands are shaking. Devon. It's a long way, a very long way. And I don't know if I'd ever be able to work with Nat.

But what are my options, here?

Seriously?

The last talk I had with Becky was about me not wanting to take responsibility for my own life. She was doing it – in a year she would have been my boss. Nat's obviously done it. And here I am, sitting on a wet step with wet hair, with a car that'll become my home in a less than a week's time.

As I said. Time to grow up.

But hang on. My shoulders slump.

'I can't, Nat,' I sigh. 'I'd never get another licence. The Council are probably taking me to court, and the chances of me getting another are slim to none.'

She frowns, and it's her turn to put her arm around my shoulders. Again, without thinking about it, I feel myself leaning into her.

'Mark, do you remember our last conversation? The last time we spoke. That night after work?'

I don't say a word.

'I've thought about that a lot,' she says. 'What might have been. The days that could have happened. The nights that needn't have been cold. It was one of those moments, you know – one of those times my life might have splintered down another path.' She pauses again, and I wonder what happened to the girl I once knew. 'Don't worry about your licence,' she says. 'My Council will talk to your Council. They have a knack of sorting these things out.'

'Really?'

'Really.'

I'm still shaking, but the cigarette's calming me down. I get up and climb down a couple of steps to look at her. Even though she's sitting there, in the wet, she looks strong. As strong as I've never known her. I crouch down and rest my fingers on the step.

'OK,' I nod. Even though it'll be hard to work with her, deep down where I don't want to look, I know I'd rather be nowhere else but by her side.

I'll do it right, this time.

She beams and stands up, wrapping me in her arms.

'Great!' For the first time, she really does look more relaxed. 'You really don't know what this means, Mark. Thank you. I've looked for so long. I never realised it would be you that I'd find. But it seems kinda right, doesn't it?'

'The world's a bit weird like that,' I say. 'Well. Who would have thought it? Mark Adams. Landlord.' Her smile falters a bit.

'Mark Adams, Landlord,' she repeats. 'It suits you.'

The two of us walk down the road to where Jon is waiting, and we start back to Porter Street where a pint is waiting to send me on my way. We sit outside the Seven Sisters and raise a glass to our departed friend. After three more drinks, we repeat the toast Jon, New Girl, Becky, and I made that final night.

'To Mark – and his plans to take over the world.'

The three of us clink glasses and, as is tradition, we look into each other's eyes as we toast. But as I make eye contact with Nat I falter, just for a second, as I see what's there.

And it changes nothing.

Look at me. All grown up.

I'll make her proud. Just you watch me.

I'll make Natasha Bennett proud.

Chapter Four
The Rain of Long Barrow Ridge

Bloody Devon. I haven't said that nearly enough in the last couple of hours.

Bloody Devon.

'The park shuts at dusk,' the woman says. 'So what are you doing still here? You come for a nice walk in the moonlight, buddy?' She steps forward and I step back. She's the height I always wanted to be, just a couple of inches taller than average, with black hair pulled up into a neat pony tail. She keeps her torch pointed at me and swipes it from left to right, checking the darkness behind the rain.

'No, no, I needed a piss!' I blurt out.

'Uhuh, I've heard that before. That's why you come to the Ridge when it's closed. It's a long way to drive just to take a leak. Maybe you just like getting your cock out in the park.' She flashes her torch at my crotch, then back to my face.

'Seriously! I'm not dogging or anything!' Do I look like a dogger? How do I explain I'm not a dogger? 'I'm not from around here! I've been driving for fucking hours, I'm really tired and I had a bottle of Diet Coke an hour ago at the services! I saw the sign for this place and drove right in. Listen, there was nothing to say it was closed. No barrier or nothing. I'll get out of your face and go, OK?'

Hang on.

Shit.

I sit on the wall, to the side of the embarrassing patch of darker concrete and the sound of the unrelenting rain becomes louder. Every so often, a drip falls from the overhanging roof and lands down my neck, making me shiver.

I don't think I really care anymore. I'm getting used to being cold and wet. The woman walks over, her with dark green wellington boots deftly stepping over the long puddle inching towards them. I put my hands to the bridge of my nose, wipe my face and look at her. She's a park ranger of some sort, if parks still have rangers, with a thick green jacket. Embossed on the pocket is a logo which reads 'Long Barrow Ridge', under which are the words: 'Jennifer Peynton'.

'Best be on your way. We wouldn't want any of your little friends turning up giving me the wrong impression would we? I'll just call the police again – they've been here three times this week already.'

'Listen. I'll be out of my way as soon as I can, It's just that my car...' I vaguely point in the direction of the car park. 'I sort of snapped the key in the lock...'

'Oh.' She glances over to the Metro sitting lonely in the distance. 'You *were* pretty desperate. There are closer trees than here, you know. You might want to try them next time.'

'Sorry, it was raining and I was brought up right. I thought the loos would be open.'

'Idiot. You got a phone on you?'

'It's in my car and it's got no signal anyway.' She looks again at the car, and looks at me. Jennifer's hard stare is slowly lapsing into one of pity – which I'm not sure I prefer. I look down at my trousers and the tops of my shoes, and realise the look of pity is somewhat justified.

'Let's take a look at your car,' she sighs. We start wandering back to the car park, her torch casting an ever moving bob of light left to right ahead of us.

'Thanks. My name's Mark, by the way. Mark Adams.' I offer her my hand. She glances at me and rolls her eyes. I wipe it on my jeans and shut up.

'Jen,' she answers. 'Watch your step.' I watch my step, and we reach the car. She crouches down by the driver side door and turns her torch to the lock. 'Yep, looks buggered. Right. Come over to the cabin. There's a phone in there where you can call the AA. You've got to be quick though, as I lock up in fifteen minutes.'

I obviously don't pass the 'Are you a threat test'. My hands go a little deeper into my pockets. She leads me to the other end of the car park where there's a little security hut. Not much: an armchair, a TV showing a DVD of a classic *Dad's Army*, a kettle which Jen switches on, and some chocolate biscuits holding down some paperwork. The whole place has a musty smell thanks to the four weeks of rain. I don't take the liberty of the armchair, but instead sit on a plastic stool by the window. Jen hands me the phone.

'There you go. You look like the sort of guy they'll prioritise.'

'Thanks.' I take the phone off her and cradle it in my hands. 'There is one small problem,' I tell Jen, as a cup of tea is put on the table next to me. 'I'm not actually a member.'

She sighs like someone who thinks she's seen everything before. 'How far have you driven today?'

'Not far.' I take a sip of the tea, which needs more sugar.

'About four hundred miles.'

Jen laughs and shakes her head. It does feel like a stupid thing to do, but with all that's gone on this week, breakdown assistance just slipped my mind. I take more tea. I hope it doesn't make me need the loo again.

'Four hundred miles? Hopeless man! I'm surprised you made it this far.'

'I would have been fine! That car's got thousands of miles left in her.'

'If her moron of a driver hadn't locked all of his stuff inside.'

'Well, there is that...'

There's a few more seconds silence than is comfortable. I stare into my tea, Jen still looks me up and down. I feel I'm on display.

'So where are you heading to, then?'

'Oak Cheating. A place called The Axe.' Jen's eyebrows raise in surprise, and she slowly puts down her drink. The look which crosses her face reminds me of Nat's, just before she offered me the job.

'The Axe? I know The Axe,' she says, and the room looks a little darker than it did a moment ago. 'I know it well. What's a lad like you doing driving four hundred miles across the country to go to a place like The Axe?'

Now, this isn't the reaction I'd hoped for. I'd hoped for a

'Wow, really?' or an 'I love that place!' But no. 'A place like The Axe' is the last thing I want to hear right now.

'What do you mean?' I ask.

'You ever been there?'

'Not yet, no. I ran into a spot of car trouble, if you remember.'

'I do. So why are you going there?'

'I'm the new landlord.' As she raises her drink to take another sip, Jen freezes, and just looks over the rim of her mug at me.

'You? You're the new landlord?'

This isn't going well.

'Yes. If I ever get there, and the place still exists.'

'But you don't even have the foresight to pay for breakdown cover. How do you think you're going to survive The Axe?'

'Hey,' I say a bit too defensively, 'I worked for a Fortnights for over a decade. I've thrown more people out of pubs than you've had cars in that car park.'

'Witty. You'll go a long way.' She looks at me in the eyes again. I wish she'd stop doing that. 'Do you know anything about The Axe, Mark?'

I shrug. 'Not much, Nat didn't go into too much detail.'

She frowns as I carry on, I'm not sure out of annoyance or concern.

'Your traditional sort of place. Guest bitters. Dimpled glasses. A line in the floor where you stand to play darts. Pub quizzes. Skittles. Absolutely no 16-year-old wankers on cheap cider and black. At a guess. It didn't have a website, and Google didn't turn up much. Bit strange, that. Hasn't even got a TripAdvisor review.'

'No,' she states as a matter of fact. 'It wouldn't. I take it when you say Nat, you mean Natasha Bennett.' I smile as my two worlds meet for the first time.

'Do you know her?'

Jen still doesn't take her eyes off me, and I shuffle in my seat.

'We have mutual friends. She does her job and I do mine. Oak Cheating and the Ridge are special places. I was able to help her out after her accident.'

'Accident? She never told me about an accident.'

In the few hours she was in Staunton, she seemed pretty

closed down, but it sounds a big thing to miss out when you're asked 'how have you been.'

'No, she wouldn't have.' She shakes her head. 'C'mon then, Landlord. It's not far. I'll give you a lift to your new castle. The Ridge'll look after itself in this weather. Leave your car here, and we'll sort something out. You would have never got to Oak Cheating without a 4x4 anyway. A lot of the roads will be washed away this time tomorrow, especially up on the moors. You won't be leaving any time soon, with or without your car.'

Five minutes later and I'm being smothered again by the imposing country roads. The canopy of trees reach in for the car and the rain keeps trying to force me back. Jen may be fearsome, but she knows the dark. She understands the moor and she leaves the Ridge fast behind us.

She remains tight lipped, even when she's in the driving seat of the Land Rover, and she still won't tell me any more about Nat. She's more interested in my background and what I've done in the past. I fill her in as best I can, but the sorry and soggy atmosphere and the way my words seem to hang gives her opinion of me away.

Guess that's one more person I have to show.

We turn left, and right, and left again. We pass the same bloody tree that I passed four times already tonight. We travel over a Postman Pat bridge and run a red light where no one was waiting. And, ten minutes after we left, we pass a small sign.

I stifle a yawn and a comment about careful driving. I look around to get a sense of my new home, but I can't see that much in the rain. The tunnel of trees has disappeared, stolen away by the dark of the moor. We climb, and the road narrows. Sharp fingers of bush and hedge scratch the car, to warn us away. Water runs down the middle of the road as we climb forever upwards, and Jen slows to a crawl to avoid the potholes cracking the ground open every few feet.

I may have cursed my child-sized bladder, but I wouldn't have had a chance getting up here on my own. The Axe really is remote.

I've gone to live at the end of the earth.

'Is this it?' I ask.

'Pretty much. There's not much here. You've just got this one road, and a couple of cottages about a mile away. They built The Axe where it had to be built, not because it'd be popular.'

'What does that mean?'

'You'll find out. Best buck up if I were you. We're here.'

We slow down. On the edge of the road is a small wooden sign, painted white before I was born, pointing to an overgrown track on our right-hand side. Grass grows in the middle, as if the imposition of nature on the broken tarmac could make the sign read true.

The second road seems, if that were possible, even smaller than the one we've just climbed, and I pray we don't meet anything coming the wrong way. But before I have time to think too much there it is, rising up on top of the moor, almost hidden by a solitary oak tree which towers over the small, squat building. The branches stare at me through the night, pointing me back the way I came, and daring me to approach my new home.

The Axe & Grindstone

The Axe has the look of a building whose memories have worn it down over the past four or five hundred years. As it grows larger, as we climb the tight winding lane which stops at the base of the oak, the rain starts to ease to a faint drizzle. There's history here, in this small forgotten part of the moor, and as we pull up beneath it, I get the strangest feeling the tree is judging whether I'm worthy to step inside. The Axe is as far from a Fortnights as is humanly possible.

Jen turns the engine off and looks to me. 'Welcome home,' she says. 'Do you need any help with your stuff?'

'Funny,' I mutter, as I look through the window. A small chain connecting knee-height wooden posts separates the small car park from a row of dying window boxes and peeling benches. Several dozen small panes of misshapen glass, connected by diamonds of lead piping, make up the bulk of two casement windows on the pub's frontage, each one surrounded by dark timbers. These timbers spread unevenly across the building, convening on a triangular porch across a heavy front door.

My front door.

The one above which my name will metaphorically sit.

I glance up at the first floor – at what I assume is my new flat – and see only two small peep holes. There to let in light, nothing else. As with the oak, the pub is looking at me, through me, and daring me to do it justice.

Well, no one dares me and leaves without seeing me try.

I look over to Jen just as she pulls the handle of her door and jumps down. I look again at the pub and do the same. The ground is wet, and I sink a little before I find the coarse gravel at the edge of the lane.

'That,' she says, pointing at the tree, 'is the Life of Oak Cheating. It's probably the oldest thing in the county and one of the greatest of its kind in the UK. They say its trunk is almost ten metres in diameter and is probably eight or nine hundred years old.' She looks at me, shivering in the cold. 'It's seen every single Landlord that's stepped foot in that pub, but not every one that's left it. If I were to give you one piece of advice, Mark Adams, and believe me you'll need it, it would be this.

'Listen to it. Listen to that which has seen your like before and guided them through what's to come. Hold it close and hold it dear.'

She looks back at The Axe, then back down the lane. 'I'll drop your car off in a day or so when I can get it up here. I think you'll find the weather's better in there anyway.' She comes over to me and gives me a hug which catches me off guard and which I'm not sure I'm supposed to give back. 'I'd best be off.'

Hang on.

'Wait,' I say, as she pulls away, opens the Land Rover door, and starts the engine. 'I'm no tree hugger, I'm a barman. And I've got no idea what you're on about, but you're freaking me out a little.' She looks at me as she closes the door and winds down the window.

'You're freaked out already?' She puts the car in reverse and mutters under her breath. 'I hope she knows what she's doing.' She takes one final look at the pub. 'Good luck, Mark,' she says. 'I mean it. I really, really hope you make this work. For all our sakes.' She nods, winds up the window, and drives off.

The lane fades into a murky darkness we wouldn't allow in town. Before me, stretching a good eight feet tall, a wooden sign on top of a post creaks back and forth in the cold December breeze. Beneath a rusted chain swings a double-edged war axe. Beneath that swings a wooden sign in the shape of a skull, its jaw hanging limply towrds the ground.

It's laughing at me. The bloody pub is laughing at me.

I walk over to the window, the glass panes distorting the shadows inside. The lights are off.

'You'd better be inside,' I say under my breath. I look over to the oak, and as I do so there's a gap in the clouds, and the moonlight highlights the branches pointing me to the door.

Listen to the oak.

What a load of bollocks.

I stand there for another minute, alone in a new village, waiting to start my new life.

There's no putting this off any longer.

I walk to the wooden front door, put my hand on the large

iron handle, turn it, and enter the darkness.

The Axe & Grindstone

Chapter Five
The Delight of Broken Glass

'Hello?'

There's no response.

Maybe I was wrong. Maybe there's no one here after all. This is awkward.

'Hello?'

I try again. Nothing.

The Axe is dark. I'm not a tall man, to my shame, but as I move through the lounge bar even I find myself having to duck to avoid the uneven ceiling and its struggling Tudor beams. The rain outside has stopped but so has the sound it made. There no longer seems any connection between Oak Cheating and the world outside.

It can't be a surprise to anyone I'm here. My trainers – not the loudest things on the world – are making enough of a racket on the rough wooden floor as it buckles and creaks under every step. I run my fingers across the dusty bar, leaving small snail tracks behind them. My rather ironic mantra at Fortnights was, 'If you're bored, something needs cleaning.' Despite the scorn I got in reply, you could always see someone polishing something.

The Axe could do with the Adams Touch.

Small brown lamps hang from dark stained walls, and their fake candle bulbs flicker and deepen the shadows which itch across the wall. Well, I said I wanted atmosphere and a place with character, wooden stools and its fair share of stories. Ghost stories, by the looks of things, but stories none the less.

I explore, and press down on the corners of the dark wooden tables arranged in no particular order as I do. Every single one of them rocks, and the sound of their rocking gives the pub a lonely heartbeat. A long brass foot rail sits proudly at the base of the bar itself. I crouch down and run my hand along it. There's not a speck of dust, and it gleams.

A small rattle comes from behind a brass cash register where a faint orange light outlines a small cream coloured door. I lift up the hatch, knowing instinctively where the lock is, and step behind the bar. Immediately the place feels a little more comfortable and I'm a little more in control. I rest my hand on the large pump of one of the guest ales. Yep. This place could be mine. This is where I belong. My own little castle.

I take a dimpled pint glass from the open shelf above my head. It feels heavy in my hand, and right. I've never served ale in a glass with a handle before, and the thought brings a smile to my face. A checked tea towel lies longingly next to the small porcelain sink, and I use it to polish the years from the glass.

'The usual, Frank? How's the wife? I haven't seen you in a few days, has your knee been playing up? You just sit there, mate, and take the weight off. One for myself? I don't mind if I do, thanks, you're a gent.' I know I'm talking to myself but I don't care. I could do this all day. I pick up an empty tumbler and, like an expert, toss it into the air. It spins around, and I catch it at just the right angle. Proper barmanship, like learning to ride a bike. I throw it up and watch it again for one, two, three, then snatch with my other hand, slam it on the bar, and mime the perfect count for pouring one shot of vodka. '£3.50, Joe, but this one's on me.' I imagine my new friend taking a grateful drink and raising a toast to his favourite landlord at his favourite local.

Oh, the plans I've got. I pick up the tumbler. One more for the road. Cheers.

Scratching.

The jolt makes me drop the glass and it smashes on the floor. What the hell was that? The feeling... in my head... I shiver, suddenly cold, and turn to the door behind me. It's small, with the top at shoulder height. I curl my fingers around the edges and slowly ease it open, the light gradually filling the rest of the pub. Rather than banishing the shadows, it makes them longer, sharper, and more dangerous.

Where the hell's Nat?

The Axe seems to creak, and small noises seep from the

walls. The carpet in the hall looks like it wants to drown me. Does quicksand carpet exist? Tonight, I get the strangest feeling anything's possible.

'Nat?' I call again. 'You here? It's gone ten. I'm a bit late. Sorry.'

A brief movement to my left, and my heart's the loudest thing in the building. I thought I saw something... but it's only another door, which used to be white, slowly inching open and closed in the breeze. Set under the stairs, with one corner cut away to fit, it's the only thing moving.

There's no breeze. And all of the windows are closed with the outside door firmly shut.

So why is this door moving when it blatantly shouldn't be?

'Nat?' One more time. Nothing.

Breathing more heavily than I would like, I take the painted wooden handle, and pull the door slowly open. Behind it, descending into darkness, are tight, concrete steps leading down to the cellar. A proper cellar, for a proper pub. Maybe she's down there?

Or maybe she's not. I could wait up here. That sounds like a better plan. I'll just wait behind the bar, where I'm expected. There's nothing to see down there. Nothing at all. Nothing until the morning when it's light and the shadows have gone to bed. I close the door quickly. There. Sorted.

Scratching.

With a blink, the lights go out and I'm standing in a black pub on a black lane in a county that's determined to hide itself from view. I freeze, every hair on my skin bolt upright. I'm ready to bolt myself, but I can't see where I've come from nor where I'm going.

Scratching.

I think it's ahead of me. No. The voice. It's all around. Before, behind. In my head. No, in front. Dammit I can't see!

Scratching.

I throw my fists to my temples. I've got to get it out.

It's eight feet tall, but inside my head. I need the release.

I need the relief. I shout out again – all hope of regaining my cool now lost – and stumble back to the bar.

'Natasha!'
Scratching and Scratching...
I fall to my knees.
And Scratching some more.
There's a piece of broken glass.
Scratching your Self and your Soul through your core.
I could end it. I could cut it out.
The Landlord will scream...
So I scream.
And a door slams. And the lights come on.
And there's silence.

Natasha's standing there with her hand on a brown Bakelite switch, looking at me on my knees with a shard in my fist.

She's beautiful. I'm an idiot, and scared shitless.

This is the best fucking cigarette I've had in a long, long time. Natasha's back inside whilst I take a 'moment' out on a wet picnic table. I've made her turn all the lights in the pub back on to kill as many shadows as possible.

The oak tree across the lane is judging me.

I'm not going crazy, am I? That was pretty intense, but the longer I smoke, the less it seems real. That's the second time tonight I've got spooked. Oak Cheating can take a running jump so far.

But still.

Scratching.

It makes me draw my nails down my arm just thinking about it. An automatic reaction, I guess. Like yawning.

I yawn.

It's been a long day.

I look through the window and see Nat behind my bar. That takes me back. It's comforting. I need the comfort. She looks business-like and professional, and even though she's dressed less formally than last week, she still walks with purpose and pace. She's now a confident woman who owns her life outright. And it's just sinking in how much of mine she now owns too.

It's also sinking in just how much I've missed her.

I stub the fag out on the gravel and wander back inside. She smiles the smile I remember.

'Better?' she says.

'Much. Sorry about that. Didn't mean to be such a wuss.'

'That's OK. Power can be a bit temperamental. We were in the cellar. Didn't hear you at first. Well, until you...'

'Started screaming. Yeah. Thanks for that. We?'

'I,' she brushes the hair from her eyes. 'It's OK. I won't tell anyone. But as a rule, try not to scream. What do you think of it?'

Do I lie and never sleep again, or do I tell the truth, get away before the floods cut off my escape, but see the look of disappointment on her face?

'Could do with more brasses, watercolours and cricketing cartoons, but am sure I'll settle into it.' I smile, convincingly. 'We'll get on OK.'

'Good. Glad to hear it.' Nat's behind the bar, and I'm not. I don't like the feeling, and even though I'm still a tad freaked out, I just want to sign on the dotted line get life back to the way it was.

'I broke a glass.'

'So I see. Were you tossing glasses again?'

'Hey,' I retort, 'I've got better since we last worked together!'

'So I can tell,' she smiles. 'Did you have a chance to look over that contract and background material I emailed you? Does everything look OK?'

'All looks good,' I nod. 'It's fine.'

OK. I'll admit it. I checked two things – salary and accommodation. That's all I care about, really. And the licence and lack of court case Nat seems to have secured.

'Great. You're doing me a real favour here, Mark, coming all this way. This will be fine. All fine.'

'Yeah, it will be,' I reply, trying to put both of us at ease. 'So, area manager of a brewery, then?' Now it's her turn to shrug.

'Yes, it's... different. It keeps me busy,' she says, and leaves it at that. She pulls out the contract and places it on the bar. It's the same one I read last week, albeit on posher paper. Someone at her head office is a fan of calligraphy.

An Established and Agreed
Contract of Employment

Between

Mark Cornelius Adams

and

The Council

'Once you sign it,' Natasha continued, 'I can give you the full tour, show you the flat and leave you to it.'

There's no real alternative, to be fair, is there? I can't come all this way not to sign, and I really, really need some sleep. I pull over the pieces of paper and quickly scan them. I haven't seen or signed a contract in over a decade, as Richard did all the legal stuff at the old place, but I'm sure the standard stuff hasn't changed all that much. I glance over the main lines to make sure nothing's different. Role – General Manager of The Axe and Grindstone; hours – as necessary to protect the establishment; pay – well, enough; accommodation – provided. That'll do.

I take the pen offered by Natasha and sign. This should be the moment where I feel elated, like I've just turned a new corner and a new chapter in my life. I should feel the sense of achievement that comes with reaching a career high. This is everything I've ever dreamed of. Everything I've ever wanted. Even though I never actively sought it, I've been working towards this minute of my life for the past eleven years.

But all I feel is a slight chill. I pass the pen back; the red scratch lines on my forearm strikingly red against my pale skin and the dark wooden bar. I notice the piece of glass, lying on the floor where I dropped it, and in my head, I can still hear the faint echo still taunting.

The Landlord will scream...

Chapter Six
The Cellar of Crossed Light

The pop of a champagne cork is one of the most life affirming sounds in a barman's life.

You're the source of someone's celebration. You're the reason behind the smile, and the master of the room. I've got opening champagne down to a fine art. A slight twist of both bottle and cork in opposite directions.

Nat's not quite as practised.

'Congratulations!' she beams, as she mops up and hands me a glass. 'Feels a bit weird being your boss...' I smile a thin smile at her. 'But we'll make this work.' She winks, and I relax a little.

'It's going to be great,' I say. 'You going to give me the tour?'

Nat breathes in. 'Of course, c'mon. The tour. Grab your stuff, I'll take you around.'

I wave at the empty space behind me. 'This is it, for the moment. Just me. Had a bit of trouble at Long Barrow Ridge – do you know someone called Jen? She's got my stuff. And my car. And probably a story she can sell to a women's mag.' Nat rolls her eyes and walks round to my side of the bar.

'Yes, I know her. She works for the Council.'

'She said you have the same employer. You can't have a council-owned pub, can you?'

'Listen,' she says, 'Are you telling me you've rocked up at my place with no clothes and no sense of shame? You haven't changed a bit.'

I laugh. 'That was only that one time.'

'Twice.'

'OK, maybe twice. At least I was on my own. I had to throw the cushions out when Becky last stayed over.'

'Bless. Do you play skittles?' She walks over to a large table by the door, enclosed on three sides with leather padding, and a large net canopy which marks the surface with diamond shaped shadows. Nine pins stand upright, made from the same oak as the table itself. Sturdy and strong.

'Never played it before in my life,' I answer, looking at the strange contraption before me. 'I'm not bad at bowling though.'

'With the barriers up.'

'I let you win.'

'Of course you did.' She pats me on the back. 'I think we'll end with the skittles, Mark. I need to fill you in on a few things first.'

Bubbles in hand, Natasha takes me around the rest of The Axe, showing me the lay of the land whilst making me think of what life used to be like. On the left, the cellar with delivery doors and apparently not at all creepy. Upstairs, a small sitting room with sofa bed, small TV and small-town wallpaper; a bathroom, and a kitchen complete with microwave and a kettle for Pot Noodles. No expense spared. There's even a drop-down Formica table in the corner. I feel quite at home.

We take a seat on the sofa bed – not something I thought I'd be doing with Nat just ten days ago.

'So, everything's in the book – it'll explain everything,' she gestures towards a small binder placed between us. Any questions?' I look around the room. I want to ask what I've missed. I want to see how she's grown as a person, whether the spark I thought was there all those years ago still exists. I want to ask her why she never called and never kept in touch. Above all, I want to ask why she turned into the same person everybody else did, when I thought she was different.

'When do I open?' I ask instead.

'You don't,' she replies, putting her glass on the floor.

Excuse me?

'This is a village in the middle of Dartmoor,' Nat explains. 'No one comes here, unless it's the summer and they're lost. I need you to keep the peace. That's all. Just keep the peace. It's all explained in the book.'

'Hang on,' I say, putting my glass next to hers. 'Have you brought me all the way down here for a *Shining* job? You know. Look after the place in the winter, until you go mad and see ghosts?'

'Oh, Mark,' she mutters with a sigh. 'They're not that bad.'

I look at her for a few seconds without saying anything.

She's kidding. She has her kidding face on. I'm sure of it. I know that look.

She leans forward on the sofa, and I don't lean back.

'This is a pretty unique place, Mark,' she says. With two fingers, she touches my arm, resting on the back of the sofa. 'Some people have what it takes to run this pub.' She reaches the inside of my elbow, making me shiver. 'Some people don't. Simple as that. But I'll give you one piece of advice. Don't believe everything you're told. Believe instead in what you can see, and feel, and touch.' She leans over and gently, with the lightest of touches, kisses my forehead. I close my eyes and realise I'm holding my breath, as she speaks softly into my ear.

'Believe in yourself. Believe in what you can do. Believe in the power of people together, coming together, in one place and one time as one community. Believe in your position as friend to all; the person to bring together different worlds and different backgrounds for the very first time.

'Believe in the magic of shared experience and communal life, laughter and love. Through you, communion. Remember those words. Through you, communion.

'You will always be the most powerful person in this building. Believe in that and be strong. Above all, you need to be strong. I need to tell you...'

I sit there with my eyes closed for a moment longer, thinking of her words and the feel of her lips against my skin. I'm captivated by her. There's no one else in the world who could bring me this far. No one who can hold my attention for this long. There's no sense of time when I'm with her. Is it my turn to speak now? What do I say? I want to ask her to stay with me, to help me in my first few days. I'm sure that's her job. I'm sure that's what she wants her job to be. I'm not just another one of her managers. I'm Mark. She's Natasha. It's meant to be like this. Finally, slowly and with control I let out a breath and open my eyes.

And I'm alone.

'Nat?' I must have fallen asleep, stupid idiot that I am. I look for my phone to check the time, but of course it's still in my car. The evening's been one Mark disaster after another and a fine new start to my new life.

She's not in the flat. She's not in the bar. Her car isn't in the car park and she's not in the lane.

She's done it again.

I stand downstairs staring out of the old and distorted Tudor panes of glass at the dark lane and the disturbed old oak, making the world outside seem bent out of shape.

Nothing is moving.

There's no wind to move the hedgerows. No raindrops to disturb the puddles outside. Nothing to disturb the musty air other than the sound of my own, uneven, breathing.

Nothing, other than a set of keys, a small A5 binder and her untouched champagne glass, to show Natasha was ever here at all.

Scratching.

There's an almighty boom and a roar, and from nowhere I'm flying backwards and falling to the floor. I land on my side and wince. The building shakes and the lights flicker once, twice, before going out altogether, plunging the room into darkness. The starlight peters through to the bar, casting shades of sharp silver onto the floor and as soon as I try to get up another almighty boom forces me back down. Jesus! There's another one, and another, and with every one that follows the very fabric of the building seems to shake in reply. Boom. An old glass lampshade shoots off a pillar to my right and narrowly misses my feet. Boom. A pint glass balancing on the bar shatters into a hundred pieces. Boom. An optic falls to the floor, filling the place with a deep and sickly smell.

I try to rise to my feet and stumble to the door. It's shaky, so shaky, but I slowly get my balance. One foot in front of the other, Mark. Not hard.

Boom.

My hand goes to the table next to me, but I'm still upright.

Boom.

Three steps.

Boom.

My hand on the door.

Boom.

Twist it.

Boom.

Twist it.

Boom.

I twist and I twist and my hand is raw against the ridges of the old round doorknob, rubbing uselessly into my palm, but it won't move. I hit the bloody thing and shout obscenities but they don't work, as they almost never do. I've got to get out, I've got to move as fast as I can. Whatever it takes I've got to get out of this fucking...

Boom.

...pub. The back door. There's a small beer garden with a climbing frame and barbeque. I brace myself between two tables, wait for another...

Boom.

...and make a run for it. I can see the exit the other side of the room. It's not far, I can make it and

Boom.

I'm on the floor. I get back up and reach the doors but before I even try, I know they won't open. What the fuck is stopping them? What sort of fucking mental thing is making that sound? I've got to get out. The front door won't open. The back door won't open. I don't know what I'm going to do and I'm going to die on my feet right here and right now without seeing another living soul ever again.

Boom.

Think, Adams, think. Can you smash a window – No, the lead lining'll stop me getting out. Then what's left? C'mon Mark, what's left – what's left?

The cellar.

Boom.

There are two doors in the cellar. She told me. Used for deliveries. I race to the back of the bar and the small door that leads to the basement. The frame's so low I have to duck my head;

the staircase so narrow and deep it's hard to take two at a time. I reach the bottom and the black is thick and cold. A thin strip of light carves through the delivery doors and lands on the concrete floor to make a cross in the centre – it's enough to give my eyes time to adjust and make my way around the room. Nearly there – climb up one step, climb up two – and my hands are on the lock trying to slide it back. It won't budge, the bastard thing won't budge.

B...

The world didn't shake. The sky didn't fall. I look back at the dark cellar and all seems quiet again. The cross on the floor is all that's there and all I can hear is my own heart trying desperately to escape my ribcage with the adrenaline coursing through it. I turn on the step, and my shadow moves across the thin strip of light cast beneath me.

I look at my shadow, turn to the gap in the doors, and back to the light it shines on the floor. One gap, one stream of moonlight.

But there's a cross on the cellar floor.

Two slivers of light.

Where the fuck is the other one coming from?

Slowly, softly, I step down from the ladder, my hands in front in case I should fall. I let one find the wall and follow it around to my left. I can feel red brick dust on my fingers – it's visceral and rough but at least I can feel it. It makes me feel more connected. Like I'm back in the real world. I can't fucking see anything, but I can touch it. I reach the left-hand wall, where the light is supposedly coming from. There's nothing there. But I can see the light cast on the floor. From the 'nothing there'. This is doing my fucking head in, and I'm not sure I can take much more. I wave my hand in front of the wall – and yes, there's the shadow of my hand, waving back across the beam of light. I need to get out of here, this is wrong. I don't care what the stories were. I don't care if I don't last long in this nightmare place, I just need to leave. But still...

There's a breeze. Not from my right. Not from the doors in the roof leading to the car park. From behind me. From the wall, coming through the very air itself, and as I watch, the air seems to split in two. Light spills before me. I shield my eyes but they quickly adjust.

The Axe & Grindstone

Don't believe everything you're told. Believe instead in what you can see, and feel, and touch.

There's another door. Over there, in the brick wall that's now suddenly stone. The thin band it once cast on the floor is now a thick slab of light casting onto the concrete, with my shadow burned into it.

'Fuck me...'

I must have missed it, but it's another way out. It must be. It's the only door in this place that's open. Slowly, I walk towards it and peer through. There's another hallway just beyond, also made of stone. I look back at the cellar one more time and step through.

My hand goes to my chest – if there's anyone here they'll hear my heartbeat, and I can't be having that. There are lights on the wall so it's this or the darkness, and I no longer like the darkness. I press down, touching the floor that's littered with straw gently to make sure it's real. The hallway, if hallway is the right word, leads round a bend to the right where a large, heavy, wooden door blocks the way. An old ring gate latch keeps it shut. I look backwards again. No way out. Come on Adams, press on. I twist the ring, the latch lifts and the door opens.

Bloody hell.

It's another room – another bar, unlike anything I've ever seen before. The walls are mottled black, with hundreds of thousands of individual crystals shining and reflecting from one to another like the entire room has been carved from polished rock itself. Pictures hang proudly from each wall, but pictures of what I don't know. They're photographs, but they've got to be fakes – there's nothing natural in the world that looks like that with a pint in its hand. He's big, and... green, for a start. The Tudor beams which hold the ceiling upstairs are again above my head, but here they seem grown from the fabric of the building, not carved and placed there, and organically flow from the ceiling down the walls to form chairs and tables and even the bar itself. Everything seems part of everything else. And there, twenty feet ahead of me, is another big wooden door, with a big round handle, exactly the same as the one upstairs.

Boom.

I jump back, but there's no shockwave here, as if the very walls around me are absorbing it.

Boom.

Boom.

Something to the right catches my eye and I turn to catch a blur of motion – and suddenly the keys on my belt are gone, snatched away by something small: a rat, a fox, something! I turn back towards the door and freeze. There, with my keys, is a short... creature, five feet tall. It's not a man, not really. Its skin is too orange and, the hair on its arms, they're downy, but dear God they look sharp. It's wearing nothing on its feet – oh God look at its feet! Its eyes are dark and piercing. I can't move. I'm rooted to the spot. Once again I really, really need the loo.

It's looking at me. Taking me in. It's wearing a black cap – turned back to front – with an auburn pony tail growing through it, a black Meat Loaf T-shirt and blue jeans. Dear God...

'You the new boss?' It speaks. Its harsh, unimpressed voice actually speaks. 'Eh? Speak up, lad. You took y'time. I thought he was going to knock the bloody door down!'

Boom.

Boom.

Boom.

'Yeah all right, all right. Keep yer bloody 'air on.' The thing takes my keys and turns towards the door.

I have to find my voice – c'mon, I have to.

'Wait!' I shout and the thing stops and turns back to me.

'What?' it asks, frowning.

'Don't open the door! Don't let it in!'

'Don't be a soft bastard. We're gonna have fun with you, all right. I've got to open the door. Arnold gets grumpy if he doesn't have his cherry brandy, and you've kept 'im waiting three weeks already!'

It crosses over to the door, slips a big brass key into the lock, turns it and nonchalantly walks past me back towards the bar.

'C'mon then. In yer come.'

The door opens with a crash, and I look up.

And up.

And up.

The thing framed in the doorway looks down. And moves towards me. It's huge. It's bald. It's made of green rock. Why can't I move? I've lost the power to speak, to run, to scream. I was right when I thought that all my days had been leading up to this one, for I know I'm now looking at the thing that'll kill me. I close my eyes tight. I don't want to see.

But it doesn't kill me. There's no pain, no smash in my skull and no stab in my chest.

The rock-man just crashes, clumsily, around me. I open my eyes, spin on my heels and watch it, still not killing me. It takes a seat, almost collapsing with all its weight onto a wooden stool growing out of the bar, with a 'humph' and a sigh, in front of the orange guy whose got a dimpled glass all ready.

'Usual?' he says.

'Please,' comes a growl. 'Bad day.'

I need a drink.

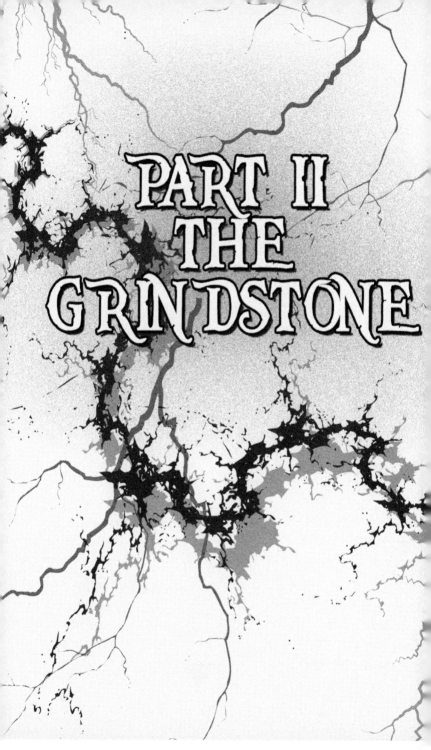

Alternate

For Screaming starts the Scratching.
And Scratching starts the Night.

The echo of the scream has long since seeped into the walls of the cold stone chamber, but the memory lingers on. It's behind his eyes when he sleeps. It taints his throat when he swallows.

It haunts him, as does the feeling this is somehow deserved, that this is right. He used to have a place in the world, and now his role is new. His name is new. He is no longer whole. He is no longer the man he once was. He is now Previous.

The surgical threads which protrude from the remains of his arm itch, but he resists the urge to act on it.

For Scratching starts the Scratching
Starts the Binding Brothers' Light.

No. He can still feel the sensation lingering in his former fingers – but he wishes to god that he can't. It'll go away, he tells himself. Soon, all the pain and the sorrow and the loss will be someone else's. There'll come a time when the new guy becomes the Previous, and he'll be allowed to slip away into nothingness and mourning and dream. There'll be nothing after that, but mourning.

And worship.

Tap. Te-tap-te-tap.
Tap. Te-tap-te-tap.
Tap. Te-tap-te-tap.

The sound of his approach makes the Previous shuffle back against the wall. Maybe this will be the day. Maybe this will be the last time the door to his cell will open. Maybe it'll be his friend walking through.

No.

He stares at the floor, so he doesn't look in the face of The Man With The Crab-Like Feet as he enters. He's wearing his black robes today, lined with crimson. He must have been praying. Pity the men he was praying with. The robes flow down the thin lines of his body, giving him volume he wouldn't otherwise have known. His presence fills the room, and the air seems to still out of respect. The Previous keeps his eyes to the stone as the man slowly walks forward.

Tap. Te-tap-te-tap.
Tap. Te-tap-te-tap.
Tap. Te-tap-te-tap.

The man walks on his toes, four pink and gnarled claws to the front with one where his heel should be, inching him forward. He moves his legs only when he has to. He doesn't have to today.

'He is young,' he whispers as a matter of fact, pausing to taste the words as he speaks them. 'Were you... ever that young?' He speaks with disdain, green spittle hitting the stone floor in staccato drops of bile. The Previous shrinks into the corner, knowing best not to respond or react in any way other than submissive respect. It's not enough. The man crouches in front of his prisoner and uses one long nail to raise his prisoner's chin. There's no other choice but to look.

'I asked you a question.'

The Previous draws shallow breaths and nods. The Man With The Crab-Like Feet drops his finger and walks away, slowly gliding across the room, the sound of his toes haunting it with every step.

Tap. Te-tap-te-tap.
Tap. Te-tap-te-tap.
Tap. Te-tap-te-tap.

'I told you God was good,' he says as he reaches the one, small window. 'Your replacement is no true Landlord. I am attuned to him, like I was to you. I can feel his... panic. This should be swift and glorious. Your prayers have been answered. It'll be all over, soon.'

There comes a small cough from the corner, as the Previous lifts his head.

'You know... you know what I think of your prayers,' he says.

'And you know what I think of your blasphemy.'

The Previous waits for his throat to stop burning and the

courage to build once more, as he sees the man walk once more towards him.

'The Council won't...'

'The Council remains a hypocritical joke!' The Man With The Crab-Like Feet shouts for the first time, launching towards his prisoner and pressing against his forehead. His skin is waxen, and his dark black eyes burn with night. He presses so hard the Previous thinks this is the end. He can feel the veins in the man's temples as they throb and beat out a rhythm of hate into his skull, and his breath forces its way into his mouth. 'They speak of friendship, when I ask them so... nicely not to.' The man closes his eyes, turning his head towards the wall. 'Why?' He brings his hands up to his prisoner's scalp and rests them there, ten thin needle-like fingers, each a sharpened pin. He flexes each finger, drumming and tapping, and tapping and drumming. The Previous holds his breath, expecting his head to be ripped from his shoulders. This is as close as he's ever been to the Man With the Crab-Like Feet. This is as close as he hopes he'll ever get again.

'I'm sorry,' he whispers, hoping it's the right thing to say. He gets nothing in reply for the longest minute of his life.

'You're... sorry? Of course you are.' The man taps him on the top of the head like a parent to a penitent child. 'Of course you are. I know it's not your fault. The Council talks of tolerance. All I ask for is one small ceremony. Just one...' The man leans back and looks the Previous in the eyes. He strokes his face, running his nails up and down, wiping away the tears almost tenderly. The fingers run down his chest: up and down, up and down. Then to his groin and his thighs: up and down, up and down. The Previous squirms as the man's fingers explore his body. 'But you know how personally I take this, don't you?' The Previous nods. The man stops his fingers half way down the other's thigh, and he leans into his ear.

'Show me your tolerance,' he whispers. 'Pray with me. Show me the god which lives within you.'

He plunges his fingers deep into the man's thigh. The Previous screams as the needles bite into him, deep into his flesh.

'Oh yes,' the man grins in pleasure as he presses deeper. 'Scream for me. Scream like that. You know that'll make it better.

Make me forgive you. Make it all right again.' He presses against the Previous again, his mouth an intimate inch away from the scream. He sucks, and inhales the other man's breath, pressing himself closer and closer. The Previous tries to back away, but there's nowhere to go. His head forces itself back against the stone wall and the man presses deeper and deeper into his thigh. The Previous screws his eyes shut as he screams again but is forced to open them by five more needles. The Man With The Crab-Like Feet glares deep into the terror he finds, and smiles.

'There He is...' the man whispers, as the Previous screams once more. 'How glorious...'

The pain grows and grows, and every thrust from the man's fingers cut further, scraping the bone. Every scream makes the man's smile widen – his open mouth grotesque and gluttonous. Finally, as the Previous feels he's about to give in to the despair he didn't know existed, the man withdraws his fingers with one final jolt and brings them up to his nose. With a long, sensuous movement he draws them along and takes in the scent. He smiles at the Previous beneath him before wiping the blood on the other man's face.

'It's OK,' he whispers as he cleans himself. 'I missed the main artery. I wouldn't want to harm you in any way.' He gestures absently towards the punctured leg. 'We'll get that sorted, like we sorted your arm. That looks fine now, doesn't it. No need to make a fuss. No need to cry about it.' He steps back. Without moving his legs, he walks over to a single wooden chair, sits, and dusts himself down. He spends a moment watching the Previous sob, before picking up the severed arm which lies discarded beneath the chair. He picks at the end.

'You scream well, you know. Not everybody I see has that talent. It's a gift you should share. When all the worlds are screaming, you'll stand out. Doesn't that make you proud? It'll make me proud, knowing you're one of the best. Knowing it's the practice that I gave you that nurtured your talent.'

He stands, and once again the tap of the nails echo across the stone floor as he walks towards the thick wooden door.

Tap. Te-tap-te-tap.

The Axe & Grindstone

Tap. Te-tap-te-tap.

'You will thank me for raising you so high. You'll thank me for making you the best. Thank me now. Thank me for the practice I just gave you.' He stands at the door, staring at the Previous, waiting for the response. 'Thank me.'

There's a thin, faint 'Thank you' from the corner of the room.

'Louder. And say my name.'

'Thank you... Thank you... Veli Khalid.'

The Veli smiles at the respect inherent in the use of his title.

'Good boy. I've seen your soul, and it is almost ready. Sweet dreams, my Previous. Dream of the Scratching and the pride it'll give your master to see you take centre stage. Dream of what your successor has to look forward to. Dream of what you'll teach him as he kneels next to you and screams.'

The door opens and Khalid steps through. As it slams into place the room is once again submerged into darkness. The Previous sits there, his back against the damp stone walls feeling the cold condensation seep through his shirt and onto his skin. He grasps his leg with his remaining hand and waits for the man who'll come to treat it, as he always comes. He kept the limb, he was lucky today.

Others won't be so lucky tomorrow.

Chapter VII
The Clean Scent of Apples

I'm not normally a fan of whisky, but it seems tonight isn't a night for normal.

I take another sip from the glass I'm holding tightly with both hands. It's warm and, dear God, it's needed.

I'm sure I'm not going mad.

I'd know if I was going mad, wouldn't I?

Snap me out of this now, please. Any time would be grand.

To use barman's language: When you're ready, mate.

I'm not saying a word. You don't want to talk to fictitious parts of your imagination in case they talk back. This one can keep serving me whisky though. This is the fourth. It's making things seem better. I'm just going to keep sitting here at the end of the bar, staring at them as they stare at me. I'm sure they'll disappear back into their fantasy world before I do. I'm real. I know that much. I saw myself in the mirror before I left Staunton this morning.

Yesterday morning.

Whenever the hell it was when I left Staunton.

I squint, to see if they're still there when I squint. Squinting makes them look funny. Squinting makes them look puzzled. That makes me smile, so I keep squinting. If I tilt my head to the left, the rocky green fat thing looks like he's sitting on a hill. If I tilt to the right, he looks the same, just the other way round. I think he's speaking. He's got a big, boomy, voice – which figures really, if you think about it.

'He's taking it very well, Emmet,' the green giant says, taking another sip of his pint of cherry brandy. 'You might owe me that fiver, after all.' The orange man with funny arms and bad taste continues to polish a glass whilst looking up and down at me.

'We'll see 'bout that, Arnold. He hasn't met Mrs Miggins yet.'

There's something terribly, terribly wrong.

I'm out of whisky.

Pretty sure squinting at the glass will make it fill up again. I squint.

I put the glass on the smooth, polished top of the bar, and slide it from finger to finger. This is fun. This is like a game.

Emmet – which is a weird name for an orange faced Meat Loaf fan, if you ask me – gives me more whisky.

'This is the only time I'll do this, yer know. Special occasion and all that. You can drink yer own profits if it'll stop you runnin' back to yer mum.'

I'm going to have to play along with this for the moment, aren't I?

'Yes. Good,' I reply. 'My profits, my drinkie.' I point at them both with the glass. 'My monster, my orange barman.' They look at each other again. The monster snorts.

'Something went wrong, didn't it, lad? She didn't tell you, did she? And I bet you didn't read yer contract,' says Emmet, cleaning his fifth glass in a row.

My God, the man's obsessed. Is that normal for orange people? Shit, sorry. That sounds a bit racist. I pull my contract out of my back pocket and scan through it again. Arnold burps and puts some coins on the bar.

'C'mon lad,' says Emmet. 'Read out the good bits. I 'aven't done this for ages.'

I sigh. If I humour him, maybe I'll wake up. Maybe I'm still on that sofa bed. Maybe Natasha's still next to me. Lying next to me...

'Fine,' I grunt. 'An Established And Agreed Contract of Employment Between Mark Cornelius – no laughing – Adams and The Council. Funny. Never heard of a council-owned pub.'

'Yeah,' gruffs Emmet. 'It means ponce and arse-headedness. Go on.' He waves a damp dish cloth in my general direction. He's a bit rude, when he's not giving me free drinks.

'Yada yada yada...' I breeze, 'General Manager of The Axe and Grindstone...'

'There yer go. Stop for a minute.'

I do as I'm told. I still don't think I'm allowed to leave, having been told to 'Sit down, stop gawping and have a stiff one' as soon as Arnold had entered.

'Say that again,' says Emmet. Arnold swigs back his brandy and shakes his head slowly.

'General Manager of The Axe...'

'...and Grindstone, yes.' They're both staring at me, as if they're waiting for some sort of penny to drop. Emmet rolls his eyes. 'Well, I take it you've seen The Axe.' He points to the ceiling. I follow his finger and look up. I nod. 'Well now you've seen The Grindstone.' He points to the other side of the bar. I follow his finger.

Oh.

I take a sip of the fresh whisky. I could slug it back like Arnold, but that'd mean I'd be out of whisky.

Oh.

I take a packet of Reds out of my pocket and wave them at Emmet.

'Do you mind if I...'

'Your pub, boss.'

Your pub, boss. My pub.

I have two pubs. It's like a two for one Friday.

Both a little weird, but in truth one slightly weirder than the other. I wave the flame of my lighter under my chin half-heartedly and light a cigarette.

'Right...' I reply, even though we all know this isn't right at all. 'So. My pub then.' There's a rumble from my right.

'For goodness sake...' Arnold doesn't seem impressed and is faster than he looks. Whilst still holding onto his pint glass with his right hand, his left flashes out and crashes into my arm.

'Ow!' I cry out. Jesus Christ that hurts! I've been given the world's most painful dead arm by a creature that only exists in my head!

'C'mon, Arnold,' scolds Emmet. 'I've warned yer about that.'

'He'll thank me,' comes the sullen reply. I rub the top of my arm in self-pity, wondering what I'd done to myself to deserve this. I haven't exactly eaten anything today (other than a cold pasty from a service station) that'd give me dreams like this.

Dreams that hurt. Hurty dreams.

Hang on.

Dreams don't hurt. Dreams make you wake up before you crash through the floor.

Holy shit.

This is for real. And to hammer it home, a thin oblong package is thrown on the bar in front of me with a thump. It's wrapped in thin wax paper. And on the top, in scrawled black writing:

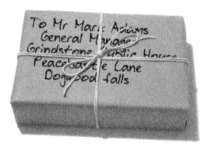

To Mr Mark Adams
General Manager
Grindstone Public House
Peacebattle Lane
Dogwood Falls

'Present for yer.' Emmet's smiling, which is possibly one of the more disturbing things that have happened to me tonight.

Peacebattle Lane? Dogwood Falls? Never heard of them. Fairly sure they weren't on the map.

But it's addressed to me, all right.

I pull at the little bit of string that keeps the wax paper from peeling off, and unwrap the unexpected gift. Inside there's an engraved wooden board. I can feel it, pressing into my fingers. This is no dream.

Mark Cornelius Adams
Licensed to sell to spirits, and all others,
intoxicating liquor for consumption
on the premises.

'Fuck me.'

'Not my type, lad. Yer too pale. Now give me yer hand.'

I'm not giving him my hand.

'I'm not giving you my hand,' I state plainly. Emmet puts down his glass.

'Arnold?' The rock on the stool raises his hand to grab mine, and I reach over to Emmet quicker than is perhaps manly. 'Cheers,' he smiles. He takes my contract, and places it on the board. He then places my hand on top of both. 'You a fan o' poetry, lad?'

'I know *Gil-Galad The Elven King...*' I start, without wanting to reveal too much.

'Never heard of it. But your job is all about the verse, so better get used to it. Now shut up. I can't do this as well as she can, so it might not work as well, but it'll do fer now.' Emmet closes his eyes, and places both hands on mine.

'She? You know Nat?' I start to pull my hand away, but Emmet pushes down. He opens one eye.

'Course I do. Now shut it and repeat after me.'

'Where is she? Where did she go?'

'Away. Things were a bit wobbly. You might o' noticed. Now repeat after me...'

'Is she alright?'

'In a way. Now shut up, lad, or your glass stays empty.'

'Sorry...'

'Now repeat after me...' he closes his eyes again.

Should I close mine? I'll close mine anyway. Seems the right thing to do. 'My name is Mark Cornelius Adams. I am licensed to sell without bias, disdain or judgement. I am the friend to all, no matter their blood. Through me communion, the Oak and Dogwood.'

Remember those words. Through you, communion. Above all, you need to be strong.

I mumble the words, with one eye still open.

'My name is Mark Cornelius Adams. I am licensed to sell without bias, disdain or judgement. I am the friend to all, no matter their blood. Through me communion, the Oak and Dogwood.'

Emmet smiles and pours me another whisky. That makes me happy.

'Good. A little background. This place – it's not yer average bar.' He's all news, this one. 'It's probably the most important bar in the entire fucking world.'

'Too right,' pipes up Arnold. 'Another brandy.' Emmet looks at me and nods.

'Do you want to take this one, boss?'

I'm still not entirely sure I can say no. I stand up – pick myself off the floor – and walk behind the pumps. It all feels... familiar, and it's crazy, but for the first time tonight I feel like there's somewhere I belong. I know. At home, he says, whilst standing next to a rude orange man with hairy arms and a troll who drinks pints of cherry brandy. I take a bottle from the shelf behind me, open it, and pour half of it into the empty glass. Arnold throws another coin onto the bar, a rough ring of gold, which Emmet snatches away and places in an old brass cash register.

'You're a natural. We'll get on fine,' says Arnold, bringing the glass up to his thick and mildewed lips.

'Thanks,' I reply shakily. 'Nice to know.' I turn to Emmet. I'm behind a bar – apparently my bar – so my confidence is slowly coming back. I can talk to anyone when I'm behind a bar, even if I do end up slurring a little. So c'mon Mark, bite the bullet. Brave new world.

'Be straight,' I say, one hand on a bar pump. 'Who are you? What's this place, where's Nat, and what the hell have I just signed up to?'

'Oh, so that's yer voice is it? Nice to hear it at last.' Emmet brings around two wooden stools; there's only a couple that don't look like they've been grown from the pub itself or are still attached to the walls or the floor. We sit, the roles now reversed. Emmet sits next to Arnold, and I'm behind the bar where I feel more real. 'That's three questions at once, lad,' he says. 'Where do yer want to start?'

I think for a moment, which is not the easiest thing after a drink or two.

Believe in what you can see, and feel, and touch.

'What is this place?' I ask, feeling the wood under my fingers. 'Why is there a pub in my cellar?' Emmet's smile widens as he blows a tuft of orange hair away from his eyes. It falls glibly back across his forehead, and for a second, it looks as if it's grown not from his head, but from his hopelessly outdated baseball cap.

'It's a good enough question, boss. We're not in yer cellar.' I look at him again, and squint. It doesn't make him look any different this time.

'I'm fairly sure we are,' I answer. I'm not *that* drunk. Emmet nudges Arnold who grunts, amused by something, and gulps from his tankard once more. The barman gets up from his stool, stretches his arms, and straightens his cap. His pony tail flicks from side to side, as if he'd somehow trained it by watching Crufts. I am, of course, still imagining all of this. He gives me one last look, turns on his trainers and, with a dramatic flourish, throws open the door.

A cold breeze picks at the corners of my contract.

Apples. I can smell apples. Why can I smell apples?

Emmet's standing just beside the doorway, looking pleased with himself. Smugly, he crosses his arms and leans back against the worn oak frame.

Through the doorway, I can see starlight.

That's not Oak Cheating out there.

Maybe I am that drunk.

I stare for a moment, before walking slowly around the bar. I keep my hands firmly on its surface. I'm not letting go. Who knows what will happen if I let go? But I have to see this. I have to check for myself. Slowly, tentatively, I let go of the bar and walk over, my footsteps making the floorboards creak under me. I place my hand on the thick wooden door – don't let go, Mark – and look up to the dark and cloudless sky. Over to my right is the moon, shining down a silver light onto... not the lane. Not the car park. Not the old oak tree which judges and pours scorn on the new guy, but brown and shiny cobbles.

Fuck me.

I step back inside and breathe out hard, my breath escaping without thought into that brave and horrific new world.

Which smells of apples.

I look at Emmet and point outside. He nods, eyes opening wide. I point again. He nods, slower this time. I think he's mocking me. I may have to have words, after I've seen...

I take a small step forward, and nothing happens. I take another, and another, and hold onto the frame of the pub which feels as real as the one upstairs. I'll just take one step outside. Just one.

The Axe & Grindstone

The cobbles are hard and steady. They glisten in the starlight, and shine with the gaze of another sky. One more step. Maybe two. It won't hurt to let go of the door frame. Emmet will catch me if I fall. I'll wake up if I fall...

Before I know it, I'm no longer holding onto the door, and five or six steps later I'm outside the pub, looking in, listening to the deep and dry chuckles of the rock at the bar.

This really isn't Oak Cheating. And what I'm looking at isn't The Axe. It's similar, don't get me wrong, but different. Squat. Like someone's tried to squeeze it into a space that's slightly too small. There's a creak to my left. I look up, breathing hard now, and there's the sign.

THE GRINDSTONE
A PLACE FOR ALL
SHAPES AND SIZES
ALL WELCOME
CRISPS AND
CUSTARD CREAMS

And there, making sure I can't miss the strange buildings in this strange lane, is a second moon. I'm really not in Kansas any more. This really is a different world under my feet. I jump up and down, feeling the impact of the hard ground as I bounce. I can't help it. I giggle. This is mad! And there! Look up there! Look at the stars

– and the moon – and the OTHER MOON! I look over to the OTHER
BUILDINGS where there should only be an oak tree and a small
track. This is Impossible – and the air I'm breathing is Impossible –
and the two 'blokes' I've been talking to are Impossible.

But is Impossible bad? Should I run away from Impossible
every time I think I find it? Isn't Impossible the one thing that I've
been looking for, dreaming away in normality. I've done normal.
I've done average. I've spent the last eleven years smoking by the
fire escape of drudgery watching normal people have fun. I laugh
again as I run my fingers through a small Impossible bush on the
side of the small Impossible lane.

Fuck me...

CHAPTER VIII
THE DEPTH OF THE SMALL PRINT

I don't know how long I've been sitting on this stone wall, feeling the wind on my face.

It's like waiting five minutes in the dark – there comes a point where it becomes impossible to tell. The sailors of old used to use the sun and moon to tell the time. I've got two moons. Two pubs. Two worlds.

'Was that a smile, boss?' Emmet asks, as he walks out and sits next to me. His feet – I'm slowly getting used to the strange six-toed trainers he wears on his feet – dangle a few inches from the ground. I try to hide my expression, but fail. I shouldn't be accepting this. I should be running a mile, I know.

'You're real, aren't you, Emmet?' I reply, knowing the answer before I speak. 'Are you sure you're real? Are you sure Arnold's real? Am I not just sitting upstairs on a shitty sofa bed above an empty pub, dreaming to myself?' I kick my heels against the stone wall and look up again. 'I mean, look at those stars. I can't get enough of those stars! I've been trying to make patterns out of them, you know, like they did back in the olden days.' I point to the sky. 'A shoe, maybe?'

'A shoe, lad? Are yer kidding? That the best yer could do? Try The Castle, The Hourglass and The Stocks and Peasant, for a start!'

I try to find each and every one of them as he points them out, but as soon as I fix on a star I lose my place and have to start again.

'In a few days' time,' he says, 'we'll see the Waning Crux – a group of stars no one's seen in a generation. And then...' he tails off, distracted by his thoughts, and slowly lowers his hand.

'What?'

He looks at me and I'm not sure, not certain, but his eyes glisten like the cobbles at our feet.

'Nothing,' he sniffs. 'Bit special, that's all.' I shake my head, trying to clear away the fog which comes from too much whisky. 'What was next on yer list?'

I look up again, and around, still trying to take it all in. I shrug at the town around me, not knowing where to start. We're at the bottom of a hill, which shouldn't be there. Small, simple buildings line each side of the lane, twenty feet apart. Each has its own style of wooden shutters covering the doors and windows. Each one is different, painted with scenes and portraits of people, families, friends. They're drawn with care and even at a distance I can see that each one is unique and deeply, deeply, personal. To the right of The Grindstone, the lane dips sharply. The stone wall we're sitting on curves to block it off. It's the only thing between the pub and a sharp fall onto the rocky face of the cliff below. The ocean – an ocean – pours off into the night, a blanket of pin-pricks and endless royal blue. I giggle again. I'm trying to be manly, but I know that I'm failing.

'Where are we?' I ask. 'Does Nat know about all this? I've got to tell her. She'd be amazed! She's got to see...'

'Aye, she knows,' Emmet says. 'She knows all right. This is the town of Dogwood Falls. You're sitting on a wall in Peacebattle Lane, and that,' he points at the pub, 'is The Grindstone Public House. Yer new business empire.'

I shake my head.

'I still don't believe...'

'Start, cos it ain't goin' anywhere. Well, not today, at any rate. And yer can't pour a brandy if yer think the brandy don't exist. It gets people cross, and it's never a good idea to do that, now.' He sniffs and wipes his nose.

'Do a lot of folk get cross about imaginary brandy?'

'More than you think, lad.'

I turn to him and grin. 'You know, back when I first got started, the smell of brandy used to make me feel sick. We'd go out on a free Saturday night; drink ourselves silly and try to be overly helpful to passers-by on Porter Street at midnight. Self-styled Angels of Staunton, me and my mates.'

'I've known you an hour, lad,' says Emmet, drily. 'You don't strike me as angelic.'

I give the orange bloke a nudge on the arm. 'I'll have you know I was the top man, back then!' I say. 'Cost me a shoe one night, a solitary shoe. Never quite worked out how, but it must have made someone happy.'

'Yer'd be surprised the number of folk who come into The Grindstone and ask for a shoe, yeah. And the brandy?'

'Every Sunday I worked – I'd have to top and tail the spirits. Pour the half bottles into each other to fill them up.' He rolls his eyes at me. 'Sorry. Worse thing on a Sunday morning with a hangover, half a litre of brandy being poured under your nose. But you get used to it after a while, don't you?' Emmet nods and looks back up at the stars. 'Like I guess I'll get used to this place.'

There's a pause, while the two of us collect our thoughts. From inside The Grindstone, my new regular impatiently crashes his tankard on the bar.

'Leave him,' says Emmet. 'He needs to pace himself or he'll get ratty.' He bounces his feet against the wall. 'It sounds like you 'ad a good team, back at yer old place.'

'Them lot?' I follow his gaze and try to pick out The Hourglass. 'Yeah, they were all right. We stopped doing that silly stuff after a while. They all moved on – to college, university, a decent job. Stops being fun, having to make new mates every shift change, even though you pretend it's OK. The ones you get close to, well...'

He turns to look at me, his dark eyes reflecting the light of the two moons.

'Yeah, I know,' he says, without needing to say more. I take out a cigarette, and wave the lighter under my chin before I smoke. I catch his look.

'Old habit,' I mutter as I breathe out. 'Back as a kid. Never won at keeping it there the longest, but I kept trying.' The smoke tastes real in my lungs, and I keep it there for as long as I can. It tastes of home, and it tastes of the world I lived in a few hours before. It tastes of stolen moments hiding from Joan, and the stolen days away from mum. It tastes of me and my life, and it's helping.

'So,' I say, breathing out, 'what about you, then? What's the story there? What's the team like?'

He snorts. 'Team?' he says, with a brisk sniff. 'Yer lookin' at yer team, lad. Just me and Fox, the past few years.' He jumps down, and starts kicking a pebble. 'Just me and you, now. And her.'

'Natasha.'

'Aye.'

'Do you know where she is?'

'I know where she's been. I know where she's gonna go. I don't know where she is right now, lad. No.'

I jump off the wall and take another smoke. The sound of waves crash over me, and I close my eyes to drink it all in. I wish she could be here to see the night sky and smell the sound of sunlit apples. When I dreamt of fairy tales as a child, I dreamt of Dogwood Falls. When I dreamt of a life worth living, I dreamt of right here, right now. I don't know what I've done to be given this chance to begin again, but you don't make it a mockery by running away.

Mark Cornelius Adams. Licensed to sell to spirits, and all others, intoxicating liquor for consumption on the premises.

Hang on.

I open my eyes and look at Emmet who's deep in thought and looking out to sea with his spiny hands clasped behind his back.

'Emmet,' I say, trying not to fudge my words. The whisky is slowly wearing off – an unfortunate side effect of not having any for the last half an hour. 'Licensed to sell to spirits?' He turns around and raises a ginger eyebrow.

'Aye.'

'Spirits.'

'That's what it says.'

'To spirits.'

He looks at his watch before mouthing the words back at me.

I nod.

Right.

Of course.

It makes as much sense as a green rock-man with a drink problem. I take a step forward and, from the other side of the lane peer back into The Grindstone. Arnold's sitting there, holding his glass upside down in silent protest.

'And all others?' I ask tentatively. Emmet sniffs again.

'Friend to all, no matter their blood.'

'Through me, communion,' I reply by rote. 'The Oak and Dogwood.' The left side of Emmet's mouth curls up into a contented smile. He thinks of himself as my Yoda.

'That's it, lad. That's it. Now,' he says as he adjusts his cap and flicks the hair from his eyes, 'you'll be a bit of a celebrity fer a while.' He looks up the lane towards the rows of houses. 'Although I had faith in yer, folk round here weren't expecting another landlord. Now Arnold's stopped crashing about, they'll want to meet you and grab a drink. Look.'

Emmet points up the hill where I can see a few people, small and distant, standing outside their homes. They're staring at the new boy. One by one, they start to move towards me.

Oh man.

'It's a bit late, Emmet,' I start. 'I mean, it must be one or two in the morning, by now. Don't you think we could...?'

'Different world, boss. Different time. We don't sync to your green witches time here, yer know.'

'Right,' I mutter back. I suppose I'd better get my game face on. 'Friend to all,' I tell my barman. 'Let's do this.'

'Watch yer back!' shouts Emmet as he squeezes behind me to get to the gin.

'Coming through!' I shout back as I let him past, a glass briefly present in both hands. It wasn't just a few people coming down the hill. It seems the entire town is here, in my pub. And they're all talking about one thing.

The Landlord has returned.

'Did you put flyers out or something?' I call, as I pull back the pump that feels so natural in my hand.

'Not me, lad,' calls Emmet as he throws a bottle to a young man squeezed against the wall. 'Blame 'im!'

Arnold takes a small sip of cherry brandy, and grunts. I crash the two pints of ale, with only the slightest spillage, in front of a seasoned old man crushed sideways against Arnold's arm.

'Anything else, mate?' I ask, as he looks disturbingly happy at me.

'One... one for yourself, Landlord,' he gasps with a smile.

'Cheers!' I toast him with the fifth pre-prepared whisky, and swallow hard, gasping myself as it adds to the others. I hold my hand out. 'That's... that's...' I look at Emmet for help.

'Six ponds.'

'Six ponds,' I shout. Three hollowed discs are chucked into my palm.

'Keep the change!' the man says. 'Good to have you here!'

I throw the coins into a bowl – I'll work all this Ponds Tirling nonsense out later. As he squeezes out, another man – proper men, like the rest – squeezes in. Of the eight people crammed at the bar, only Arnold is facing it. The others press against each other, their fingertips marking their place in the imaginary queue.

'Who's next?' barks Emmet, as he points at a man in a dirty linen shirt, his mind made up. I like him already, despite his pony tail. He spins on his feet as he's given his order, and cups two pint glasses under two taps with one hand. He holds them at the perfect angle for the perfect head, bops them up and down to finish and slides them into the man's hand, like a pro.

'When you're ready, mate!' comes the cry two from the left with a wave of a shiny pond coin. The more things change...

One by one, they peel away from the bar, leaving only Arnold to delicately sup from his third pint of cherry brandy. His granite fingers pinch the glass, and the only clue he may not be the monster I see before me is the sight of his 'little' finger pointing upwards whenever he takes a drink. A monster with class, it seems.

The bubble of noise in the pub rolls over in waves, as conversations merge and swell like the impossible ocean outside. My regulars seem normal, for the most part. Ordinary men and women, their clothes simple, yet a world away from the local Primark. I could be in The Axe upstairs, if it weren't for my spikey orange friend and the mountain on my barstool. There's smiles, and laughter, with regular glances my way, but I get the feeling these are people who haven't seen each other in a fair few weeks.

Look at them. Coming together, sharing stories, growing friendships, just because we simply gave them a place in which to do so.

Through us, communion indeed.

They drink ale, for the most part; simple hops and barley which they grasp with both hands and treasure as they sip. Initially, they all clawed in to see me, goggle eyed and new. Slowly, the excited handshakes have given way to furtive glances. They've come to see the Landlord, but am I what they're expecting?

I spin a bottle in the air, catching it effortlessly before whipping out my Fortnight's leaving present and slicing the cap off into the small plastic bin, hanging from the bar at my hip.

'Wass'at?' asks Emmet. I wave the small metal gadget at him.

'Waiter's Friend,' I reply as three more ponds are placed into my hand. 'Don't you have them in space?' He tilts his head and narrows his eyes. 'Corkscrew and bottle opener in one. Never go anywhere without one, Emmet. Call yourself a barman?' The last unserved customer goes and sits with his friends by the door, glancing at me as he compares his first impression with theirs. I pass the Waiter's Friend over. Emmet turns it over in his palm, feeling it for weight. Like others across the country, this one is made of metal, blue and about three inches long with a thin contoured hinge for opening bottles. A corkscrew nestles against the body, ready to be snapped into a T-shape whenever the bottle runs dry. A small serrated knife hidden away in the handle. It's my one piece of Staunton, given to me by Jon and the Bouncers before I left. It makes my barman smile as he reads what's written on it.

'Yer know, this is almost prescient. Arnold, take a look at what's written 'ere,' He shows the inscription to the mountain, whilst I take the opportunity for another shot. I'm liking this 'My pub, my alcohol' malarkey, and I shake my head to keep me going.

'Meant to be, Emmet,' comes the sound of granite and dust. He brings his hands up to his head and slowly twists his elbows, stretching them with an everlasting crack. 'Maybe she did good.'

'Now... now don't the pair of you go reading anything into

that,' I say, pointing vaguely in their direction. 'I know what you're going to say. It was just my mates taking the piss, that's all.'

'Really, lad,' deadpans Emmet.

'Really.'

He hands it back to me with a hum. 'You look tired.'

'It's been kind of a long day. And the whisky. The whisky makes me look tired. Bad whisky.'

'Most whisky's bad whisky.'

'Don't be racist against whisky.'

'I'm a barman at The Grindstone, lad. I'm not racist 'bout no one.' I grab a tumbler and pour myself a glass of water. It tastes clear and soft.

They're still staring at me. The people. With a thin smile I give the table by the window a wave. A middle-aged man nods back, and toasts me with a pint. He brushes a black strand of hair from his eyes and stands, calming the noise in the pub with his hands.

'Name's Benjamin,' mutters Emmet as he wipes a chequered tea towel around the rim of a glass. 'Nice fella. Fisherman. Can do you a good price if yer ask nicely.' The room quietens as Benjamin flicks the edge of his pint and starts to speak.

'Well,' he says in a voice worn by salt. 'I know a lot of us didn't expect to be sitting here a few weeks ago. We've all been through a lot, but I think times are changing.' There are a few calls of 'Hear, hear' and tankards raised in support.

'When Fox was... taken, we thought we were done for. I know many of you think I'm a daft old thing for saying so, but you've all thought the same thing. No more Fox, no more Protection of Dogwood Falls. But Natasha's done us proud, hasn't she?' The crowd raise their drinks to me once again and cheer. I wave back – a little cautiously.

'Who's Fox?' I whisper to Emmet.

'Bloke before you.'

'What does he mean, "taken"?'

'I'll explain later, boss.' The noise calms down once again, and Benjamin continues as I steady myself on the pump.

'So here we are again,' he says, 'back where we all belong. Arnold at the bar, the bravest GeoTroll of them all and the only one that's ever seen sense. Arnold, we salute you. You saw through the Brothers and stood by us. For that we're forever grateful.'

There's another cheer from the crowd and Arnold's shoulders slump. He pushes his glass towards me with a finger, and I top him up. Benjamin keeps going. 'To Emmet, the keeper of the keys, and the best barman in town, back in his rightful place by the Landlord's side. May you stand by him and may your... gifts keep him safe.'

'Safer than the last one!' comes a heckle and a laugh from the side of the room. I've never seen an orange guy blush before, and Emmet's eyes dart to the floor.

'And finally,' starts Benjamin, as the others start to pound on their tables, 'to the Landlord himself. What's your name, sir?'

'Mark. Mark Adams.' I say, before randomly pointing to the licence behind me. 'I have... I have a sign and everything.'

'So you do, Mark,' he chuckles, 'So you do. You must be a special, special, man for Natasha to recommend you to The Council.' I shrug, and smile.

'Well, you'll have to ask Nat how special she thinks I am.'

'There won't be a need for that,' he smiles. 'If she says you're the one to save us from The Scratching, then that's good enough for me.' Another cheer.

Wait.

What?

'To the Landlord of Peacebattle!' he cries as the pub explodes with noise. I take a step back and look for answers in the eyes of my barman. What's going on, I don't understand. He looks at me, and what's potentially pity crosses his face.

'Yeah,' he says after a moment, looking back across The Grindstone towards those with so much expectation. 'Probably should have mentioned that, boss.

'Welcome to the town where screams are holy. I reckon yer've got about three days to save it.'

The Axe & Grindstone

Chapter ix
The Cold Light of the Morning

One small ceremony.

Just one.

It is almost time.

I'm not moving. How can I not be moving? I'm running as fast as I can – how the fuck can I not be moving?

Dream of the Scratching and the pride it'll give your master to see you take centre stage.

I look behind and he's still coming. I can't see his face, but I don't need to. He's still coming and he's getting closer. I've got to run faster. Why can't I run faster? All I can hear is the tap tap tapping of his feet as he runs. It's unnatural. Nothing on earth makes that sound. Nothing on earth.

Earth...

The ground beneath my feet falls away with a crunch and I'm running on air that's thin but as thick as soup. I try to move my arms to give myself extra push as I run, but they're as heavy as barrels and as fluid as treacle. This isn't Oak Cheating. This isn't Staunton. I'm running through some strange sky above a strange land, and he's getting closer. His feet are still making that impossible sound, like ten tap shoes on ten toes one after the other. I'm getting slower – I swear I'm getting slower – and it's taking all I can to drag the foot behind me into the front. C'mon Mark, you've been doing this since you were a kid.

Dream of what your successor has to look forward to. Dream of what you'll teach him as he kneels next to you and screams.

It's no good. I'm trying. I'm trying my hardest but I can feel his breath on the nape of my neck. And that moment I feel ten needles wrap themselves around my throat...

The Landlord will scream...

...I wake up, screaming, and sit bolt upright.

Mustn't scream. She said don't scream. He'll hear you if you scream.

That's not on. That's not normal. It's not me. I'm not the sort of man who wakes up in the middle of the night clutching the air in front of him. I don't hug pillows for comfort or cry out for Joan to tell me it's OK.

Not for a long while anyway.

I try to catch my breath – my head's all clammy and I wipe it with the back of my hand and look around. I don't recognise this. Where am I?

Oh.

Oh yeah.

Shit, my head hurts. The memory of whisky and dreams. Dreams of... the man. The Man With The Crab-Like Feet who stays in my mind, even now I'm awake.

The feeling is fading but still familiar. The feeling I had on the last night at Fortnights. The feeling I had the night of the fire. The feeling's connected with *him*.

I want to shout for all I'm worth and leave this behind – this strange place with strange responsibilities I never asked for. The dream is still in my head. Running. Running from a dark place and running from a scream which wasn't mine. Running to escape the dream before I become another... what's the word? It's at the tip of my tongue but it's fading as dreams do when you start thinking of reality. Dammit Mark, what's the word? Escape before you become another in the long line of...

Previous.

I crash down onto the sofa as the word hangs there and I stare at the ceiling. I keep staring. Staring is the only way I'm going to make sense of this.

Staring and not moving.

How much was memory and how much was dream? The last thing I know for certain was sitting on this sofa with Nat. Her glass is still sitting there, abandoned, on the floor. I must have slept all night. Was she bored of me? Did I fall asleep and make her think I didn't care?

Did she know? Did she bring me all this way on purpose? No,

don't be silly, Mark. There are dreams and there are dreams. You just fell asleep and she left you again. She does that, remember? She waits until just the right moment and then walks away.

I shake my head and run my fingers through my hair. There's no need to start thinking like that. No need to go down that particular road again.

I wonder if I can stay on this sofa all day. The room looks normal. I like the room. I can relate to the room. Could do with a telly, but otherwise it's fine. There are no monsters or goblins or any of that shit in the room. The room is calm. The room is beige. The room is above The Axe Public House.

I'm the new Landlord of The Axe.

Nothing more.

All else is whisky.

I need my car. I need the pills inside which'll steady my head. I need my phone so I can call Jon and have him talk sense to me. I need a big fuck-off sausage roll to grease the cobwebs away.

I pull myself off the sofa and try to get steady on my feet. I walk over to the window and stand on tiptoes to see out. The sky is grey and casts an unending shadow across Dartmoor. I can't see a single soul, but at least it's not raining. At least I think it's not raining. I can't hear the raindrops hammering into my head.

Right.

A plan.

Walk to Long Barrow Ridge. Try not to get lost. Talk very nicely to Jennifer and get my car back. Take pills. Find garage and eat sausage roll. Talk to Jon. Kip on Jon's sofa for ever. It's this sort of plan which makes it worth getting up in the morning. Let's do it, and forget this sorry place ever existed. 'Make Natasha Bennett proud', of all things. Well, if she can't hang around when it gets weird then neither can I.

The Landlord of Peacebattle, indeed.

Saviour of the town where screams are holy.

I don't do responsibility, and I most certainly don't do screaming.

I open the door onto the landing and look out. It's quiet, with nothing moving. This is a good sign. The stairs sneak down to the right and round the corner to the ground floor. Everyone knows if you keep to the wall, you make less noise, so that's what I do. Step by step, foot by foot, I creep down. Don't make a move, don't make a sound, or the man will get you.

I get to the bottom of the stairs, and there it is, still and unmoving. The door to the cellar. Still no sound, and still no sign of anything out of the ordinary. I try and keep as far away from it as possible as I inch around, stuffing a couple of packets of crisps into my jacket as I do. It's fine. It's OK. Nothing's coming out. Nothing'll get me. I step behind the bar of The Axe and breathe a little easier. It smells musty and old, like it's held its breath in anticipation of a new Landlord for so long. I rest my hand again on a beer pump.

What a shame. This could have been good. If she'd have been straight with me, it would have been fine. I would have had games nights. Become friends with my regulars.

The friend to all, no matter their blood.

I might have even learned to play skittles. Slowly, I walk over to the skittles table, odd thing that it is. I could knock a few over now... no, Mark. Get out. Just get away.

The front door opens first time, thank God. Whatever fused them together yesterday is no longer working, and the cold December breeze invades my – no, the – pub. I do up my jacket, tightly. No turning back. Just walk.

I close the heavy door softly so as not to disturb anyone, and step out onto the gravel. The rain's not long gone, it seems, and the air is damp and fresh. Keep going. With purpose, I stride onto the lane, not intending to stop until I reach civilisation. I don't want to pause, but I do, just for a moment.

There's a sound, a quiet, deep and golden sound, and it's coming from the oak. The Life of Oak Cheating. It's calling to me. Breaking my hangover. It's judging me.

No.

I stride past and walk down the lane. The canopy of trees either side block out the cloud, and it seems twice as dark as it did a moment ago. Tiny streams of water flow down it, and the road's edges are coarse and torn. Every few steps I have to avoid a large pothole – gaping wounds in the earth. The lane gets steeper and narrower as I descend. Once or twice I almost lose my footing. This is mad, why am I doing this? The streams of water surging down the lane get thicker and deeper, as if all the water that's fallen on the moor has only this road through which to escape. The land seems to have sunken with the weight of the water, and mud and bracken litter my path.

I reach a corner, and it's impossible to go any further.

Shit.

The bridge, the Postman Pat style thing I faintly remember driving over, is underwater. Bits of branch and tree sweep past, and there's no way I can get over it.

Merry Christmas, Mark. It looks like you really are stuck in Oak Cheating for a while.

The oak looks smug as I shuffle back up the hill. Bastard thing. The Axe is still there, waiting for me to return, as a light drizzle starts to fall again. I don't care about the rain. It seems so small, compared to everything else. I'm not going back inside. Not just yet. I walk around the back of the pub, kicking every stone in my path, and take a seat on the soaked bars of the climbing frame in the beer garden. There are no birds, no wildlife, nothing to suggest there's anything alive nearby apart from me.

And a crash from the cellar. A barrel being dropped. I know that sound.

Do I go back inside?

Couldn't I just wait here?

I'm really beginning to get wet...

The steps to the cellar are just as steep as they were last night.

'So you're real, then. I didn't dream you?' I shout before I get to the bottom.

'Let's not go through all that again, lad. Thought we had enough of that last night.'

I turn to look at Emmet, standing in the shadows. I nod.

'How long have you been there?' I ask.

'Long enough. Changed a barrel. Had a couple after you went back last night. And my boss drank all my whisky. Bit of a bad head.'

'You and me both, mate.'

'I thought so.' He walks over to the wall and kicks a brick at thigh height. I step back again as the air seemed to crack in front of me and the door to The Grindstone appears. I can feel my fight or flight reflex kicking in yet again, but nevertheless I keep still. I can feel my hands clenching, trying beyond hope to make myself appear cool and fine with this.

'We need to talk, boss. There's a reason I needed a snifter last night. I wanted to let yer in gently.'

'...gently? You call that gentle? I thought I was crazy!'

'Gently. Yer sat down. Yer 'ad a drink. Met a few folk. But yer need to get up to speed. And quickly. Get your boxes in from outside and in yer come. I'll get yer a brandy.'

'I'm all right here, thanks. And it's nine in the morning, Emmet.'

'I've a shit load o' headache pills out back.'

'Fine. But no brandy.'

Emmet smiles. 'Coffee then. And bacon. And pills. I think we still have some. Just don't be too long. Yer know the way by now.' He disappears into the gap in between the air and The Grindstone. Yes, I know the way.

I take my time.

So it seems I wasn't going mad, and it was more memory than dream after all. There's a slight tingle in my fingers as, fifteen minutes and three cigarettes later, I follow Emmet back through to The Grindstone. The brickwork gives way to mottled stone, and the air tastes faintly of apples once more. I know what's behind the door at the end of the hall, and that may be what's keeping me from going through it. My fingers brush the black iron latch, but I need a moment if I'm going to lift it like I should.

I can hear him moving on the other side, and I can hear the sound of the heavy front door as it opens to the town of Dogwood Falls.

'You're early,' comes the muffled voice of my barman.

'Not early enough it seems, Mister Savage. Half the town is talking of the new Landlord. God knows what he thinks. Scraping the barrel a little, this time, wasn't she?'

The voice is lined and clipped, and speaks with the experience of an age spent in command.

'I'm sure he'll do,' says Emmet. 'He had a good rapport with folk last night, and he took his Licence well enough.'

'I see. Two arms and not three? Did she do that much right? And I expect you've got the Protection up again?'

'Secure. For the moment. The lad had a brief moment when he first arrived at The Axe, but it passed when Natasha and I got to him. And, yeah. He's just got the two arms. I checked.'

'Small mercies, I'll take them where I can. And where is Miss Bennett? I take for granted she briefed him before he arrived, did she not? Time is of the essence, as I keep trying to press onto the pair of you.'

There's a pause, and I try to keep my breathing still and quiet. I press my back to the wall and crouch so I can hear the answer.

'I don't know,' says Emmet. 'There were a shift in the balance and I haven't seen her since. The poor lad knew nothing when he arrived. First thing he saw was bloody Arnold in a grump.'

'For the love of God!' There's a crash as the old man smacks something – a stick, a cane – onto one of the tables. 'You are to keep him here at all costs, do you understand me, Mister Savage? He is not to step one foot outside that door. They'll come for him, you realise. He can invoke the Protection but it won't last long outside these walls and then where will we be, hmm?' Three more crashes on the table. 'Lost. Once. More.'

'I can't keep him here, Gorman. Not if he wants to go exploring. You should have seen him last night. Brave new world out there and all that.'

'Don't start with me, Emmettaman Savage. I remember where we found you, do you? The Rout of Ket? The Slaughter of the Gifted? Consider your place. We are days away from another Hundred Holy Wars and this Landlord of Peacebattle must be kept safe. Do you understand?'

I press my ear closer to the door as Emmet lowers his voice.

'What happened to Fox wasn't my fault.'

'Well it certainly wasn't mine. You, the Last of the Gifted, left him alone when you knew they were coming.'

'He told me to.'

'He was a fool.' The visitor – Gorman – sighs. 'And it cost him his life, and the lives of countless others both here and in the other place. Don't let it happen again. When will the GeoTroll be back?'

'Soon,' mutters Emmet. 'But he's not been the same since the Brothers converted his clan. He'd drink this place dry if he could.'

'I know,' says Gorman. 'But needs must. He'll help you protect the Breach whilst the boy learns the ropes. I'm convening the Council at the market on the harbour to try and get as many people off the island as we can. Then, we'll head to the Gate to stop this once and for all.'

'But the Incorporeal...?'

'Dammit, man!' There's another crash on the table. 'One job. Do you hear me? One job. Keep the boy safe. Protect him from the Scratching and stop it from leaching onto others. Do a better job than before. Do I make myself clear, sir?'

'Very.'

'Good. The *Book of Blackwood* is a hateful piece of spite and poison, but it gives a glimmer of hope there's a way out. Now I have work to do. And so do you.'

There's a shuffle and a slam. I crouch for a moment longer and contemplate lighting up in the hall. If I don't move my head doesn't hurt, and I don't have to understand the world.

The Scratching. He called it the Scratching, like I always knew he would. I rub my left arm, the scarlet thin lines still there from last night. Memories and dream. One and the same.

I don't know how, and I don't know why, but slowly I stand and place my hand on the latch. More than coffee, more than pills, the man on the other side of the door has a mission that's far more important and for the first time I know that all of this is real.

Emmettaman Savage. Last of the Gifted.

Protect me from the Scratching.

Chapter X

The Protection of Dogwood Falls

'So,' I say, as I step through the door. 'Bacon.' My barman looks at me and blinks his eyes in puzzlement.

'Bacon?' he asks, cleaning a glass with another from his endless pile of tea towels.

'Bacon,' I reply. 'You promised.' Emmet puts down the glass and sighs.

'Aye, so I did. Sorry, lad,' he says tossing the towel onto his shoulder in time-honoured tradition. 'I got distracted by something.'

There are two green mugs on the bar, chipped and patterned with fingerprints and watermarks. Inside each is a thick black liquid which looks like it's been piped from the ground. I point at it.

'Coffee,' says Emmet with a nod. 'Special brew. Good for the head.'

I take a tentative sniff, which widens my eyes and dulls the ache. Fine, I'll take whatever I can get. It tastes deep and bitter and remains in my mouth for longer than it should. But straight away I start to feel a little more human.

'Thanks,' I say to my inhuman friend. 'It's good.'

'No it's not, but cheers fer the thought.'

I sit on one of the stools facing the bar, as Emmet restarts his polishing. In the light, The Grindstone looks different, if no less strange for a different sun streaming through the windows. A Jacob's Ladder of peach and gold almost bounces off the wooden floor, bathing it in puddles of light that seem to struggle staying put where they fall. It's mesmerising. I think I'm almost glad I'm not going mad. Which, if you think about it for too long, can itself be one of the first signs of madness.

I take another sip of coffee. Whilst the light is enchanting, the atmosphere is not. I stare at the bar rather than meet my barman's eye. No. Enough of this. I can't be doing with silence.

'These mugs,' I say as I struggle for some other form of words. The elephant remains in the room.

'Aye,' says Emmet. 'What about them?' 'For an orange bloke who can't stop polishing shit, they're a bit grubby.' He puts down the glass and picks up his coffee.

'Don't bring the colour of my skin into it, boss,' he says as he takes a sip. 'You're supposed to be above that.'

'Sorry...'

'Right.' Another sigh. 'That's Fox's mug yer drinkin' out of. Mugs ain't for polishing. Not like glasses. Yer not supposed to see the whites of yer eyes in a mug.'

'You have no whites of your eyes, Emmet.'

'That's beside the point.' There's thirty seconds of more silence as I feel him looking at me, almost weighing up the sums in his head. This time, however, it's him that speaks first.

'He weren't much of a coffee drinker, was Fox,' he says as he places a glass in the rack above his head and reaches for another.

'No?'

'No. He said you could get too used to it, and before long you weren't at yer best unless yer'd had a shot. He used to say the Landlord o' Peacebattle needed to be focused all the time. Anything which distracted from that had no place under this roof.'

'He sounds a right barrel of laughs,' I mutter.

'Aye,' says Emmet. 'And he were my friend as well as my boss, so no pressure.'

I sniff as I put the mug back down on the bar.

'Well, this Landlord needs a smoke. Do you mind?' He shakes his head, and I'm soon drawing it in. There are times for manners, and there are mornings like this. 'So what happened to him?' I ask.

Another glass is brought down and checked for watermarks that aren't there.

'He called Time. Everyone's is called at some point. But I tell you this, lad, it's a Landlord's privilege to choose when to ring the bell.'

'And did he choose?'

'I fought with 'im no end, but aye. He chose. Sent me away. Sent Natasha to you.'

Neither of us says anything as I stub out the fag and finish the coffee. I push Fox's mug back across the bar towards Emmet. It sits there, and waits for us.

'How?' I ask, finally. He looks at me, and the coal of his eyes blink twice.

'What do you mean, how?' he says.

'I mean, How? Why did Fox choose to call Time? Why am I now here, talking to you? Why did she come looking for me, and what's happened to her?' I look at him and keep my voice low. 'It's time for answers, Emmet. The bloke last night. The bloke this morning.'

'You heard?'

'I did.'

'Yer weren't meant to.'

'Bit of an oversight, given the coffee you'd made me.'

'True,' he says. 'I guess Gorman's voice does carry a bit.'

I rub my arm, the stings from the scratches not as angry as they were yesterday but just as distracting. Emmet nods at them, and his eyes tighten.

'Y'know, all things considered, boss, yer not doing badly so far.'

'What do you mean?'

'Yer arm. Last night I were in the cellar when you arrived. Lucky, really. He must have attuned himself quicker than ever.'

'Who?'

He waves his tea towel at me. 'Fox always said it came to him in the quiet seconds between breaths. Just at the back of his mind, y'know? And in the darkness before he went to sleep. He said there were whisperings he finally got under control, but it took him time and more than he wanted.' He takes another glass and begins to polish. 'I were brought here soon after he was,' he continues. 'Just after it started.'

I go to speak but Emmet raises his finger. He goes on. 'He couldn't cope at first, even though he'd got more of a briefing than you. Things were a bit more normal back then, of course. Less stressy. The Council were a bit calmer.'

'The Council?'

'The Council of the Wounded. Our employers. The chap who was in here earlier – Gorman Duran, their Chairman. He's never been an easy bloke to impress, but one of these days, y'never know.

'Anyway,' he says, moving his attention to a stubborn mark on the bar which refuses to leave, 'This were all about thirty years ago – so you can see why folk wanted to see the new Landlord on yer first night – but I can still hear his screams. It got into his head, like it got into yours.'

'The Scratching,' I say, lighting the cigarette. It helps.

'The Scratching,' Emmet replies. 'No one knew what it was, back then. Took us all a bit by surprise and no one more than Fox. We just thought he was mental, at first, until he took the fruit knife from behind the bar. Did you hear the words, lad? In yer head?'

I think back to last night, when all was new and the future was Dartmoor, and nod. Emmet stops his cleaning and walks around to my side of the bar. He sits next to me and rests his elbows on the aged wooden surface.

'It eventually died down, with me here able to control it. The Scratching's a Remnant from the Hundred Holy Wars. There's a few left here and there, haunting the wilderness between worlds. Elemental forces to be shaped and forged if yer know how – and there are folk out there who've been working on them for years. It's a dangerous one, this Remnant. Y'see, it's the manifestation of the urge to...'

'Harm yourself,' I say without thinking. 'To make yourself scream until it's the last breath you take.'

'Aye,' says Emmet as he reaches for his cold coffee. I put my head in my hands and stare at the floor. I can see where this is heading.

Becky.

None of this makes any sense. Elemental forces and shit. Remnants. But I think back to when I woke up, and it feels real. I rub my arm once more.

'You can cope though, boss,' says Emmet as he puts his arm around my shoulders. I can feel the downy hairs on his arms bristle, and I feel a little stronger for them. 'You and me, we'll cope together. That's my job y'see. To protect the Landlord o' Peacebattle from shit like that. I've got a bit of a gift.' He taps the side of his head. 'Works a treat. Fer the most part.'

'For the most part?' I reply, with a raised eyebrow. He shrugs and I stretch his arm away and walk to the window. My hand rests on the cold iron handle as I stare at my crooked reflection in the lead-lined glass.

All that stares back is me.

'I'm the Landlord of The Axe. Nothing more,' I say, looking into my own eyes and ignoring the world beyond them. 'And then only until the flood dies down. After that, I'm gone.'

'Yer the Landlord of Peacebattle, lad. An Embodiment of the Union – the representation of peace through knowledge.'

I spin round to face him. 'What does that even mean?' I shout. 'You keep calling me that – the bloke last night called me that – but it's all shit isn't it?' I wave my arms around. 'All this, it's not right. It's bollocks. I'm a bloke from Staunton who finally, finally, did something different. They told me to move on, and I did. Look where it got me. I tell you this, mate, the next time I see Natasha Bennett, I'm going to bloody kill her.'

At the mention of Nat's name, Emmet's face falls to the floor and he shakes his head.

'She...'

'What?' I ask.

He stands and walks over. His eyes cast over me, head to foot. He twists the handle and opens the door. The scent of apples washes in, and the sound of the waves sweeps away the tension.

'You're a Landlord all right,' he finally says, as he closes his eyes and breathes in the air of Dogwood Falls. Do you know how long I've been working alongside them?' I shake my head. Besides the bad Meat Loaf T-shirt and the faded baseball cap on his head, Emmet's face is oddly timeless. He has a couple of lines around his eyes, and those you'd expect around his mouth, but nothing to give him away. I shake my head. 'Coming close to a hundred years now, thirty of them behind that bar.'

He sniffs as he registers the surprise on my face.

'You're...'

'Comin' up to middle age now, aye,' he says.

'And I thought I'd been a barman for too long.'

'You ain't seen nothing yet, lad, so trust me when I've said I've seen a lot.' He walks out into the street. Cautiously, I follow. The breeze comes in from the cliff and runs through my hair. I shiver and thrust my hands into my jean pockets. Emmet walks to the wall across from The Grindstone where he turns to look at me.

'Peacebattle Lane, Dogwood Falls. The spot where it started and the spot where the Hundred Holy Wars came to an end. All your fault, of course.'

'My fault? Fuck off, I've only just got here!'

He shrugs and adjusts his cap, straightening the cuts of orange hair that poke from the front.

'Well, sort of your fault. The Book says he was a bloke like you, from a town called Babworth.' He looks up, as the blue morning sky begins to darken. He frowns. 'Ichabod Blackwood called himself the First Pilgrim. Some say he'd been bewitched. Others say he was the devil himself. Who knows? What we do know is that him and his band – through the power of prayer, they say – cracked nature apart on that very spot.'

I turn to look at The Grindstone. The squat little building looks older than it did a moment ago, with the inside a dark mess of shadows fighting for light.

'Inside the pub?' I ask.

'Well, it weren't a pub back then, this were hundreds of years ago.' Emmet grunts. 'Can you imagine? Maybe it would have changed things if it had been.' There's a clap of thunder and I look up. In the distance, there are clouds forming. But these aren't grey, or white.

They're purple.

'We ought to get inside,' he says. 'They're building again. They probably know you're here now.'

'I'm a popular chap,' I say. 'But carry on. I asked for answers, Emmet, and I'm not going back in there until I have them.'

'Really?' he says, pointing at the clouds forming on the horizon. He takes off his cap and runs his arm across his forehead. 'Because the Incorporeal aren't going to wait for you.'

'Emmet, this is what I'm talking about! Incorporeal?'

He stabs at the clouds with his finger.

'I'm not worried,' I shout. 'I have you to protect me, don't I?'

'Get back in the pub, Mark.'

'No.'

'Please, boss!'

I take a couple of steps up the hill towards the clouds which are forming and reforming above us. The purple smoke swirls and flows, surging towards us on tidal flows of wind.

'What are they?'

'They're converts, and they're hungry for more. You don't want to be converted, lad, believe me. You'll be killed, but still be alive. You'll scream and keep on screaming. Screaming starts the Scratching...'

'...and Scratching starts the night,' I mutter.

'Yes!' he shouts. 'You know the words, they're inside your head! Now come on!' I look at him and hear the rumble getting louder in the sky.

'The Landlord of Peacebattle...'

'Protects the breach Blackwood opened! He started the Hundred Holy Wars – so fierce every nation from every world hated each other. He thought he'd found Eden, Mark, and everyone here was a gift from God put here to service him and his followers. Blackwood's been dead fer hundreds of years but his followers remain and they're growing. The pubs are there so folk can interact and know each other again. Like I said, you're here to spread peace through knowledge, now come on back inside!'

The clouds have reached the top of the hill, and they're falling, rolling across the ground and relentlessly coming towards us. I get this now, we have to move. I allow Emmet to take my hand and drag me back towards The Grindstone. The rumble's become a roar that's nipping at my heels as we leg it towards the solid door of the pub. Emmet races through first, and I fall on the ground by his feet. He slams it shut, and the roar subsides.

Safe.

I try to catch my breath, but every one I take seems forced and laboured. 'That...' I gasp.

'Yeah,' Emmet says as he leans against the door. 'Don't worry, they can't get in, that's what yer Licence is for.' He catches his breath, and slides down to sit on the floor. Soon, all I can hear is our breathing. 'Answers,' he says, finally. 'Yer a plug. The protection of Dogwood Falls, keeping the link between the Oak and Dogwood. Remove the Landlord, remove the protection. The Scratching gets through to Oak Cheating and then to yer world. Perpetual screaming, forevermore. Everyone you know and everywhere you look. Blackwood's descendants, the Binding Brothers, removed Fox's Licence, and now they'll be after yours.'

'I think I'll have that drink now, Emmet,' I say.

'I think I'll join you, boss.' He gets up and pours us both a drink, which I take with both hands and return to the window. The Incorporeal have returned to the sky, and swirl above our heads. They remind me of a swarm of starlings, moving as one and dancing silently above us. They're vultures, waiting for the carrion hiding in their public house.

I raise the glass to my lips but pause. Something's...

Scratching.

The glass smashes at my feet, as I lose control and fall backwards. I raise my fists to my temples to block out the sound. As my head crashes backwards, I sense Emmet rushing towards me but he's failed, I know beyond hope that he's failed. As my fingers begin to draw against my skin, the only sense I have is the voice in my head of the Man with the Crab-Like Feet.

> *Scratching then Scratching then Scratching some more.*
> *Scratching your Soul and your Self through your core.*
> *The Landlord will Scream and his Screaming will call*
> *The Brothers that Bind. Oak and Dogwood will fall.*

CHAPTER XI
THE SONG OF THE GRINDSTONE

The dreams are milky this time.

At the edge of mankind, all nature will weep.

There's a mixture of voices, and it takes a moment to realise I'm hearing one for real.

For the blood of the Landlord will flow thick and deep.

The patterns of light float in the darkness and slowly, to make sure I know how to stay sane, I open my eyes. 'There you are,' says Joan as she puts a bacon sandwich on the living room table. It's Sunday. Of course it is. She's wearing her sermon collar and blouse. 'I was beginning to get tired of tip-toeing around the sofa. What time did you get in last night?'

'I don't know,' I murmur and sit up, wiping the sleep from my eyes. 'About three, I think.'

Three hands he will have, and two voices to cry.

The sandwich oozes brown sauce. I remember dreaming of bacon. How did she know? 'Do you have any coffee?' I ask.

'Of course,' she sings. 'What do you think I am?' She takes a leather placemat from the pile by the fireplace and puts it on the table. A couple of seconds later, there's a mug of black coffee sitting on it.

'Thanks,' I manage between mouthfuls. Joan takes a sip of tea but keeps moving, picking papers from every corner of the room and not showing any sign of slowing down despite pushing sixty.

'Drink up,' she says, as she stuffs four hardback study guides into her black holdall. 'You've been asleep forever. You need a shower before church. I'm leaving in about ten minutes, and you can grab a lift if you're quick.'

I slump back on her well-worn sofa, the ends frayed and the pattern faded. This doesn't get any easier. She pauses briefly as I yawn, to fix the small silver crucifix I bought her ten years ago around her neck.

At the sign of the cross hanging deep in the sky.

Joan takes another drink and sighs, resigned to my look. 'Well, if you're not coming again, then at least can you do the washing up? I've invited the Donalds round for Sunday lunch. You'd be a great help if you'd get the potatoes ready for me.'

'I'll try,' I say, 'but I'm back at work again at twelve.'

This time, she stops. 'They're working you too hard.'

'I signed a form. It's fine.'

'No it's not. I worry about you.' She walks over, places her bag down on the floor, and sits on the arm of the sofa. 'You're practically living at that place these days. It's not good for your health. You'll end up killing yourself if you're not careful.'

I run my hands through my hair. Maybe I do need a shower after all.

'It keeps me busy,' I say, as I lean away from her, conscious of my breath. 'And I enjoy it. I feel I'm helping people.'

'Hmm,' says Joan, pursing her lips, and repressing a smile. 'Mrs Donald wouldn't approve, so I won't tell her if you peel me some spuds.' She taps me on the nose.

'Yes mum,' I grin.

'And don't call me mum.' She stands, adjusts her dog collar, and pulls her bag onto her shoulder. 'How do I look?'

'Sunday best,' I smile. She moves to the door, but I call just as she walks into the hall. 'Joan?' She pops her head back into the living room.

'Whatever it is, you can tell me on the way, you know.'

'Still working.'

'I know, but I have to try. What is it?'

She's double dried her hair today. There must be a Christening or something. I take a deep breath.

'They've offered me the room above Fortnights. They say I can move in next week.'

Joan takes a moment to place her bag back onto the floor, and crouches in front of me.

'Are you going to go?'

I pause and look at her. 'I think so, yes. If that's OK.'

She glances down for the briefest of moments, and smiles. But I've seen that smile before.

'Of course it's OK,' she says. 'You have to do what you think is right, Mark. And if that place will make you happy at last, then you should take the chance. But think about it, for a few days, will you? There's more to life than that pub, and you've got a future beyond Porter Street, despite what you think now.' She stands, after some trouble, and kisses me on the forehead. 'And you know you've always got a bed here. If you ever decide to use it.'

I smile and squeeze her hand. 'I'll peel your potatoes,' I say, 'but no talking to Mrs Donald about me.'

'Be good and I won't have to!'

I wave her goodbye and watch her drive away. A couple more hours until I'm back behind the bar and king of the pub lunch.

I've a good feeling about this. I think they're finally taking me seriously at the pub. Time to get off this sofa and make something of my life.

There's time for a quick nap, right?

Just a little sleep.

Scratching.

'I need to see the Landlord.'

The voice is deep and coarse. This is no longer Sunday.

'He's resting,' says Emmet. 'He's new, so give him a break. Now what can I get you?'

This is no longer Staunton. I keep my eyes shut.

'You can get me a Landlord. I've heard he's here, the new one.'

I slowly open one eye and adjust to the light of The Grindstone. Emmet lay me down on a bench by the door after the last attack which ended as abruptly as it started with a flash of Emmet's eyes and a press of his palm. Gifted is an understatement. It's true. Emmet's the one who gives protection to the Protection of Dogwood Falls.

The man's breathing is erratic, and his palm opens and clenches every few seconds.

107

'Please,' he rasps. 'You don't understand. I've seen it. I've seen The Book and now I've...'

Emmet raises one finger and the man stutters to a halt.

'Firstly,' he says, 'yer need to calm down a little.' He gestures to the stool in the middle of the bar. 'Sit.'

'But...'

'Sit. Yer in my bar. Now sit.' The man shuffles his feet forward and collapses onto the stool which groans – for a brief moment – before adjusting itself to the man's weight. It grows upwards, until he's at the perfect height to rest his elbows on the bar.

'Good.' Emmet glances over to me in the shadows and briefly shakes his head. 'Secondly,' he says as he pumps a heady ale into a dimpled and expertly polished glass, 'steady yer hands on something. Here.' He places the ale in front of the stranger. 'Drink up. It's as new as the Landlord. Now what's yer name?'

'Darion. My name's Darion.'

'I thought it was. Yer Anya's son, aren't you?' Darion nods. Emmet picks up a tea towel and a new glass. 'I were sorry to hear of yer father. He were a good man.'

'He was too young,' Darion whispers, clutching his glass with both hands. 'He was supposed to retire, and spend his life in the garden.'

'Aye,' nods Emmet. 'There's many that were. Yer not the only lad that's sat where you are now, lamenting what might have been.'

'But I'm the only one that's going to do something about it. Have you seen them? The Incorporeal? They're swarming.' Darion's voice grows. 'It won't be long now, you know. It's happening and there's only one thing that'll stop it!'

Emmet raises one more finger and there's silence.

'Now, lad,' he says. 'Enough of that. How have you read The Book? No one's read it outside The Brotherhood or The Council in generations. And I know yer not in the Council, and you don't look the religious type.'

'There was a rubbing in my dad's things. He was a historian with links to the old days.'

'Yer should be careful of links to the old days,' Emmet says, taking time over each word. 'The old days keep track of those who remember, and never let 'em forget.'

'But the old days will stop the new, barman. Unless I see the Landlord right now. I mean it, you spikey haired...'

I cough, politely.

Darion spins round on his stool and leaps to his feet, poised and tense. His hands spring open and shut, open and shut, as he stares at my shadow.

'Can I help you, sir?' I state plainly, finding the voice of a Friday Night Staunton.

'Were you...'

'Sitting right here? Yep. You should look around before raising your voice. Some of us were trying to sleep.'

'You?' He looks me up and down, wiping the sweat from his brow. 'You're the Landlord of Peacebattle?'

'Apparently so.' I look at Emmet and catch him rolling his eyes.

'I was expecting a hero!'

'And I was expecting a dartboard and *Country Life Magazine*. I'm not sure of your point.' Darion turns to look behind the bar, where Emmet nods approvingly, and crosses his arms.

'They can't be allowed to get you,' says Darion. He begins rocking on his heels, one foot in front of the other.

'They won't.' I tell him, trying to believe the words as I say them. 'I've got the best staff in Dogwood Falls.' I keep eye contact with him, but sense Emmet rise by an inch.

'You need to leave,' he mutters under his breath. I take a step forward and he takes one back.

'Tell me about it,' I say. 'But I can't at the moment. There's nowhere to go.'

'One way or another,' Darion growls, 'you have to go.'

He reaches into his dark and muddy jacket and pulls out a six-inch blade. The hairs on Emmet's arms spring upright and glisten sharply under the lights of the bar. I step back as Darion paces the room in front of me. There's a crack of thunder outside.

'You hear that, Landlord?' he shouts. 'They're getting ready for you. They're preparing you! I've read it. I've seen it and know.

You've tasted the Scratching. Tell me, you've tasted the Scratching and lived!'

I nod, backing away to the door. Emmet starts inching his way to the end of the bar, his arms on guard.

'Put the knife down, lad,' he says with a grim and fateful tone. 'You don't want to start a fight in here. No one starts a fight in The Grindstone. Anya should have told yer better.'

'But I've no choice!' the man shouts, swinging the blade between us with one hand as he wipes tears away with the other. 'It's written. I saw it.

'At the edge of mankind, all nature will weep, for the blood of the Landlord will flow thick and deep. *Your* blood, Landlord! We have to stop them, so I'm spilling it first, y'hear? I'm going to save the world!' He lunges at me, but I dart out of the way, and throw a stool into his path. Emmet swings from a bar post and swipes at him, catching him with two sharpened arm hairs which impale deep into his shoulder. Darion cries out and takes a thrust at Emmet, but he ducks and rolls over to the door. I hold my palms in front of me.

'Darion, we can sort this out, mate,' I shout, as he upends a table from the centre of the pub. We dance around each other in a circle, Emmet trying to advance but stepping back with every wave of the knife. Darion rests one hand on his injured shoulder and matches us step for step until he stands with his back to the open door. The sky crackles with thunder, but without lightning to precede it. There's no sky beyond the dark purple mesh of the Incorporeal circling overhead.

'Quick,' says Emmet. 'Yer Licence. Use it!'

'What?' I turn to him, a moment distracted, and Darion's on me, wrestling me to the ground. I feel the knife on my throat, but Emmet pulls him off, another few spines impaled in his back. Darion cries out in pain and the thunder replies.

'Use it!' shouts Emmet, gasping for breath. 'Say the words! For discord and schism, for those you have scarred.'

I pant on my knees, clutching my throat.

'Do it!' he cries.

'For discord and schism,' I wheeze, 'for those you have

scarred... The Grindstone disowns whom the Landlord has barred!'
I raise my hand towards Darion. 'The Grindstone disowns...' He
looks at me, and his eyes search for pity.

'Please...' he whispers. 'For my family. For yours...'

'Whom the Landlord has barred!'

The black crystals sunken into the walls of The Grindstone
glimmer and gleam like a thousand eyes all staring at Darion. The
shadows deepen and the glass starts to sing with a solitary note
that seems to shine. Emmet stands and his hairs flatten against his
body. He folds his arms and shakes his head.

'I'm sorry, lad.'

The song of the glass rises in pitch and Darion drops the knife.
He clasps his hands against his ears and spins to look at the door.
The wooden frame starts to warp and grow, distorting itself as
if seen through the uneven windows either side. It stretches the
building, making the walls melt and seep in to make room. When
the door reaches the roof, it stops.

And there's silence.

Darion takes one, impassioned, look at me.

'No...' he whispers.

With a boom he's snapped through the door, an elastic puppet
strung too tight. He flies backward at impossible speeds, until he's
lifted over the wall and disappears the other side of Peacebattle
Lane.

I fall to the floor as the door returns to normal and The
Grindstone returns to peace.

'What the fuck just happened?' I ask, looking up at Emmet as
he brushes himself down. He frowns as he picks out the new holes
in his T-shirt, but crouches down in front of me.

'Last bit of yer induction,' he states. 'Are yer good in a fight,
boss? There's a fair few to come.'

'I... I... I used to have doormen,' I say, eventually. 'Policy was
to let them...'

'Yeah, never mind, eh?' He stands up, and rights the table and
chairs. 'Yer protect the Breach between worlds, Mark. Yer need
to be able to chuck out anyone that might harm you, or anything
this place stands for. The Binding Brothers removed Fox's Licence,

so they removed him. You still have yours, so you can remove anyone who troubles you.'

I sit for a moment. I need a cigarette.

'Is he alright?' I ask. Emmet adjusts a chair and pats it with an apologetic tap.

'Oh he's fine,' he says eventually, getting my drift.

'The thing... the magic thing...' I rub my eyes, 'it whacked him out a fair way.'

'About a mile.' He returns to the bar. 'It lands them in the harbour. Dogwood Falls ain't a town, it's an island, and you've just sent Darion for a little swim, that's all. He's fine – but he can't set foot in here again. That's the rule. Once you're barred, you're barred forever, unless your Licence is revoked.'

I slowly get to my feet and run my fingers through my hair. I need a drink – I've no idea what time it is, but I don't care. I grab a tumbler and knock back a whisky.

'Is there anything else she didn't tell me, Emmet?' He looks at me for a moment, before taking a glass himself. He holds it to the light and inspects it for fingerprints. He gives a satisfied grunt and pours himself a glass. He knocks his against mine.

'I think we're there, boss.' He downs the drink in one. 'I think we're there.'

Chapter XII
The Soul of Days Gone By

Around year six or seven of my old life, my former boss – a chap named Adrian with mousey hair and a guilt complex – sat me down for a career chat.

He started doing this three or four times a year. It was, he said, part of his own 'managerial objectives' to see me grow as a person.

He tried quite hard, bless him.

A couple of weeks a year I'd cover for his holidays – my own pub to play with, my own army of students to order around. Every time, Adrian would come back for a debrief. What did I do whilst he was away? How did it feel to be in overall charge?

I'd shrug my shoulders. It was fine, nothing happened. Once or twice I'd have to give 'the talk' to someone. 'Don't be late again or I'll tell Adrian.' 'If I hear you call a customer a fucktard again, Adrian will know.' Nothing out of the ordinary.

He'd sigh and ask me why I didn't want to do anything with my life, and time and again I'd tell him I'd got where I wanted. I was perfectly happy. Just let me be. And his message was always the same.

'Show leadership, Mark. Make the right choices. Take charge.'

I'm not going back inside, I've decided.

Leadership. Choices. Charge.

The Axe's whisky supply is surprisingly large for a pub that's perpetually closed.

It's Christmas next week. You wouldn't really know it, to look at this place. I wonder if they actually celebrate Christmas in Dogwood Falls.

Probably not.

Leadership. Choices. Charge.

I think, if I play my cards right, I can sit under the Life of Oak

Cheating for ever.

When I was 17, my mother told me smoking would kill me one day. She found a packet of reds in my jacket pocket whilst looking for a lottery ticket. It turned out the craziest I'd seen her so far wasn't actually the craziest she could get.

There were several things thrown at me that night, and it would be the last time, of the many that had come before, that I would slam the door to our flat behind me. I didn't speak to her for two years after that. There was no more of her emotional blackmail. No more reporting in at all hours of the day or night, and no more pans thrown at my head on one of her bad days. I'd moved on. I'd made the hard choices and taken charge of my life for the very first time.

Leadership. Choices. Charge.

Of course, the next time I did speak to her, two years later, she couldn't speak back. It was the calmest conversation I'd had with her since I was a little boy.

Clare and I turned off her life support machine a few minutes after I'd spoken those final few words: a soft, gentle explanation of why things had turned out the way they did.

She knew how I really felt, of course. Deep down, where it mattered, without the usual shit that came out whenever we spoke. I didn't have to say it, but I did anyway, quietly. At the end of the day I was her son and I think what scared her most as she stood on the stained concrete balcony that last Sunday together, was that she knew I could be as stubborn as her. Once we'd dug ourselves in and bunkered down then that'd be it. Come hell or high water we weren't going to change. She'd smoked all her life, and out of sheer pig headiness she kept on smoking precisely because other people were telling her to stop. And, likewise, because she told me to stop I never have done.

I'll stop when I want to.

I'll 'develop myself' when I want to.

Get a new job when I want to.

Take charge. When I want to.

'The cigarettes will kill you, Mark.'

I doubt that very much.

The Axe & Grindstone

It's just before half four in the afternoon, and the meagre sunlight has pretty much gone. The base of the judging old oak tree has long since grown warm with my body heat, but now the chill's beginning to really bite. But still, I'm staying here, nestled in between two roots which grow, thick and strong, as an oval seat on the ground filled with moss and wood chippings. The branches, even though their leaves lie discarded and forgotten all around me, still form a tight knit canopy above my head. It's my new shelter from the world – from the worlds plural. The Life of Oak Cheating has seen a lot. It's survived a lot. Maybe if I stay cuddled in its base like this it'll protect me too. It's worth a shot. I've got to pick up these things where I can.

I'm still not going inside.

The corkscrew of my trusted Waiter's Friend snaps back and forth with a solid click. It feels secure and an extension of my hand. From the top left-hand side, I pull out the inch-long serrated blade, used to cut the seals from wine bottles, and run it along my finger. The power of the Scratching's weak, but still at the back of my mind. It taunts, with the never-ending question. What if, Mark? What if?

I snap it shut and wedge the tool back in my pocket. The inscription written by my friends burns as it rests there, hidden and false. I won't be needing it anytime soon.

Leadership. Choices. Charge.

The sad thing is, I could do it if she were here.

Joan always said she brought out the best in me. I remember the first time I saw Natasha Bennett – one of the only people at Fortnights I didn't personally employ. Two hours into her first shift, and she owned the bar. Every pint, every bottle, every drunkard.

Every barman.

They say I have a purpose now. They say I am the dream. They say I'm the one to bring the world together and stop it from screaming.

But this dream no longer has a dream of his own.

On a hazy summer's day, we sat under a tree like this one, old and gnarled. Rounders wasn't her game, and it sure as hell wasn't mine, so while the other bar staff got sweaty, we sat in the shade eating mini scotch eggs and drinking spirits out of cans. The sun was warm, and the park was full of endless possibility. The afternoon stretched on until the gin ran dry, and the memory remains as crisp and as vivid as the colour of her lipstick that day.

She had something on her mind, so she was there but distant, and no matter of teasing would get her to share. People used to think we were a couple, you know, and that afternoon surrounded by laughter and games it was a little easier to pretend. As the sun set on our picnic, it was my best chance to make it a reality.

Show leadership. Make the right choices. Take charge.

No. She was gone a week later.

It's starting to rain again, as if the sky thought the dry spell was boring, but I don't care. I'm not going back inside. The pub is cursed as is the damn breach of nature in the cellar. I'd rather get wet than have another freak threaten my life, or try to end it myself. No. There's a line, and I'm never crossing it ever again.

A breeze rustles the branches above me, and something drops into my lap. It's small, cold, and... shining.

It's an acorn.

What the...

An acorn. In December?

I stand up, pushing my hands against the tree. The tree is warm – not through the transfer of my heat to its bark, but through something else. What the...

I step back and look at the acorn in my hand. It glistens, and it sings. It glows in my head, and the song draws me to the tree. I place my hand back onto its trunk, its hard mottled surface scratchy against my palm. It's warm. A warm tree. I place both my hands on it now, at chest height, at head height, to the sides above and below and all around as I walk in a circle pressing myself into it.

Leadership. Choices. Charge. I place the side of my face against the bark. I know it seems weird, but at the same time it seems weirder not to. There's nothing more natural to me right here and right now than to do this. My ear presses against the side, then my cheek, then my nose and I close my eyes. In the cold December afternoon, it feels like that warm June day, with the sun beaming down on my skin. Once again, I feel wrapped within it and it seems to slowly draw the cold and the gloom and all the bad thoughts from wherever I've been storing it inside. And there's a sense – what is it? There's a sense of...

Leadership. Choices. Charge.

Strength. Security. Steadfastness.

...strength and security. Of the Life of Oak Cheating, an unmovable object standing watch throughout the years. Years and years of Previous before me. Of choices being made. Of steadfastness through unsurmountable odds. And most of all, of warmth. The warmth of community, of breaking bread, and breaking barriers. The warmth of making friendships and, more importantly, of being the person through whom other friendships are made.

Years of history course through me, through sense and smell and thought, and I suddenly start to understand. This isn't something you walk away from. I could run down that lane and keep running through the dark. I could run through the flood waters and across the moor. I could run for ever – the Landlord of Peacebattle who never again sets foot in Peacebattle Lane. I could be stubborn once more and say that as I wasn't given the choice, the role isn't mine to play. I could dig in and do whatever the opposite of what's expected of me.

I could do all of this, but I know I'd lose my very soul.

I gasp for air, and step back. I can still feel its touch even through I'm now a foot away.

Woah.

I stand for a minute. Two minutes. The timers on the outside lamps of The Axe flicker on, and as the orange bulbs start to warm through, their glow starts to cast my shadow onto the two roots which made up my moss-covered seat. I step forward again and touch the nearest branch but get nothing but hard, cold and damp wood. I step forward again to try and replicate that feeling – the feeling that's picked me up and shaken me so much. But the touch of the tree just brings memory now. It's almost like its message has been delivered, and now it has to rest. It stands there, as it's always stood there, and looks down on me: its newest son and its newest ward. I look at my Christmas Acorn, grasp it in my fist, and place it in my pocket. It'll look after me. It'll be there for me. The Life of Oak Cheating with me wherever I am. It's sung to me. I know it to be true.

Show leadership. Make the right choices. Take charge.

Right. Pucker up, Mark.

I run down the stairs to the cellar, two at a time, stride into the darkness and switch on the light. All normal, nothing out of place. Without breaking my step, I walk over to the back wall and kick the brick at shin height. Ow – there's got to be an easier way to do this. The air crackles and sings with the smell of old brick dust as it once again splits in two and reveals the back corridor to The Grindstone behind it. One foot forward, then another, then another and I'm back behind the bar. Deep breaths. Strength, security, steadfastness.

'Arnold. The usual?' I don't stop. I can't stop. Pint glass, on bar, fill with cherry brandy. God that man is huge. I twirl the bottle – my equivalent of an A Level and a second-class degree – and drop it back perfectly into place without a drop of sweat.

The GeoTroll just looks at me.

'Ta,' grunts Arnold, finally as he picks up the glass.

And that's that.

'Where's Emmet then?' I ask my regular, trying my hardest to look him in the eyes.

'Out,' says Arnold, his large green-grey forehead crinkled with lines.

'That it?' I reply. 'You don't say much, do you, fella?'

'Nope,' he flatly states whilst bringing the pint glass in his huge hands up to his chapped, coarse thick lips.

'And he left you in charge, did he?'

'Yep.'

'Right.' I can't let myself be distracted, or I'll procrastinate. 'I need to see Emmet. I have to see this Council of his.' Arnold looks at me and slowly places his empty glass back on the bar.

'Good,' he growls. 'Work to be done.'

'What work?' I ask. 'This is the kind of thing I need to know. Emmet says my Licence keeps me safe for the time being. But fuck it, it's not good enough. I know what's at stake now. I know about the Scratching and – more than that...' I trail off, thinking about the acorn in my pocket. 'More than that, I know my part in it. The convener. The man through whom friendships are made.'

I can still feel the warmth of the oak tree, and the sense of community. It's new, yet old. A feeling you'd never find anywhere but behind a bar which straddles two worlds and brings them together.

'And it's me, isn't it? I'm the one they must get past in order to infect everybody. The papers were asking all sorts of questions about it. Said something must be causing it. And if I'm right, then it happened just as Fox was taken. Three weeks without a Landlord in place. Three weeks with no plug. Three weeks where the hole in the sink hasn't been filled. It's out there already. And this is my first time as an Embodiment. Expect I'll be a little... leaky.'

'Leaky's fine, lad. Fer now.' Emmet stands in the open door, a pile of papers under his arm. 'Leaky will do for the moment. You'll do alright.'

He comes in and drops the papers on the booth by the door.

'I want to see your Council,' I say to him. 'I need to know what their plan is.'

'Maybe you don't need to know the plan,' he says, trying to bring himself to my height. 'Maybe your part of the plan is to stay put and stay here.'

'And maybe that plan isn't working. Didn't seem to work for the last bloke.' I walk over to the door of The Grindstone and take a deep breath as I see another purple cloud roll across the sky. It's time to explore this new world and embrace this promotion. It's time to meet Gorman face to face and get the answers I'm due.

It's time to take charge.

CHAPTER XIII
THE SCREAM OF THE HARBOUR'S EDGE

His instructions are clear. No sightseeing. No distractions.

Just go forward, always forward, and watch your step.

The acorn shines in my pocket and sings in my head. The tune is that of Joan, Clare, Chloe and Ella, Jon, Becky and Nat. Go forward in strength and security, it hums.

I've still no idea what I'm doing, but at least I'm doing something. If I'm a part of somebody else's larger plan, then I've got to hear from the people that wrote it. If my role is just 'serve brandy, don't die 'til we've figured it out', then that's fine. God knows I can sit tight, and not make a fuss until it's all blown over. That's my forte – it's what I do.

It's what I did.

'He's not going to be impressed, y'know', says Emmet as he pulls on his faded leather jacket two minutes after he'd taken it off. 'You heard him.'

'I know. You are to keep me here at all costs,' I repeat, as I walk over to the window. 'I am not to step one foot outside that door. But you know I'm going to anyway, Emmet.'

'Aye,' he says, as Arnold shuffles off his stool with a thump, 'but yer an idiot and a fool.'

'Perhaps,' I sigh. 'But one with an Arnold and an Emmet beside me, right?'

Emmet looks at the GeoTroll sitting at my bar, as he downs his brandy and crashes to his feet.

'Right,' grunts Arnold.

'There'll be Incorporeal,' says Emmet, looking into the stone eyes of the rock in front of him. 'It's been a while. Are yer sure you can...'

'I'm fine,' he mumbles.

121

'You could stay and protect the pub?'

'Pub's just a pub,' Arnold says as he extends one jagged finger towards me. 'Protect the Landlord. Protect The Grindstone.'

'But...'

'Incorporeal won't get close. Not if they know what's best.' Arnold's fists open and clench, leaving small lines of green-grey brick dust to float to the floor. 'Besides,' he says, nodding at me, 'he needs to see for himself.'

Emmet closes his eyes, and for ten seconds just stands there. Eventually, he lets out a long breath and looks at us both.

'Fine,' he mutters. 'The Council are at the harbour. They're trying to convince people to leave before they make one last stand against the Binding Brothers. They won't be pleased to see yer, but technically they can't turn you away neither. Heaven knows what you want to achieve.'

Leadership. Choices. Charge.

'I just have to look in his eyes, Emmet,' I say, as I pull on my own jacket. 'Will Nat be with them?' Arnold glances at the barman.

'She might, aye.'

'Then that settles it. We leave.'

Emmet walks over to the bar and picks up the keys he snatched from me that first night. 'Just remember,' he says, 'Keep yer head down cos there's a price on it. We can do this cos he don't know yer face. In here, yer an Embodiment. You're safe – for the moment. Out there, you're a bloke who don't know his left from his right.'

'Fine.'

'And no screamin' like a girl.'

'No screaming,' I say.

'Good,' he nods again. 'Glad we got that sorted.' He turns to Arnold. 'How quickly can we get to the Falls?'

The GeoTroll folds his arms. 'Twenty minutes in the old tunnels,' he grates.

'No,' Emmet shakes his head. 'Tunnels are blocked. Have to go overground.'

'Forty, then. If we're quick.'

I walk over to the door, unlatch the lock and swing it open.

'Then let's make a start,' I say, as I turn once more to look at the sky.

And the stars shine down upon me.

The night is dark, and the inky black of the strange other world highlights the growing shadows of Peacebattle Lane. The Castle, The Hourglass and The Stocks and Peasant all hang in their place, unfettered by cloud, and untroubled by ghosts.

The Incorporeal have gone.

A line crosses Emmet's brow as he joins me in the doorway.

'Well that makes it a little easier,' I whisper. 'Right?'

'Hopefully,' he murmurs. 'There's always room fer a little hope.' He beckons to Arnold, and I step onto the cobbles outside so he can get out. I feel a chill I'm not convinced is the breeze, and button up tight.

'Mark,' says Emmet as he turns the iron key in the lock. 'Put your hand on the door.' I give him a puzzled look, but do as he says. 'Now repeat after me.' He stares into my eyes as he chants the words, and my stomach knots as he does.

'Where once was war, where all shed blood, through me communion: The Oak and Dogwood.'

I take another deep breath. It feels the more of these words I say, the more I become trapped by them. 'Really?'

'Don't mock,' he says, slowly. 'Not out in the open. It's an extension of yer Licence. It's mainly superstition, but every little helps. Every time yer lock the pub up, yer have to say the words. Think of it as yer security alarm. Besides, it's bad luck, otherwise.'

I take a moment. Just the one. She'd said it before she left The Axe. 'Remember those words,' she'd said, and when I repeat them, I stumble. '...through me communion...' I take another breath, 'the Oak and Dogwood.'

I'm expecting a tingle, or some internal song from the acorn or Grindstone. All I get is one approving nod from Emmet.

'That were well done, lad. Now that really is everything you know. You spoke The Landlord's Motto well.'

'Obviously a natural,' I reply, as I turn to the hill. 'Right. Lead on MacDuff.' Arnold tilts his head, quizzically. 'Never mind.' I sigh. 'Shall we go?'

The Axe & Grindstone

'Let's move,' grunts Arnold, as he strides in front and I struggle to keep up. Yesterday, I sat on that wall and marvelled at the strange night sky. Now, my eyes are fixed ahead, with quick glances left and right only holding my gaze on one spot long enough to take in the sights.

No sightseeing – I know – but this is my first good look at my new town. My new world.

We're the only people on the streets but, now and again, I see shapes peering out from their painted shutters to see what we're doing. There's still not a cloud in the sky, and the air is fresh and warm: a far, far cry from the Dartmoor clouds which blanket Oak Cheating in cold December rain.

'The people. They should be at the harbour,' gasps Emmet as he runs behind us. 'I don't understand why they're not.'

'They've met the Landlord,' states Arnold, who's markedly less out of breath. 'Why would they leave?'

We climb up, and round, all the while not losing a step on the carved cobbles beneath our feet. On every corner of every street there are obelisks. At their end, the lanes merge with three or four more in large circuses, with a more prominent obelisk at the centre of each one. I point at the nearest. Emmet gets my drift.

'Memorials. Remember I told yer. Dogwood Falls were where the peace treaty between nations were finally signed. Each one of 'em represents a race who fought and lost something of 'emselves.'

'But there's so many of them.'

'It weren't called the Hundred Holy Wars fer nothing, lad. But I've served each and every nation that's carved here in The Grindstone, and got to know 'em all, one by one. When you look at those names, look at yer duty to do 'em justice.'

We keep striding, our pace increasingly hurried. We pass more and more obelisks, each with its own unique symbols and each with an oblique verse or two from some obscure text. As we move further on, the texts become harder to read, defaced and smeared with paint.

'That's new,' says Emmet. 'They're obscuring any text that ain't their own.' We move faster and faster, until I'm almost running to catch up... and then nearly crash into Arnold when he suddenly halts dead in his tracks.

He holds up one heavy hand – stop.

I crouch at his feet as all seven feet of rock towers above me, and he looks down. Behind the inky black of his eyes are two small flames, impossibly lit from within the dark mass of his skull. There's a faint roar coming from inside him, as if gas burners had suddenly switched themselves on and were powering up, ready to drive Arnold's hulk to full strength. His words burn themselves out of his mouth and even though there's no heat, I can feel and taste the scorching of the air coming out of his mouth.

'Wait.'

Emmet crouches beside me, his hairs poised, upright and sharp. At the side of the road there's another small wall, and he runs over to peer over the edge.

'Smoke,' he whispers as loudly as he can. 'From the Harbour Lodge. Quietly, edge round the next corner to the lookout point, and keep your head down. Arnold – that means you.'

Shit. My heart's beating and I swear they can all hear it. Whatever's out there is going to be drawn to us by the sound of my panting and my heartbeat.

I'm going to get us all killed.

Leadership and taking charge can go screw themselves.

I crouch down as low as I can and use Arnold for cover. If they can't see him, then they can't see me. The three of us turn the corner and reach the lookout at the top of the hill.

Beneath us, reaching off to the horizon, lies the harbour of Dogwood Falls. There are boats, ships, junks, dotted around haphazardly moored onto any scrap of land or jetty. Wooden huts meet them, to obviously sell goods. At the far end of the cove a waterfall flows into a pool surrounded by wooden bridges and ornate carved buildings at three different levels.

One of the buildings, on the top level, is on fire.

The sound of a distant bell tolls through the air. It rings out by a young lad in an alcove near the fall. People are fleeing – more people than I've seen all night – from the buildings into the boats and casting them to sea. It's panic. Sheer, unadulterated, panic.

The Axe & Grindstone

Emmet turns to Arnold. 'What can you see?'

Arnold lifts his head above the wall, and the fire in his eyes reflects the fire in the harbour. The gravel in his voice is more pronounced than before.

'It's the Harbour Lodge. They're after the Council.'

I strain to see more. Although the majority of people are fleeing the harbour, three or four are standing still. They're hard to pick out at first, but as the fire grows so does the light, and the outline of black and crimson robes. I know what they are without being told.

'The Binding Brothers,' I whisper, as I press my back to the wall and thrust my head in my hands.

'How did they know?' grates Arnold, the roar inside him growing in depth and fury.

'I don't know!' says Emmet. 'They've kept themselves hidden away for so long. Even when they took Fox they never dared move against the Council.' He mutters to himself, calculating reason and motive whilst shaking his head. He points to the harbour, and I turn to look at the scene once again. The furnace inside the GeoTroll rises in pitch, as the familiar purple cloud of the Incorporeal sweeps over the Falls.

The Brothers outstretch their arms in welcome as the ghosts pour through the buildings below. They hover above the water, blocking any escape to the ocean beyond. The few boats struggling off shore start back to berth, and the black smoke from the increasing number of burning houses is consumed by the arriving ghosts.

Through the wisps of the darkening sky, I can see an unlucky few on the crackling floor at the water's edge. The villagers nearest to the Brothers are on their knees. They claw at their own skin. With one haunting finger, one robed figure turns to the boy ringing the bell and a man races towards him with a club in his hand. From this distance his cries are bestial.

'Fuck off from my son!' he cries and the voice slams into my head. Benjamin. The first man to toast my new position. The Brother turns to him and raises an arm to the sky. Without stopping, Benjamin smashes his club against the edge of a mooring post, splintering it in two.

'No!' I shout, but too late. With one hand on a splintered spear, he thrusts it into his arm and begins to scream.

The Screaming starts the Scratching,

And once again it's in my head...

And Scratching starts the Night.

...and I shake like never before...

For Scratching, starts the Scratching

...I can feel all three of them holding me down...

Starts the Binding Brothers' Light.

...stopping me from hurting myself like I know I must.

But I don't. Strength. Security. Steadfastness. Through me, communion. Fuck off out of my head! THROUGH ME, COMMUNION!

And it's gone. I shake my head to make sure. Nothing. Both of my friends look concerned, but relieved – even Arnold whose fist is drawn next to his ear, looking ready to punch me at any second.

'It's OK. I'm OK.' I look at Emmet and his hand on my shoulder. I feel his power course through me and know that I'm fine. He nods and smiles weakly.

'Good lad. We need to get out of here. Now.'

'Agreed,' growls Arnold, pulling down his fist from the side of his head and scooping it round my waist. This is not going to be comfortable. I steal one last glimpse at the harbour.

But God, oh I wish to God that I hadn't.

There, at the base of the flames, surrounded by an altar of self-immolation, he's standing. Staring at me.

I can hear him walking in my head.

Tap-te-tap-te-tap.

Tap-te-tap-te-tap.

The razor-sharp toes of The Man With The Crab-Like Feet clack along the ruined wood of the bridge. He's staring at the lookout where I'm kneeling fifty feet up. The lookout where I screamed when I promised I wouldn't.

It's him.

The man from my dream.

He's real.

He's looking straight at me. Wanting to scratch out my Soul

The Axe & Grindstone

and my Self through my core. And now he knows my face.
   As one, we run.

CHAPTER XIV
THE COUNCIL OF THE WOUNDED

And we keep on running.

On and on and on. Around every corner and across every single bloody cobble in Dogwood Falls.

Arnold's got me tossed over his shoulder, and all I can see is what we're running away from.

They're coming.

At first, I think it's smoke from the fire – but that's over a mile away by now and the black smoke still rises to the west, choking the perfect night sky I've still not gotten used to. One by one it blocks out the tiny pin pricks of light, darkening the night around us.

But it's not that. It's not rising harmlessly into the sky. It's travelling broadly flat against the ground through the trees, two metres high rolling through the wide streets and narrow lanes of Dogwood Falls. It flows around them, sweeping across the horizon like a crimson red tsunami, rolling over everything in its path but leaving it intact. There's only one thing here worth destroying now.

Me.

Arnold roars underneath me as he uses his free hand to swing round an obelisk into a side street in between the main lanes leading back down the hill to The Grindstone.

'The cloud! It's gaining!' I shout, to a grunt from Arnold. I think he knows. I don't think our plan is working out as well as he expected, as his right hand keeps having to readjust its grip on me to make sure I don't slip off his shoulder as he runs.

Scratching.

'FUCK OFF WITH YOUR SCRATCHING!' I yell at the oncoming cloud, more for effect than affect, as it makes no difference other than to banish the irritating voice from my head. We have to get back to the pub. It's the only place with the protection we need against the Brothers. I'm beginning to get this now. As I'm staring right at them.

The Man.

The Man With the Crab-Like Feet.

He's been in my dreams. How? How is that even possible?

Without thinking I put my fingers to my throat – I can feel five needle pressure points about to break the flesh on my neck. It was just a dream. Surely it was just a dream? Dreams don't hurt. Dreams don't want to make me saw my own arm off like the man in the basement did...

A door opens to our right and a young woman with short blonde hair and an old patched sweater looks out. She sees us running and I wave my arms at her, gesturing like a mad man for her to get back inside. She turns, puzzled to see what we're running from... and screams. In an instant the cloud turns from crimson to a darker, deeper blood red, and speeds up. Her hand goes straight to her mouth to stop herself and slams the door tightly shut.

A couple of seconds after we pass, the cloud engulfs her house.

Rather than pass over it, as it does the others, it enters every way it can, forcing itself through every gap it can find. Through the chimney, under the door, beneath the windows, and through the beating in my head I can hear her screaming again and again through the tormented stone walls.

Don't scream. I remember. It likes the screaming. Screaming starts the Scratching, and Scratching starts the Night.

Something clicks in my head and I grow colder, if that were even possible. I know. I don't know how I know, but it's deep inside and once the thought has lodged itself inside it's impossible to ignore.

The Binding Brothers have an army of the dead – an army of ghosts – shapeless and formless and inhuman. There must be hundreds of them, all rolling and charging towards us as we try and make for safety. Emmet's voice rings out, knowing what I was thinking.

'When did the Incorporeal get this strong?'

He looks back – and at once his downy hairs are upright and poised. 'While we were sleeping and pretendin' nothing was wrong,' he shouts.

'Can we get back to The Grindstone?'

'Trying,' grunts Arnold, the roar in his belly doing its best to drown out anything we say. We turn down another lane – nothing more than an alley, this one. We're not going back the way we came and I lose sight of the cloud, beneath the overhanging roofs of the buildings either side of us.

'It's almost on top of us!' I cry, as I look up and the sky starts to turn red. Wisps of red smoke appear round the chimneys, and as the wave starts to spill over, I cry out... and fall.

And with a sharp pain, the world turns black once again.

Shapes.
Incoherent shapes.
They fade in, then fade out.
Inky patches of colour bleed into the black.
And the black seeps into colour, blotting them out.
And the cycle continues.

I can... sense you now.
I know your... face now.
You cannot... run. You... will not hide.
Soon... you will scream... for me.
And the scream will be... delicious... inviting... in...toxicating.
I'll make you scream forever.

The voices are merging, one on top of each other. Incoherent Noise. Incoherent Shapes. I can't concentrate on them all – why don't they realise?

'...fault...dead...safe...plan...'
'...Council...lead...safety...darkness...'
'Brothers...Landlord...Oak...Dogwood...'
'Emmett...Arnold...Mark...Natasha...'

The Axe & Grindstone

'Natasha?' I murmur the word, softly. I can talk. This is a good sign.

'Shhh,' comes a voice. I can feel something cold against my forehead. What is that? A towel? 'Gently does it. Gently now.'

'Gently now,' I repeat. Repeating is good. Repeating makes me feel safe. Safer. Have to keep talking. Talking will clear away the fudge in my head. Stop it swaying. Stop me feeling sick. 'I don't want to scream forever...'

'Shhh,' says the voice again. 'No one's going to make you scream forever. Just you see.'

'Just I see. Yes. Tired.'

'I know you are.' The voice is soft. 'You need to wake up now, Mark. It's time for work.'

'I don't want to go to work. Phone Richard.' He'll understand. Bad head. Scary dreams.

'You don't work for Richard any more, Mark. You work for me, now. Remember?'

I remember. The shapes blur and then focus in on themselves. The voices converge on one. I open my eyes, and Natasha's kneeling beside me.

'There we go,' she says with a smile. 'And we're back.'

'Nat!' I say, blinking myself awake, 'You're... here. You're alive! So much... so much to tell you!' I lift myself onto my elbows, but suddenly get dizzy and crash onto my back once again. 'My head... what happened?'

I look around – we're in some sort of tunnel. Curved brickwork surrounds us and in front of me sit a group, dishevelled and dirty, huddled around a small table in a makeshift camp. Arnold's a few feet away, and turns towards me briefly.

'Sorry,' he says, bluntly. 'Mis-judged gap. You've got a big head.'

'Fair enough,' I reply, not knowing quite else how to answer. I've never been knocked out before. Punched a fair few times, but never actually knocked out. Chalk one up to experience. I look back at Nat. 'I thought you were dead... Where are we?'

'Beneath the town, in an old munitions tunnel. They used them back in the war to move supplies around Dogwood Falls –

so people didn't have to move them above ground once they'd come off the ships. They're all on one level under the town, so no worrying about moving heavy goods up and down the hills and cobbles. It's also a convenient hiding place if things get... heavy.'

An older woman, looking like a 1950s starlet, comes over and also kneels beside me.

'You alright there, dear? I'm Estelle,' she says, offering me a glass of water with a pink pill slowly dissolving into it. 'We were a bit worried there for a minute. Arnie can be terribly clumsy when he's under a bit of stress, can't you Arnie?'

'Guess...' comes a gruntled reply from across the way.

'Now drink this all up, Mark, there's a good lad. Will help with the concussion. The pill's a bit old, but it'll do you OK. I had a fair few of these when I were dying, so I know they're good.'

'Dying?' I prop myself back on my elbows. 'What do you mean, dying? I'm not dying, am I?' I feel around the back of my head for bleeding or other such injury. Nothing, apart from a large lump on my scalp. Estelle looks shocked and puts her hand to her mouth.

'Oh no... sorry, dear, I didn't mean you were dying! Gosh, how me and my mouth. No, goodness no. I mean, you only banged your head dear, well, I mean, Arnie banged your head, that's to say you'll have a bit of a lump and a headache for a minute or two, but if you drink this, you'll be all right. I didn't mean to suggest you were in any sort of danger, dear. Well, not anything out of the ordinary. Well, when I say ordinary...'

'Estelle,' interrupts Nat softly, with one hand on the other's forearm. 'You're babbling again, honey.'

'Yes. Sorry, Natasha. Ran away with myself for a second there. Good to see you again though, girl.' She looks sadly at me and I smile at her, hoping it's a nice smile and not a grimace. She passes me the water and, swilling around the last of the pink sediment until it disappears, knock it back. The water tastes an odd mixture of cherry and cheese. Not a fan, but then I don't have a choice. At once, I can feel the dull thud in the back of my skull start to fade. I nod at Estelle and she smiles, relaxing a little. Nat presses her hand against my forehead and turns to her.

'Could you give us a moment?'

Estelle looks back at the party round the table, and nods. 'Just a moment, though Natasha. We've got to move again now Mark's back with us.' Estelle reaches over and kisses me on the forehead, before getting up and walking away.

'Hello again,' says Nat. 'How are you feeling.'

'Better,' I say, sitting up. A couple of people in the larger group I don't recognise look my way. Upright, I have a better view of where we are. In the curve of the tunnel two metres above us is a hatch – presumably the one we dropped down. The tunnel itself isn't that wide, perhaps two or three metres across, and lit with a thin string of small round white beads, each about a penny's width in size, down the left-hand side. Only the beads immediately in front of, or behind us, are lit, leaving the rest of the tunnel in dark shadow. The lights highlight Nat in profile, showing every curve and fleck of hair falling onto the left-hand side of her beautiful, beautiful face.

'So...' she begins, before trailing off.

'So...'

'Getting on OK?'

'Axe is a bit quiet. You left out a couple of things.'

'Yeah. I might not have been straight with you about everything. Thought I had more time. Sorry.'

'Bit out of the way as well. In the middle of flood country. When it's flooding. You know.'

'Yeah... Again with the sorry...' There's a pause while we take each other in. I'm not going to be the one to break it. And I'm not.

'Listen, Mark... I didn't have a choice. We were running out of time. I was going to explain everything when you got here but...'

'But what, Nat? You thought it best to let me find out on my own? You were with me, upstairs and then... what? You just left? One minute you were kissing me. It felt, well, you know how it felt. It felt like it used to. Then you left me. Alone, hanging there, waiting for you. But... you were gone. Just like the last time...

'The next thing I knew my world just fell apart. You know. Literally fell apart. There was this... quake, I dunno. Scared me shitless and I couldn't find you anywhere. I couldn't get out, I couldn't do anything and at the end of it all I found... this.' I gesture at the tunnel. 'Turns out it was the mountain over there banging to get into the secret pub in the cellar. Which you knew about but didn't tell me.' Nat nods.

'Yes, I knew. I got interrupted. Once you signed the contract you disturbed the new status quo the Binding Brothers had hoped would last. There was a shift in the balance between Oak Cheating and Dogwood Falls. It pulled me back here and meant the shockwave from Arnold's knocking echoed into The Axe, fusing the walls the doors and the windows. It didn't last long, but it knocked me for six a bit. Which is why I couldn't come back and see you. I'm sorry.' She takes my hand and because of this, I immediately accept her apology. I just don't tell her.

'And, no pressure, and everything. But the Landlord of Peacebattle?' Nat looks down, not wanting to meet my eyes. I get up and wipe the dust of the tunnel floor from my jeans. 'Thanks for that. A job description with a life expectancy. That's new. You should put it in the advert next time. I don't know what to say to you, Nat. I really don't.' I crouch down by her and raise her chin up with my finger so she meets my eyes.

'Be honest with me, from now on, OK? Cards on the table. Straight talking. Like the old days.'

'Like the old days.'

I don't say anything. I can't say anything. I notice we're both blinking back tears. I have to do something to stop myself breaking down. I stand and walk over to the group by the table. Behind me, I can hear Nat getting up and doing the same. On the table are groups of papers written in several different languages, not all of them English.

'So,' I say to the group, more confidently than I feel. 'Mark Adams. Hello.'

The wispy-haired man with Estelle walks around the table towards me. He's a couple of inches shorter than me and walks with a cane. It's black and wrapped around the top half of it is a large eel. At least, I think it's an eel. An eel or a snake. They look alike.

'Mr Adams,' he snaps at me. 'Why the hell are you here?' I

can't deny it, I'm slightly taken aback.

'I was looking for the Council of the Wounded,' I reply, addressing not just the old guy, but the group as a whole. I look over at Emmet, who's sitting on a sack against the wall, away from the others as if he didn't belong. He doesn't look happy. 'I'm the new Grindstone Landlord and was looking for some answers. We saw the fire and...' I pause, wanting to find the right words, '...were spotted and chased down here. I take it we're protected.'

'We are,' says the man. 'For now.' With a start he jams the cane into my ribs, making me double up. 'You are an idiot, sir.' He waves his cane at Nat. 'Is this the best you could do? Someone strong, we said! Someone who'd give us half a chance against the Brothers, not some young boil-popper who's spent the last ten minutes asleep on the floor.'

'You know my hands were tied, Gorman,' Nat retorts, the hard edge returning to her voice. 'Everyone I approached ended up dead before they could take up post. The only way Mark could get here was if I told him nothing until he signed. And even then the balance shifted before I could fill him in. So don't blame me.'

Gorman sniffs with a haughty 'hmmf', before turning back to look at me. 'You knew you were safe at the inn, Adams, yes?'

'I don't know anything. Which is the point I'm trying to make.'

Another 'hmmf'. He turns and points his stick at Emmet.

'Emmettaman Savage. It was your job to perform the rituals and invoke the protection. I take it you've done that correctly?' Emmet stands, and shuffles on his feet.

'Yes, sir. He's got his Licence. As long as he's safe, they can't enter The Grindstone.'

'As long as he's safe? Are you trying to fool an old man into not beating the spines out of you, sir? It was your job to keep him safe. It was your job to tie him to a barrel, if needs be, and keep him inside The Grindstone at all costs.'

'Too much sitting around,' gruffs Arnold from behind him. 'Too much waiting.'

'Exactly,' I add. 'Too much waiting. I was told I had some part to play in a larger plan. I needed to find out for myself what that larger plan was. Take charge.'

'Take charge, indeed? Take charge of what, exactly? What is there to take charge of, anymore? Certainly not the Council!' He waves his arms at the band of people around us. They're hurt, and bloodied, every single one. This is the Council.

'Hundreds upon hundreds of years we've kept the peace between nations! Never have we been challenged! Never slain, never hurt, never admonished. Never! You think you can come to us, first day on the job, and demand what you like of us? Don't you think we have bigger things to worry about than you? On tonight of all days? When we've lost so much, so many, and the enemy is so strong? All you have to do, young man, is sit tight and perform your duty.'

'Sit tight and perform my duty? Until what? Until you fail and I'm carted off to scream for some man's pleasure for the rest of time?'

'Oh, what do you know of screaming? What do you know of pain? I know about you, Mr Adams. I know you'll sit back and let others do the hard work. Maybe Miss Bennett here was right. Maybe you are just the man for the job. Pass your time cleaning glasses whilst the world around you changes. Makes it all alright, doesn't it?'

'What do I know of screaming? I felt it all in my head. Heard them all cry out. I'm sorry for your friends, really I am. I'm sorry for the horrible, horrible, things I saw tonight and all the people that got hurt, or killed, or worse. But I felt it all. All the screaming. Every single one of them.'

'Impossible, boy. Don't you lie to me.'

'The man. The Man With The Crab-Like Feet. Five bare-footed claws on each foot which he scuttles around on. The man that was there tonight, at the fire. I can see him. In my dreams. And he can see me.'

Gorman stops and leans on his cane, staring at me, squinting to see if he can see through my eyes. The rest of the Council, sat on stools and sacks around us, look at me. It seems I've now got their attention.

'Khalid? What do you know of Veli Khalid?'

'Is that his name? Not a nice bloke.' There's a barrel in front of the table. Although squaring up to a traumatised old bloke in an underground tunnel was at the top of the list of my things to do today, getting knocked out whilst jumping into it makes it tougher than I'd hoped. I sit down and take a moment before continuing.

'The moment I set foot in Oak Cheating I felt him in my head. Like someone speaking and drilling hot needles into my skull. Scratching, always scratching. It kept on and on. Scratching starts the screaming and screaming starts the night. Screaming starts the screaming. Starts the Binding Brother's Light.'

Gorman leans further inwards on his cane.

'Impossible,' he whispers. He turns and sweeps his cane at Nat, Estelle, Arnold and Emmet. 'And you, none of you told him this?' Emmet raises his hand.

'No, sir. It's why we didn't stop him when he said he wanted to see yer.'

'Hmmf!' He turns back to me. 'You may be a true Landlord of Peacebattle yet, young man. Do you know the rest of that prophecy?'

I think back. Prophecy? I've tried to get it out of my head, to be honest. But I've failed, and the words hang in front of my head as harsh as they were when they were first shouted at me earlier today. I can recite this one word for word.

'Scratching then Scratching then Scratching some more, Scratching your Soul and your Self through your core. The Landlord will Scream and his Screaming will call. The Brothers that Bind. Oak and Dogwood will fall.'

There's silence, as members of the Council look amongst themselves. Only Gorman keeps his eyes on me.

'Yes... yes... that's it. It hasn't been spoken for a generation. It's passed from one Chairman to another. No one in this room has ever heard that spoken, or read it from the *Book of Blackwood*, apart from you and me, Mr Adams.'

'Oh. Right.' I'm glad I've sat down. Nat puts her hand on my shoulder, as Emmet walks over to me.

'Mister Chairman, if I may, Mark here says the Scratching's reached his world already. He told me earlier today, after it got him for a bit. Not strong, cos we'd got him on board by then but...

Well, tell him, Mark.'

'Out with it, boy, c'mon.'

I sigh. The pill is doing its job of clearing my head, but not as quickly as I'd like.

'It's been all over the papers and the news. Mass suicides all over the country. People taking knives and scissors, throwing themselves off bridges, you name it. Past three weeks, you can't have read anything else. People were blaming it on social media, forming groups, cults, that sort of thing. Didn't pay much notice until my friend killed herself. Proper mental. But, thinking about it, and according to what Emmet told me, it happened around the time the last Landlord got taken by Khalid.' I feel Nat's hand squeeze my shoulder.

'We were right, Gorman,' she says. 'It's out there already. It's how I found Mark. He had this... inkling, and I knew it was him we were looking for. They've started. It's why they've got the strength to go after the Council. They're going to use that strength now to break Mark's Licence and complete their cross-over completely. They'll break it far, far quicker than they did the last one. Now Mark's in position their power in Oak Cheating is weaker, but still as strong here now they've fed. We need to get back to The Grindstone. If we follow the tunnels to the Social Quarter, we should be able to get back to the pub with little trouble. The plan we were using – to get to Khalid and break him – is now useless. The Scratching's fed too much. Everything that's happened tonight tells us we need to rethink.'

Gorman looks around to the remains of the Council, who one by one nod agreement at him. He sighs.

'We were so close. So close,' he murmurs. He lifts his cane and brushes all the papers off the table onto the floor. 'The bloody drawing board's got nothing left on it.' He looks up, at all of us looking at him. 'Well?' he bellows. 'What are you waiting for. Christmas? If I'm to think of a new plan, I need a bloody drink!'

Seems they do celebrate Christmas over here, after all.

The band gather the remains of their belongings and start walking, slowly, down the tunnel into the dark. As they pass a new set of lighting beads, they switch on automatically and the light then snakes with us – an extra welcome constant companion. After five or ten minutes – I've never been able to count time underground – my head has cleared completely and, although I might be imagining this, the lump on the back of my head seems to have disappeared.

Along the walk, I start chatting to a few members of the Council, and hear stories of Dogwood Falls when The Grindstone was packed from dawn until dusk. People of all lands, colours, races came together to share stories and drink together. Forget their differences – with the Landlord of Peacebattle at the heart of it all. Friend to everyone.

Through me, communion.

'He was a nice bloke, the Previous, always there with a smile if you'd had a hard day,' says the chap I've been talking to for the last ten minutes.

'Previous. I've heard that before,' I say, wracking my brain, with that sense of dread I felt before – when Khalid clapped his eyes on me for the first time. 'It's a funny term.

Why use it?'

'Oh, it's just an honorary title, really. Given to the last Landlords. On the obelisk nearest your pub is an inscription: 'In honour of the Previous Landlords of Peacebattle. Inspiring peace through knowledge, laughter, and real ale.' And a roll call. Your name will be up there one day. We need to get the last one's name up there, really, but since he died, people have been too scared to venture out that much.

Previous... Previous...

I stop dead.

Sweet dreams my Previous. Dream of the Scratching and the pride it'll give your master to see you take centre stage. Dream of what the Landlord of Peacebattle has to look forward to. Dream of what you'll teach him. Dream of the screaming he'll do and the exquisite pleasure it'll bring me.

'He's not dead.' The company all stop walking and turn to look at me. Gorman walks up to me.

'What? Who's not dead? What are you on about now, Adams?' I turn to face him.

'Fox. Fox isn't dead. He's alive. I've seen it. Last night. I saw him in my head. Khalid was... he was...' I can't put the image into words, not with all these faces looking at me. 'Fox is hurt. Badly hurt. But he's alive.'

Emmet and Nat are back at my side straight away.

'I don't understand,' says Emmet, looking up at me. 'That were never the plan. That's not his style. Why keep him? What's he doing to him?'

I look at Gorman, into his eyes. He knows. He realised at the same time as me.

'He's enjoying keeping him,' I say. 'He has a larger plan. No idea what, though. I tend to wake up when freaks tear into my dreams.'

'But if that's true, it means something else, doesn't it, Mark?' says Nat.

Oh God.

I know.

Don't ask me how I know, but I know. I feel... what do I feel... I feel as if the exam I've been expecting to sit is now, by mistake, the advanced paper I'd never prepared for that only the very smartest will pass. I feel as if I've been pushed onto the world's largest stage on opening night without a script. I feel as if someone's placed the world's heaviest stone in the pit of my stomach and its weighing me down so hard that I can't move any further.

There are two Landlords of Peacebattle.

This should make me happy. This should release me – let me go back to Staunton and claw back my old life. But it doesn't. Because... Because...

'It means we have to go get him, doesn't it?'

Gorman stands for a minute, his brow twitching as all sorts of thoughts cross through his mind. How, what, where, how, how? Finally, finally, a grim smile passes his lips. It's an odd look, for a man who it seems hasn't smiled in a long, long time.

'He'll never make it out of wherever he is, of course.'

'Nothing to smile about,' gruffs Arnold, who's watching us both from behind me.

'No, of course it isn't, but it doesn't matter, do you see?' I can hear the furnace inside the GeoTroll begin to light, and without looking back, place my hand on his chest to calm him. Incredibly, it works, and the gentle roar dies down almost as soon as it's begun.

'As long as we get them together, we can hold back the breach. Licence in Perpetuity! It's never been done before, but my God, we could do it. Two Landlords... I never thought it possible. It's not supposed to be possible. But... his Licence was forcibly removed: for the first time, they managed to rip a Licence away from someone. Which allowed us to give you one, Mr Adams, of course – one Licensee at a time and all that. But because it was taken, it can be given back. He doesn't realise. Of course! He doesn't realise! If he knew he'd kill him on the spot! We need Adams and Fox together. Adams – we can change your Licence at any time – of course we can – so we carry out a short ceremony for the both of you. A joint Licence, twice the power, and whatever is barred under it cannot enter The Grindstone or pass through the breach under any circumstances – even if one of you dies.

'You'd need to go of course, Mr Adams. Sooner we get you two in once place, the better. It probably means Fox's cell, but we can sort that out in a bit. My God, we've got a plan. Now we just have to work out how not to get you killed before it's done.'

He grabs his stick and walks off ahead of us, faster than he looks, with a new purpose and a new spring to his step. The rest of the Council follow him, chattering excitedly to themselves and drawing up plans.

The five of us hang back.

'Well,' I say after a second or two.

'No pressure, lad,' says Emmet.

'I need a drink,' gruffs Arnold. 'Stop myself hitting him.'

Nat puts her arm around me, drawing a sideways glance from Emmet.

'You sure you're up for this, Mark?'

Leadership. Choices. Charge.

The Landlord will Scream and his Screaming will call.

'Better be a bloody good plan,' I say, walking off towards the light.

The Brothers that Bind.
Oak and Dogwood will fall.

The Axe & Grindstone

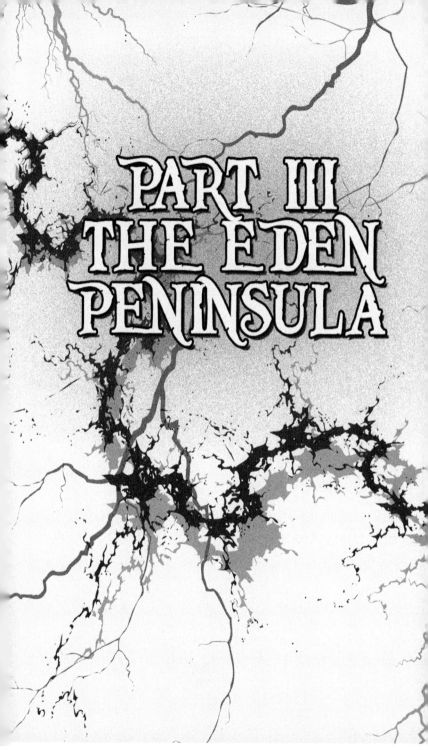

PART III
THE EDEN
PENINSULA

The Axe & Grindstone

Alternate

This Landlord is younger. He will scream longer.

Veli Khalid holds the burning man's head close to his own as the flames start to wake him. The man starts to struggle, but the bindings around his body constrict his movements and tear into his tender pink skin. His body tries to twist from side to side and lift himself another inch or two from the heat. It doesn't work. With horror, he realises where he is and knows the legends were true. He's lying, suspended by thin black ropes at a forty-five-degree angle above the Fire Pit of Gehenna.

He cries out, and Khalid, lying prostrate on a platform above the pit, grips his head harder. He forces the man's eyelids open wide with his thumbs and presses their foreheads together so he can feel the man's heartbeat through his temple. Khalid smiles a broad, gluttonous smile and drinks in the moment. He ignores the smell coming from the man in his grasp and allows himself a second of inner thought, closing his own eyes to calm his mind and steady the temptation which burns within him with the heat of the coals below.

And with that, to work.

He pulls his head an inch away from the poor man before him and stares into his eyes. The man's face is streaked with tears, and as he struggles in his bonds, his bottom lip streams with blood where he's bitten it in a bid to stay strong. But eventually, as with all the others, the strength to stay quiet finally fails.

The screams echo around the circular chamber, seeping into the porous rocks and chilling the super-heated air. Khalid breathes in deep, his mouth close and intimate and his eyes locked fast upon his prisoner's pupils.

'There. There we go...'

The man's eyes start to roll back in their sockets, and the Veli lets the eyelids screw themselves shut. He releases the man's head and it twists and turns violently.

And the screaming starts the screaming.

On and on and on. Even after he's passed out, and Khalid signals the overseer to raise him out of the heat, the screaming haunts the pit where five other Brothers peer into the naked souls of five other captives, desperate to get away. Later, when they too have passed out, been raised, and taken to a small chapel on the edge of the Cynobium, they'll wake. They'll see and feel the scorched skin blistered and blackened on their bones, and they'll scream again.

And the Binding Brothers will pray.

The stone tunnel echoes with the tap-tap-tapping of the claws of The Man With The Crab-Like Feet. As he walks back to the chapter house, a young man with newer, less tarnished robes, runs up behind him.

'Veli Khalid. Sorry. Could I have a moment of your time?'

The man looks down, in respect and fear, unable to make eye contact with his elder. Khalid stops and slowly turns to face him.

'Veli Amastad. Congratulations on your initiation. I trust all went well with the... ceremony?' Amastad nods quickly.

'Yes, yes, yes. It went well. The Elders were pleased with me.'

'You may look me in the eyes, Amastad. You are no longer initiate-elect. You do have that right... now.' Slowly, Amastad raises his face and, at the last moment, raises his eyes. Khalid continues.

'Good... good. Embrace your Brotherhood. You are one of us now. You passed your initiation. You are wholesome. We looked deep into your soul and found you pure and... intricate.'

'Do the...' Amastad looks down again. 'Do the scars heal, Veli Khalid?'

Khalid raises the younger Brother's chin back up with one of his needle-like fingers. 'Do you want the scars to heal, my Brother?'

'I, I...' He touches his left arm involuntarily, unsure of the correct answer.

'A man's scars remind him of his screaming. Don't they, Veli

Amastad.'

'Yes, my Elder.'

'And a man's scream...'

'...is the doorway to his soul. I know.'

Khalid nods. 'And by finding a man's soul, you peer into the glory of God. So remember your scream, Veli, embrace your scars... and through them become holy.'

'Thank you, Veli Khalid. As ever, your wisdom is an inspiration to us all.'

'Your faith in me does you credit. Now what can I help you with.'

Amastad shuffles with his hands, unsure what to do with them. He flicks away his black hair, which keeps flopping carelessly in front of his deep blue eyes which once again fall to the floor. He wants to rip his eyes away from Khalid's feet, but finds them hypnotic; each dirty pink heel a couple of inches off the ground, each supported by a claw of five finger-like toes resting on five razor sharp nails. One toe starts tapping impatiently.

'The Brothers brought back many converts today, Elder,' he says, when his silence becomes awkward.

'We did indeed. It has truly been a historic day.'

'I was wondering... well, I was wondering whether such numbers were normal. The screams... there's just so many screaming.'

'And isn't it joyous? Do you not find all those souls... invigorating?'

Amastad nods, but the slight hesitation causes Khalid to once again lift the younger man's chin to look him in the eyes. 'You have your first Enlightening coming up, don't you?'

'Yes Elder. I'm ready to see the face of God.'

Khalid frowns, and bends down, his face close to Amastad, who finds himself trying not to breathe on his mentor.

'Are you... sure? We do not have time for people who are not... sure, Amastad. God does not have the patience for people who are not fully committed to his purpose. And neither do I. God is counting on you, Amastad. He has chosen you to share his being with the world. God has chosen you to share his being with the next world. Does that not make you... happy?'

'I've waited for this moment all of my life, Elder.'

'He wants you to look upon Him, Amastad. He wants the world to look upon Him. He wants the next world to look upon Him. You will find Enlightenment. You will look into the eyes of a screaming man and into the heart of his soul.'

'I will see the face of God. Yes, Elder.'

Khalid stands upright again, his demeanour suddenly calm and serene, and without a hint of malice.

'Good man. You wouldn't want to join the Incorporeal. They have such a... disappointing existence. You should have seen them earlier. So excitable to be let out. Goodness knows there'll be no stopping them when we cross the breach and let the Scratching loose. All that screaming. All that opportunity to bask in the glory of the divine. The face of God everywhere you look.' He stands for a second, looking at the man who now looks back at him. He'll learn. He'll take one look and know the Glory. He'd better.

'Now, Veli Amastad. I believe it's customary for new initiates to spend the evening in service and prayer. I believe you're required in the refectory.'

Amastad runs his hands through his hair, again flicking away the strands which pass in front of his eyes. He murmurs a thank you and heads off back down the dark stone corridor a little too quickly to convey the sense of confidence and tranquillity he perhaps should have done.

The Man With The Crab-Like Feet stands there for a second, his toes tap-tap-tapping on the cold and dusty floor, and his hands flexing wide and clenched, wide and clenched. He murmurs to himself, as the light around him fades.

'I know you can hear me, Landlord. I know you can... feel me. You'll feel me for real soon enough.

'The Council can't protect you like they couldn't protect the Previous. The Landlord will scream and his screaming will call... the Brothers that Bind. Remember those words and mark mine. My brothers will pour through you, and through you into the world that you love. You will learn to love the world that I leave behind. It'll be pure, with no lies... no betrayal... no dishonesty.

'I'm coming for you. I'll show you how beautiful pain can be. I'll show you how perfect man can become when all else is stripped away.

'Oak and Dogwood will fall, and in their place will be Heaven.'

The Axe & Grindstone

Chapter XV
The Place of the Landlord

The glass which used to hold rather a fine 12-year-old malt whisky (my third) misses my left trainer by about an inch.

They're expensive trainers, these, bought with my last pay packet from the outlet village on the Staunton High Road. I've had them just long enough to fade the laces. There's only so many days it's acceptable to walk around with white laces before people start to take the piss.

'Everything all right, Mark?'

A call comes from the other side of The Grindstone – one of the Council, I forget what he's called. Sitting on my stool behind the bar, I pour myself another glass and raise it to the group still talking about me behind my back.

I'll try not to drop this glass. I'll pick up the broken one in a minute.

I'm not entirely sure why I dropped it. I mean, I'm not normally one for failing to keep a firm grip on my alcohol.

I got distracted for a minute, that's all.

As you do.

It's normal. Perfectly normal.

Everyone day-dreams.

The Landlord will scream.

It only took a second of dreaming before the jolt. The kind which wakes you up a second before you hit the ground. The kind which lingers in the back of your mind as you try to ignore its memory.

I'm coming for you. I'll show you how beautiful pain can be. I'll show you how perfect man can become when all else is stripped away.

I know him now. I know it's not normal.

He was there, again, in the back of my mind like an echo or a song which keeps repeating itself until it drives you crazy.

One day I'll have the gall to answer back, to tell him that I'm not afraid of him, his threats or his Scratching.

I'll do that as soon as I stop being afraid.

They're talking about me. I can tell.

They've spent the past hour talking about me. They talked about me as we walked through the tunnels for an age and a half. They talked about me as we legged it through the lanes to the pub.

In truth, therefore, I should be used to it – I am used to it – so I'm just going to let them carry on for a while whilst I have another whisky and try not to think of the call of The Man With The Crab-Like Feet, and his whisper in my head. I saw his vague movements behind my eyes and his belief surge through my stomach. Sometimes I see him, sometimes I hear him outright. Other times I just kind of sense him and perceive him directing his thoughts towards me. Just now it was a glimmer in a day dream. That jolt to bring me back to clarity and thought.

I grasp my little December Acorn in my left hand, and feel it reassure me through song in my palm.

Gorman is banging papers on one of the tables with his stick. Bit rude of him, truth be told. I know I haven't been here for that long, but they still feel like my tables. He's looking cross again, but then in the couple of hours I've known him that's not saying much.

I'd be cross if I were him.

I'd be cross if I'd been through what he's been through tonight.

In truth, though, I'd probably be rocking on the floor in a corner. Sitting behind this bar is calming me to some extent, the replacement liquor calming me some more. But it doesn't stop me thinking about all those people tonight running for their lives, and all the ones who never got the chance.

I sniff my T-shirt, now stained by the smell of burning. I was so far away from those poor people at the Falls, yet I can still smell them on my body. The trouble is, I'm not sure whether what I can smell is real life, or the haunt of a memory I haven't lived, or seen, but felt instead.

The smell of a vague memory – a man above a pit, dying but not allowed to die. The smell of a man who's forced to open his soul through his scream. I need some air.

'C'mon, Mr Savage. Get your arse in gear. What's up?'

Emmet frowns at me, the shadows crossing his face making him look like an extra in a silent film.

'Mr Savage is me father, not me, lad and you'd best remember that.'

I sigh, worn out. 'Are you coming, or what?'

I leave him at the top of the stairs and flick on the lights in the main bar. One by one, each corner of The Axe is lit by dim pools of magnolia light, cast upwards from dusty chocolate coloured crimped lampshades. They cast shadows on the textured walls, and the unlit areas feel left out and old. I find a packet of menthols in an old cardboard box underneath the till, rip a match from its comb and whip it against the tired striking strip.

Emmet steps into the bar.

'This place is bigger than The Grindstone.'

'It's quieter too, isn't it?'

'I think the pint glasses are safer, aye.'

Strike four of the third match lights my cigarette and I take a jealous, hungry drag and smoke in silence, watching my breath rise upwards and disappear into the shadows. Smoking behind a bar, in this day and age, is a guilty pleasure and one I take as often as I can. Neither the law, nor my boss – who's downstairs plotting to save the world – are likely to complain in this forgotten part of deepest, darkest, England. As the smoke passes through little islands of light on the uneven wooden floor, it's as if this part of Oak Cheating has its own house ghost. The smell makes it seem that little bit more like home.

After a couple of minutes when neither of us speak, I turn back to my barman. He's found the one tea towel in the pub and is polishing a wine glass with the delicacy and passion of an apprentice jeweller with a diamond ring.

'So how come you're an Axe virgin?' I ask.

The Axe & Grindstone

'Fox weren't too much of a fan of letting us up here – certainly not through the cellar. He liked to keep his worlds separate. "The Grindstone is the place for folks to get to know each other," he said, "not The Axe." He used to say that every man needed to know his place in the world. The greatest feeling a man could have was to know his place, and his role in the greater scheme of things.'

'And Fox's place – his role – was the Landlord of Peacebattle?'

'Easy to think that, lad – the Council certainly do. But he considered this bar his place, not The Grindstone. Yeah, he took his responsibilities seriously and all that. Everyone else thought he were the best bloody Landlord for years. More people made more mates from more cultures than ever before. Everyone had a great laugh and Nat and Gorman knew the pub were in safe hands. But secretly, this were his place. He just used to sit by the window, he'd say, look up at the stars he'd known since he were a kid, and know his place.'

The stars. It's dark again – God knows what time it is up here – and I have a sudden urge to have a look at those same stars. My familiar, beautiful stars – the ones I've looked at all my life and escaped into when I've closed my eyes at night. The space the Robinsons got lost in, the second stars to the right which led straight on 'til morning. The ones which the poor burning people of Dogwood Falls know nothing about.

'Let's get that fresh air,' I say.

'Hang about a second, lad. I'm trying to tell you about a man's place in the world. It's a lucky man, him that knows it. Aren't that many that do.' He picks up the tumbler and starts to polish it again. 'Arnold's the only one of his kind not totally crackers, which is tough fer him. But he made his decision, stuck to it and is happy in his place. Estelle's his wife...'

'His wife?'

'Aye, and she knows her place; right by his side. Gave up everything for him when the other GeoTrolls went nuts. You've got half a tonne of guilt drinking yer cherry brandy downstairs.'

'Why are you telling me this?'

'Because place is important,' he says. 'It moulds who you are, shapes your thinking and the way you look at the world. It anchors you. It's why the Protection of Dogwood Falls works so well. You are your place. You are The Axe and Grindstone.

'Fox's Licence,' he says, looking me in the eye for the first time since we left to see the Council.

'What about Fox's Licence?' I ask, pulling the Red from behind my ear, and resting it between my lips.

'It were ripped away because he felt his place were in Oak Cheating, not Dogwood Falls.'

'And?'

'Well, which pub would you choose, if you had the chance? The Axe or The Grindstone?' I look around the dusty shadows of my new home. 'For all the good he did as Landlord, I think Fox would have chosen The Axe – his place – and that's why his Licence was ripped away. Do you get it, lad?'

I sit on the edge of the table where I expect Fox used to sit when the craziness downstairs got too much for him. Yeah, I get it.

'You don't think their crazy plan is going to work, do you?'

Emmet shrugs.

'The Binding Brothers ripped Fox's Licence from him, even though he'd been Landlord for years. He'd made friends, he'd got a life. He knew us, and he knew the pub better than I think he knew himself. He'd made his promises, he'd sworn his oaths, he'd thrown out enough soldiers, and GeoTrolls, and drunken preachers. But it weren't enough, Mark. And you think they won't be able to rip yours from you, having been here two days?'

I light the cigarette. He goes on.

'He'd left me in charge, the day he were taken. It weren't a big deal – wasn't like he were a control freak or anything. He just didn't do it that often. You walk into The Axe, you expect the Landlord, an open smile, and an open bar bill. You don't expect me on my own. Should have known something were up. 'We'd had a bit of a falling out. Not a big one – nothing to make me want to up sticks and leave. I'd made a small comment about this girl who couldn't pay her bill. She was from a small island about three miles west of the Falls. We let her off, of course – there's a fair few who can't pay their bills lately but make them up later – but I'd made this joke in passing about all girls from West Anand being easy with everything but their cash. Fox thought it racist, even though it blatantly weren't.'

Emmet looks at me, urging me to agree. I shrug, which seems the right thing to do and he continues.

'I told you the last time I saw Nat, I were running out on her, right?'

'You did.'

'Greatest mistake of my life, bar one. I mean, what sort of message does that give? But it were the first time any of us had seen the March of the Binding Brothers made real. The Council – well, everyone in the town – had heard the Velis had somehow managed to covert a load of Incorporeal. There's a fair few around.

'Some people invest so much in the war that they can't leave if it's their time. They say that, for a while after you split your being, you can't be killed – temporary invulnerability is pretty handy in a war. But it's not a nice life – and if you don't snap back immediately you're like that forever.

'There was talk the Brothers had managed to convince the Incorporeal that the way to be released – the way to properly fucking die – was to look into the face of God and plead.'

'So they have an army of ghosts who need to make others scream, as they believe that's the only way to get to God and get to heaven? That's a bit fucked up.'

'Ain't it just, you're learning. The combined will of the Veli's prayers, plus the intense longing of the Incorporeal, focused by the Brothers' leader, equals the Scratching.'

I sigh and look out the window to the stars. Of course I can't see them – it's fucking raining again, like it always is around here.

'What's the best way to stop that from happening?'

'Simple really, boss. You kill them before they kill you.'

I snort – I do that when I laugh suddenly.

'Kill them first? Yeah right – of course I will. A load of warrior monks and their purple army of the undead.' I think I'm going hysterical. I knew it would happen eventually. It's just surprising it took this long. 'I can see it now – come and have a go if you think you're hard enough. I've got half a shandy and a packet of crisps and I'm not afraid to use them! I see your evil Scratching, and raise you a pork scratching and packet of dry roasted. Genius.'

Emmet puts down his glass, walks around the side of the bar, and comes to stand in front of me.

'Has It sunk in what they're asking you to do?'

'Only the suicidal bit. Is there anything else I should remotely care about?'

'Think about it, lad. What do you reckon a Licence in Perpetuity is?' I sigh and bury my head in my hands. I don't know and I don't care. This is all going over my head. He sees the slump in my shoulders and comes over to me. 'Your Licence is your hold on the Protection of Dogwood Falls,' he continues. 'You can bar someone from the pub, you can physically and powerfully remove them from harming the breach between our two homes. But a Licence in Perpetuity, so much more powerful...' I look at him intensely. I should work this out for myself – he's testing me.

'You say my Licence physically removes people.' He nods, slowly. 'I say a few words and "poof", they're removed.'

'About a hundred foot, aye. And they can't get back in.'

'So, a more powerful Licence... the range of any banishment will be greater,' I eventually say, calculating the implications as I speak. 'How much greater? The maps – the ones I saw in the tunnel, the ones they've got downstairs... this is a small island isn't it?' Emmet nods again, but doesn't answer. 'Guessing more than a hundred foot. Two hundred? Three hundred?' He still says nothing. 'A thousand? So anyone we use the Licence on will get cast out to sea? Hang on, is that right?'

'Yep,' he nods, darkly. 'The Council want you and Fox to use the Licence in Perpetuity on the Binding Brothers and all who follow them. Inside or outside, they'll be cast at least five miles out.'

They'll all drown. There's nothing but ocean that far out.

Shit.

I can't see his eyes. I can't see the look he's giving me when he's urging me to risk my life. I'm not the killing sort. All I've wanted was the quiet life. Drowning loads of people – admittedly loads of murdering bastard people – isn't my thing. People with loved ones. Somewhere. But still...

The Axe & Grindstone

Is this what my granddad went through in the Second World War? Enemy ship. Target. Fire. It doesn't make you a murderer if the other side is after you and your country, does it? You don't see Her Majesty laying wreaths for murderers on Remembrance Sunday every year.

I'm not going to have a gun in my hands. I'm not going to look someone in the eye and pull a trigger. I'm going to say a few words in the presence of a tortured man. That's it. I'm not going to be convicted in any court I know of. I can't see it coming up on the six o'clock news, I can't see it reported in any newspaper. But it means if I do put my life in the hands of the Council, I may be able to walk out again. What sort of choice wouldn't I make?

I came up to The Axe for fresh air. I need the fresh air, rain or no rain.

'Give me a second, Emmet.'

I get up from the table and walk over to the heavy dark wooden door, unlock it, and step outside. The cold is bracing – I hadn't noticed the temperature in Dogwood Falls, but this is clearly your typical dark December night in southern England. The sound of the rain on the canopy above the door is almost punching its way down to the ground below, and even though I'm standing beneath it, I'm still getting wet – soaking wet. But it makes me feel that little bit more alive because of it. Besides, I can't move because I can't believe what I'm seeing in front of me.

My car. My bloody car is in the bloody car park of my bloody pub.

I don't have to deal with any of this anymore.

I'm going home.

CHAPTER XVI
THE STARS OF DEVON'S NIGHT SKY

The more I seem surprised by whatever's chucked at me, the less surprised I actually am.

I mean, the last thing I expected right here, right now, was the sight of my beautiful blue 1984 Austin Mini Metro staring at me in the car park. So, naturally, there it is.

'What the...'

I run over to her, placing my hands on her hood just to make sure she's real. Yep. Real. I run all around her – I don't care how wet I get. She's all right – I can't get my head around it. My car – but I left her in Long Barrow Ridge. All my things...

Hang on, she's not all right. She's wearing a Staunton Bin Bag – sorry, by which I mean there's a bin bag draped over the driver side window. The universal sign someone's lobbed a brick at her. Why would anyone do that to my baby? The fucking bastards.

'Who's a fucking bastard?'

Did I say that out loud?

Emmet's come out of the pub and is looking at the sky and the relentless rain that's pouring down on me. He has one of his disapproving looks on him, but I can match him stare for stare this time.

'Always imagined Oak Cheatin' to be warmer. Less damp,' he says, with a sniff.

'And eight out of ten cats prefer Dogwood, I know.'

'You what?'

'Never mind – this is my car. This is my stuff. The fucking bastard's the one who smashed her up.'

'Oh aye, so they have.'

'Your concern's touching, mate.'

'Are you done with yer fresh air? You've got my world to save.'

'Not just yet, I haven't.' I gently run my hand up the cold door handle, take a breath, and lift. The door opens, the lock's been fixed, and the familiar fake fresh pine means I'm immediately home. I get in and close the door behind me. I think I'll stay here, cocooned in my little shell. Everything'll be fine if I stay cocooned in my shell. With my boxes and my partworks and my free binders with part two. My iPhone's out of juice, of course, but I can soon fix that. Everything'll now be fine.

There's a note on the dashboard.

> Hey Adams
>
> Dropped your car round – mate of mine has a flood-proof tow truck & owes me a favour (well, several favours) so here we are. You weren't around, and I'm not going to poke my nose around when I know how busy you'll be downstairs. I know my place in the grand scheme of things. Hope you're settling in.
> Your key's in the glove box. Worked some magic with a bit of superglue. Should be fine. Roads are a little clearer than they were – ought to be drivable if you're careful. Just don't drink anything before you get in your car, as I may deck you next time you're caught short.
> Jennifer
> PS – Guess you now owe me a Christmas drink, so call me.

Well, well. Jennifer Peynton. I smile an embarrassed smile at the thought, and then feel a little guilty. Even she knows her place in the world – even if that place is a little scary and possibly involving a drink or two. Maybe I didn't come across as quite the arsehole I thought I did. Or maybe she likes arseholes? I could be her perfect arsehole – a phrase I really hope I didn't utter out loud.

I open the glove box and take out the makeshift key. This is it. It feels cold in my hand, unnatural. The end of it feels sharp, like it could puncture the bubble of Oak Cheating and Dogwood Falls and let the me sitting inside, slowly escape. Hey, look at that, it fits in the ignition. Half of me thought it wouldn't. I could turn it, to see if it works. That's what people do when they have a key in the ignition. That's what normal people do, in the normal world, right? I turn to look at Emmet, who's slowly shaking his head. I feel as transparent as the glass he's just been polishing. Well, he would be shaking his head, wouldn't he? I look down the drive. The weather doesn't look that bad. Sure, I can't see past the ridge in the lane, but if I drive slowly through any floodwater I'm sure I'll be fine. But then...

Then my eye is drawn to the tree. THE tree. The crazy, warm headfuck tree.

Leadership. Choices. Charge. Show leadership. Make the right choices. Take charge.

Dammit.

Slowly, and with the sure, calm, realisation that I'm doing precisely the wrong thing, I take the key out of the ignition and sit for a second with my hands resting on top of the steering wheel. After a couple of seconds I rest my forehead there too, and close my eyes.

A few minutes later, I find Emmet under the oak, looking up at the stars, through the intertwining branches of the canopy of twigs and broken wood above us.

'You've got pretty stars,' he mutters, eventually. 'A load of them are dead now. We can still see 'em burn though. If there are good Brothers out there – and I can't see it, to be fair – then the people that matter will still see 'em long after their gone. They may stick around, like Nat did. I don't know. You got family, boss?'

'A sister, two nieces. Four and five.'

'You think they'll burn in the sky? Be remembered long after they're gone?'

'Of course. They're not going anywhere soon.'

'Not if you buck up, lad. It's your choice whether they burn bright in their lives, seen and remembered in hundreds of years, or whether they're burned in the fires of their family – like the souls at the Falls.'

The key in my pocket is becoming heavy. I can feel it getting warmer – I'm sure it isn't, but in my head I can feel it getting warmer. Calling me away. The Metro is sitting, bathed in the vague half-hearted external lights of The Axe. If I jump in the car, I can (probably) leave. But then what?

He's right. Of course he's right.

Leadership. Choices. Charge. I'm the sodding Landlord of Peacebattle – not for the randoms in the pub downstairs, but for Chloe and Ella.

And if I have to make the Binding Brothers scream in order to look into the face of God and ask His forgiveness for what I have to do, then so be it.

Chapter XVII
The Taste of the Incorporeal

'Where is he? Where is the fatuous little shit? Does he not realise the importance of his task?

Have none of you worthless drunkards explained the urgency in our mission? Dear God, no wonder we're facing the end of the world.'

Gorman's voice travels through the stone corridor towards the crack in the air.

'Do you think he might be the scariest part of this plan?' I whisper.

'I dated his granddaughter once. You have no idea.'

'You're a brave, brave man, Emmet.'

We walk the rest of the way to the sound of Gorman's stick thumping my tables, and I stop in the doorway. The Council stand around the side of the room, looking at him as he paces up and down. Arnold's sitting at the bar with his back to me, but I can tell he's got his arms crossed and wearing an annoyed expression. He could be thirsty. You know, even as that crosses my mind, I find it weird the thought of serving a GeoTroll comes so naturally. Nat's standing by the front door, and as Gorman waves his stick at her, she glances at me, puts her hands on her hips and raises an eyebrow.

'Did I not make it clear in the tunnels that he was to remain here?' Gorman continues. 'But, yet again Miss Bennett, you let him out of your sights. Inconceivable for a woman in your position – a position I shall be reviewing the moment you return from the Monastery. Will you stop pointing, woman, whilst I am trying to talk to you? Oh...' He's turned and sees me watching him, leaning against the doorframe with my own arms crossed. 'Mr Adams, what a delight. We were worried about you for a moment there. I was about to write you a card and send you flowers.'

'What a shame. Shall I go back upstairs and wait for the delivery? Could do with something pretty up there.'

'Brandy,' says Arnold, plainly. Without taking my eyes off Gorman, I go behind the bar, pick up a pint glass and empty the rest of the bottle with a flourish.

'It's on your tab, Arnold.' He looks at me, one rocky eyebrow raised in question.

'Tab?'

'Yeah. I'm sure you don't need a reason to get me back here alive, so you've now got a tab – a clean one too. No pressure or anything.' I slide the glass over to him, again not breaking eye contact with the old war-horse leaning on his stick. 'Emmet, please chalk up a bottle of cherry brandy to Arnold here. Arnie, you can pay it back next week.'

The old man clears his throat. 'Are you quite finished, sir?'

'Doing the job I'm paid for, sir.' I sling a towel over my shoulder and walk over to him. 'Unless you'd like to find someone else to do it.' I break eye contact and glace at Nat. 'Nat, any chance of a pay rise, given the extra responsibilities not in my contract?'

Gorman bangs his cane on the floor. 'Your contract states you do what the Council deems necessary to uphold the Protection of Dogwood Falls, Mr Adams. Nothing less.'

'Natasha?'

'I'm sure I can work something out, Mark.' I break into a smile I'm not sure I feel and turn back to the old man.

'Good. Well, come on then, Gorman. Did no one explain to the Council the urgency of our mission?' There's an uncomfortable beat, and this time it's Gorman who moves first, muttering under his breath as he turns on his heel and walks over to the table by the door. He gestures to Nat, who beckons me over to a map.

She places one delicate hand on my shoulder. As she does so, from the corner of my eye, I see Emmet start polishing something as he listens. I don't think discretion was ever one of her strengths. She points at one corner of the map.

'I am, under sufferance, taking you here to the Gate of Fourteen Fellow Men, on the Eden Peninsula.'

'Bit of a pretentious name. What's the Gate of Fourteen

Fellow Men when it's at home?'

'The Ancestry always went in for pretension. That generation always believed you had to link place to history, so everyone who knew the history knew their place. Peacebattle Lane – the place where the final battle brought peace. The Gate of Fourteen Fellow Men – the place where a jury of fourteen tried and executed Ichabod Blackwood and swung his body for eighty days and eighty nights to prove a point. These days, it's the entrance to the Cenobium – the Monastery of the Binding Brothers.'

'Right,' I say, 'and you're sure I can't stay here? Things to do, glasses to clean...' Emmet puts once down on the bar and picks up another. '...possibly...'

'Sorry Mark.'

'Just checking. Fox is there then, is he?'

'We think so. Would make sense. It's hard to be sure. Once a year, a member of the Council dines with the Brothers in order to keep the peace. Last year they requested Fox. He took a guest.'

There's a crash as another glass smashes behind the bar.

'Yer not serious?' The barman stands there, staring.

'You've been there before Emmet. None of us have.' Nat walks over to him, and places her arms on the bar, leaning across it. He must have a great view. 'You have to be our guide.'

'Bollocks. Buy a map. I can't go. That were never the plan. He'll...'

'Emmet, it's been a long, hard, day and we're all very tired. It would make me very grateful. You know what's at stake here.' He looks at her, and I can see the conflict in his eyes, as he looks into hers. Slowly, he nods. Nat smiles, thankfully, and gives him a small kiss on the cheek.

'Good man.'

I catch Emmet's eyes, as he sits back down on his stool. He looks shaken. I guess his place turns out to be by my side. I guess it's the way it's meant to be.

'Right,' I turned to Gorman. 'Let's do this.'

Natasha, Arnold, Emmet and I step out of The Grindstone onto the wet cobbles outside. The sky, once full of the strange and distant stars which shone upon my first night in this strange and distant land, is obscured. The night is blindfolded by a stifling purple mist which seeps from above.

The Incorporeal. Hovering above The Grindstone and Dogwood Falls like an ever-present cloud of vultures waiting to feed upon the empty remains of the town, once the living have left.

'And what do we do about them?' I say, pointing up.

'Can't punch them,' grumbles Arnold. 'Shame. But I guess I have to stay and make sure they don't do anything stupid.' Estelle goes over to him, stands on two petite toes, and kisses him gently. She says all she needs to with one brush of her fingers against his arm, and then turns to me.

'Landlord's Motto, dear,' mutters Estelle.

'Yeah,' he says on cue. 'It's more than superstition, lad. I may have sold it a bit short, earlier. It's still a part of yer Licence though.' I look through the door to the remaining members of the Council standing inside.

'Will the Protection work with you inside when I'm not?' I ask Gorman.

'Don't fret, Mister Adams. Defending the breach is our life's work, and the GeoTroll here will make sure that's remembered. Don't you forget that – or let us down. Get to Fox and get out. It's that simple. Banish the bastards who want to crack nature apart and evangelise your land through pain and suffering.'

I look at him, and keep looking at him.

'And if I fail?'

'Don't. For the sake of your family. Don't. For the sake of all living things who refuse to believe screams are holy. Don't.'

'No pressure.' I sigh. Guess this is it then. 'Emmet,' I say calmly. 'Close the door please.'

The heavy oak door closes slowly, and definitively as if it knows it's doing it for the final time, so has to make a special effort. I take the iron key from my belt, place it in the lock, and turn it twice. My palm is sweaty and wet, so I wipe it down my jeans – only slightly ashamed to do it in front of Nat and Estelle. Oh well. I place my palm on the door.

'Where once was war, where all shed blood, through me communion: The Oak and Dogwood.'

This time, although I'm expecting no tingle, I feel a glowing warmth in my hand and the threatening cloud above me swirls counter-clockwise and moves away – only slightly, but there's a definite movement.

And there's another, to my left coming down the hill. Jesus, they're fast. Three men storming towards us and they're not stopping. They're after me. Shit – they're coming to kill me. I haven't even stepped out of the porch and they're going to kill me. Their yells and guttural cries are screeching their way into my skull and they're going to kill me. Arnold pushes me aside and runs towards them. Emmet stands in front of me, poised like yesterday with his hairs razor sharp, upright and glinting, but all that means is I can't see the men who are going to kill me.

I fumble for my keys but drop them – of course I drop them. Shit, shit, shit, and I'm on my knees as I scoop them up.

'Don't open the fucking door,' growls Emmet.

'What do you mean – don't open the fucking door? They Are Going To Kill Me!' A fair way off, I can hear grunts – and the sound of knife on rock – as Arnold tries to take them down.

'Bar the fuckers!' Emmet shouts.

'What?'

'Use your fucking Licence! Bar the fuckers!'

'Fine!' I shout, thrusting my arm towards the men for dramatic effect. For discord and schism, for those you have scarred ...erm... those blokes over there, the Landlord has barred!'

The grunting stops, and I can see my would-be killers rise through the air as if a huge shockwave of silent sound has swept them off their feet – carrying them beyond sight over the top of the hill at the end of the lane.

Wow. Think about the power that'll have if both Fox and I use it at once. A Licence in Perpetuity, huh? OK, if my mind wasn't made up before, it is now. It really is me or them.

There's a knock at the window. It's Gorman.

'Are you still here?'

Nat stands for a moment, hands on her hips, and exhales.

She turns to Estelle.

'Right, honey. Am I really going to do this?'

Estelle pauses, her hands gracefully bend her back. 'Yes, dear. War requires a lady to be, shall we say, a little less fussy when it comes to dignity.'

'No such thing as dignity any more,' Nat mutters under her breath.

'How's this work?' I ask.

'With discretion. Emmet, I know what you're like. You keep your fingers and your thoughts to yourself once we're on our way, all right?'

'Of course! Yer think I'm some sort of pervert?' Nat sniffs, and ignores the question.

'Mark, what we're about to do is painful – and, well, sort of taboo. So if we get through this, we shall never speak of it again, understand?'

'Yes, boss.' There's no other real answer I could give, really.

'And when I said I'd told you everything, I may have held back. It's kind of personal.'

'What do you mean?'

She nods at Estelle, who acknowledges her, and takes one look back at The Axe. Slowly, Nat's face begins to lose shape, and her features blur and wave into the familiar purple mist.

No. Not my Nat.

I can't think about it. I mustn't. I can't take it in. I can't focus on this right now. My head's too full of stuff to register this lie...

Jen tried to tell me. After her accident...

It all rolls through my mind again. The laughs. The drinks. The dancing and the smiles and the jokes and the kiss. No. I raise my hand to my head again and I can sense Emmet flinch behind me. Nat. Poor Nat. My Nat – no, not my Nat any more. Never just my Nat. Just... Natasha.

She'd died. She'd become one of them.

Her face loses focus until I recognise nothing more about the Nat I knew from so long ago. She floats in front of us, mixing and flowing so I'm not certain where the air stops and she begins. She forms a ring around us which grows in height, and soon neither Emmet nor I can see anything of the lane or the pub behind us. We look at each other as the world around us seems to revolve.

Nat's spinning, faster and faster, and I feel like I'm in the eye of a storm about to be swept up. The wind sounds hollow, and it's getting louder and louder – an unholy roar which seeps through my soul and even though I'm pressing my palms against my ears I still can't stop it getting in.

'Nat!' I cry out, but it's no good, I can't hear myself shout. I fall to my knees next to Emmet, who's trying to act calm but also failing. I want to stop now. Is it too late to stop now? This was a stupid plan thought up by stupid people. I'm their Kenobi flying into their Death Star, and Kenobi gets killed. The wall of sound and noise is getting closer. Emmet and I nudge closer together until we're almost touching, but we're still too far apart.

'Natasha!' he shouts, 'What yer doin? You never said you were gonna do this.'

'Do what?' I shout back. 'Emmet, what are they going to do?'

'Brace yerself. This ain't gonna be nice.' The purple cloud is turning redder and redder as she speeds up. The wind is whipping my face and, oh my God, there's nowhere to shrink to, nowhere to move. If I tilt my head even an inch to my left, the storm's going to rip it off. I don't know what's going to happen, I don't know what to do.

The choice is made for me. With one, final, roar the ghost of Natasha Bennett snaps shut the last remaining space and she courses through me – through my skin, through my mouth, through every porous inch of my body. I can feel her in my stomach, I can feel her in my head. I can feel her flowing through my blood and my brain and the space between the cells which keep me together.

And I feel her start to rip my body apart.

I cannot cry out, I cannot scream for help for there is no air in my lungs but Her. I cannot reach to Emmet, or see him, for She is blocking the signals to my arms, and my eyes. I cannot run away for She is now my legs, and one by one She starts to dissolve my toes. I can't feel them any more – dear God I can't feel anything any more. I can't see anything any more. It's dark – darker than anything I've known in my life and although I've lost feeling I have sensation. New and abhorrent sensations of drowning whilst afloat, helpless – so helpless. Everything I am. Everything I've grown to be is afloat and not here, stolen from me until all I have left is this voice. And I wonder when this will be taken from me.

'Mark.'

Her voice. My voice. The same.

'Natasha.'

'Mark, it's OK, it's over.' I can sense her voice. I can sense her calming words and for the first time believe it might be OK.

'What's happened? What is this? Where am I?'

'You're part of me, the two of you. It was the only way. I had to reach into your bodies and realign things a little.' She pauses, and I can sense what she's going to say before I feel her words.

'Mark, Emmet. I'm sorry. I'm Incorporeal. And now so are you.'

CHAPTER XVIII
THE GATE OF FOURTEEN FELLOW MEN

The world is dark, but getting brighter. Sensation becomes light, and awareness becomes sound.

My thoughts are still jumbled up like my sock drawer on a Saturday night, but I've drunk Overproof Rum so it's not as unusual as it sounds.

She – We – She – says it's only temporary. I'm not dead, and not technically a ghost. Well, OK, I think I'm technically a ghost.

Perhaps.

Oh, God, I'm confused.

We're currently flying – which makes me laugh in itself – slowly over Dogwood Falls, in amongst the 'other' Incorporeal. I can be put together again, I think. God, I wonder whether I'll keep my clothes. They're not part of me, are they? I never thought. Am I going to be dumped in the middle of an evil monastery with no clothes on?

No, Mark, you'll have your clothes back. They're just atoms at the end of the day.

Jesus!

Sorry.

Will you stop doing that, Natasha?

Sorry. This is new for me as well. I've never had anyone in my head before. And you wondered why I was against this plan.

It's a bit... intimate, isn't it?

Just a bit.

Not that that's a bad thing – I mean, well, I always wanted to know you better, and everything. Didn't expect it to be like this though. I mean, as intimacy goes, it's not a fumble in a flat above a pub on what turns out to be your last night in town, but...

Mark, you're babbling.

I know. I'm sorry. I just have to keep talking, or whatever this is. It's the only way I know for sure I'm still here.

You're still here.

Good. Glad to know. Seems the right time for a fag. It's what they do in the films, right? Hang on, the colours are getting lighter – and I can actually see colours! That's new.

You're becoming more entwined with me. You'll soon be able to see what I do.

Well that's a start.

Hang on. What happened to Emmet?

Yes, I'm here. The buggers lied to us. I want to get off now.

I second that. Getting off is good.

That's not the first time you've thought that, is it Mark?

Nat, that's rude.

Sorry again.

There's definitely light now. Light and shapes – and a moving world that's forming around me. It's a bit tricky to make out everything, well, anything, at the moment, but everything's getting clearer. The sensations are different, soft and flowing, and known. I know these sensations. The heat of the currents, the certainty of the poles and the attraction of warm air against the cold. We're rising – we're definitely rising with the air, forming and reforming like it's the most natural thing in the world. Why don't more people do this? It's not like it's difficult or anything. I think left, and we turn left. I think right, and we turn – well, not right just yet, but I'm still a beginner and I'm sure I'll get there eventually. There are three of us in here, after all.

I just have to concentrate on the flowing lines. I assume they're lines. They're the things moving in front of us – below us, around us. Come on Mark, you can do it without them. Concentrate on the lines, the lines, and the... grass. It's grass, green green grass, and you're flying over it like a pro. Just keep doing what you're doing and don't stop. You're Incorporeal, you can feel the wind course through you – that's what it's there for, to give you something to move through. Grasp it, reach out to every single molecule and push it through you to move forward.

What a pro.

Dogwood Falls stretches out around me. Without turning my

head – for I have no head, it seems – I can see the valley and the coast behind us, and the dark saucer of Incorporeal circling The Grindstone in the distance. Beneath us, empty roads and empty fields make up the majesty of the island. The maps and drawings laid out in my pub have done no justice to this place at all. Dogwood Falls is a collection of small hamlets, kept small and manageable by a network of interlinking cobbled roads which meet in circular junctions, all with the commemorative obelisks we ran past to and from the harbour. The harbour itself can still be seen – a thin column of dark smoke contrasting deeply with the pink and vicious clouds surrounding it. For a moment, the harbour itself looks ugly against the beauty of the ghosts around it – and I have to concentrate hard to stop myself admiring the beauty of my own kind.

"Do you always talk to yourself in yer head, lad?"

Not always, but often.

"Explains a lot, boss."

Leave me alone.

I shift my focus to the direction in which we're heading.

Up ahead, far up ahead, I can see the Eden Peninsula – at least, I assume that I can. In the distance I can see water on the left and the right, and there's a gap in the horizon where the sea seems banished. On that scrap of land, on that three-sided island, is supposed to lie the Cenobium, and Fox. The peninsula seems disparate – as if it's part of Dogwood Falls, but apart from it. As if the people that first settled there did so because they wanted to be special.

"I know what you're thinking, Mark."

I know you do, Nat. You have a knack at the best of times.

"The Eden Peninsula has been marked and fallow ground for generations. If Peacebattle Lane is seen as the embodiment of community and friendship within Dogwood Falls, then Eden Peninsula has come to represent the opposite to everyone but the Binding Brothers."

Don't tell me, let me guess. Connect a name to an event, right?

"Right."

"I taught the lad everything he knows."

Hang on, I'm talking here. Sort of. Eden Peninsula – it's where Ichabod settled, isn't it. The place he thought was his god-given right. Where he started to rename everyone living here as if they were his to rename. What else would he call his home, but Eden?

"The people fought for so long, Mark. They tried to keep hold of what was true, but they weren't that used to it. The hills and valleys of Dogwood Falls aren't natural. They're the grave mounds of those who died to protect their way of life."

"Some of us fought and died, lad, and kept fighting. Some of us were there at the beginning. This is the third peace I've lived through now – well, if you pardon the term. It wasn't until Fox came along, and then Nat, that I sat down for an actual drink with people from your world. You weren't a bad lot, after all, all things considered."

And now, Emmet?

"Now I'll live through the fourth."

His voice is insistent. He's got faith in me. He knows beyond doubt he'll survive.

Little else to say, really, for a while. The currents once again lift us high above the island, and, if I squint, I can see my first glimpse of Eden. I remember the stories from Sunday School – inconceivable paradise protected from the barren wasteland of the rest of creation by a large wall, guarded by angels to prevent Adam and Eve taking back what once was theirs.

This Eden is slightly different. It's not paradise, for a start – there's no green land past the large wall which cuts it off from the rest of the Falls – and there are more than two people milling around. There are hundreds. They're all walking towards an amphitheatre in the middle of a muddy field. From this height, they're tiny, but as we descend, they grow and become clearer. Hunched and tired faces never look up, and never smile.

Where are they going? I think out loud.

"Not sure, lad. I'd have been long gone if I were them."

"There's nowhere to go. The people can't wrap themselves in their houses for ever, and no one'll go to the harbour. Not after last night. They're going to church. If the Binding Brothers tell them

prayer'll help, you'll find an awful lot of people suddenly willing to pray. Faith is like energy, you can't create it, can't destroy it. It just changes form. You can have faith in peace, and faith in the Council to protect that peace and keep you alive. If the Council's no longer there, and you no longer believe in the peace it represents, you transfer that faith to something else. Faith you'll live, faith in your family to protect you. Sometimes faith you won't be next if you walk to the wall.

It's at times like these I regret taking those Sunday shifts at Fortnights. Perhaps a little more faith in my life may have been somewhat helpful, right about now.

The amphitheatre is filling up, and the air surrounding it is misty with Incorporeal. They float and shimmer around the people, who ignore them, sit down in silence and stare at their feet. In front of the sunken structure, in the view of all those gathered, stands the only opening in a wall – that must be ten feet in height – which separates the Eden Peninsula from the rest of creation. Now we're coming up, it fills the entire horizon. I need to fly close.

You sure?

Yes, Nat. This is incredible. Just look at it. It's like the Great Wall of China, or something out of Mordor.

Where?

Never mind. We sweep to the left and join a cloud of Incorporeal who run alongside its outer breadth. This is the first time we've come up close and it's unnerving. Can everyone else hear that... that chatter? That noise? The sound of, not voices, not people, but souls... I'm not sure I like that. I'm not sure I like that at all. If I can sense them, then they'll be able to sense me, us... me.

Ignore it, Mark. Remember to focus.

The wall now takes up all of my vision – or rather, the majority of what I can now sense is the wall. And it's magnificent. Carved into every huge stone is an epic scene from Sunday School. The banishment from the Garden. Lot's wife turning to salt. The plagues of Egypt. To put it bluntly, all of the righteous things from the Bible without any of the lovely stuff.

Hang on, lad, you recognise this art?

Yeah, doesn't everyone? Nat?

"Sure."

It's your basic Church of England upbringing. You may have escaped it here. Guess the details kind of got lost, what with the wars and the forceful door-to-door evangelism that must have gone on. I'll explain later.

We fly on for another couple of minutes, not wanting to think too much out loud in case we're overheard. Eventually, we come to the amphitheatre, and the centre of the wall where one half stops and the other begins. Running up the entire length is a gilded, golden gate, almost obscene in its brilliance. The sun reflects thousands of glimmering shivers onto the barren soil around it, and casts small tears of light onto the hundreds of people that gather. Dwarfed, in between the gate and the amphitheatre, stands an old, weather beaten gallows on a small platform. No prizes for guessing why that was built – or, thinking about it, why the amphitheatre was built in front of it.

The Gate of Fourteen Fellow Men, and the place where Ichabod Blackwood took his final breath in front of hundreds of grasping onlookers.

"There's a problem, guys."

"I can sense it too, Natasha."

"No idea what you're on about, the pair o' you."

Nor me. What's wrong, Nat?

"We can't get past the gate. Even though there are gaps between the bars, we can't slip between them or over the wall. Look, no other Incorporeal is getting in. That was the whole reason behind this ridiculous plan. We'll have to think of something else. All the other ghosts are falling into line behind the amphitheatre – I suggest we do the same. Something's going to happen."

We float down with the others and hang behind a woman and her little boy hugging themselves on the damp seats of the stadium. They look nervously around, and the mother pulls her young son towards her.

'You said we didn't have to come, Mum. You said we could go see Grandma.'

'Shhh, I know, Jason. I know. But all the boats are broken, aren't they, remember? All the boats that would carry us away to

Grandma are broken.'

'But I don't understand. They weren't broken last week. I went to see them. The one with the tall mast was the tallest boat in the world!'

'Yes, honey, I know. But that was last week, wasn't it? Things were different, last week. We had a Council last week to take care of us. We had a school, and a shop, and our friends...' She raises a hand to her eyes and turns her face away from her son as she wipes them.

'What's wrong, mummy?'

'Nothing. Nothing, sweetheart. Just wait for the man to come out. He's going to make it better, don't worry. He's going to tell you how brave you can be, and how much you're loved. He's going to tell you the stories of how we'll all come together like the olden days. Do you remember the stories I used to tell you, of all the soldiers and the men from the other land? Well, all the soldiers are gone now, and only the men from the other land are left. So we have to be good and listen to them, OK? Are you going to be good for me?'

'Yes, mummy.'

'Good lad.'

Not all the soldiers have left.

'Remember,' continues the mother, 'we're just stories when all's been said and done, so we have to make sure we're the hero, right? We have to be the person other little boys and girls look up to. We have to be the brave ones, the handsome ones, the ones who make the right choices and save the day. Whatever happens, sweetheart, however this story ends, you're my hero all the way through.'

There's a large boom, from beyond the gate – a drum? Thunder? I'm not sure – and it starts to open, slowly. The woman holds her son close to her and watches as the slivers of sunlight dance across the faces of the crowd. The subtle whispers which had washed over them now dry up, and all is silent.

Apart from the singing.

It's distant, and drifts along on the wind so faintly I think it's a stray thought from Nat intruding once again into my own mind.

But no – it's there and it's real. The tunes lilt and wane in the air. It's haunting, but reverential and the mismatch of sound causes a ripple through the audience. They all know what's coming.

From the foot of the wall, through the gate, they come. One by one, the men walk slowly out of Eden towards the scaffold where the old gallows watch over their audience. From the left and the right of the gate, Incorporeal meet and escort the line of Brothers, a line either side of the men who sing as they march. As they progress towards us, the clouds change form, their mists solidifying into the seven-foot silhouettes of... what are they?

Who's guarding the Brothers? They're all reforming into... GeoTrolls.

I can hear the roaring of the fires within them as they form two columns either side of the monks. No one told me I'd be up against an army of GeoTrolls! Monks, OK, purple ghosts at a push. But GeoTrolls? I've seen Arnold when he's angry! I've seen him run after those he's pissed off at! I've heard him shout at me, and I've been scared.

It makes sense. I remember now. He's the last of his clan. They're his family.

Shit. No wonder he drinks.

The roaring of the Geotrolls gives the singing an urgent bass line, and the noise grows in volume as the troupe nears the platform. The little boy throws his hands over his ears. Slowly, and gently, his mother removes them.

With each step felt by the people watching, the Brothers fall into line on the scaffold. They stand side by side facing the crowd, singing at us and drowning us with their hymn. I've never been a big fan of Latin at the best of times. Today is not the best of times.

I can't make out all the words – I'm not good at things like that – but it's getting louder and louder, and as they sing the brothers slowly raise their hands to the sky. *Faciem dei, faciem dei*, over and over again until after a final cry all is quiet.

The brothers stare at us. We, as one, stare back.

Do they know that I'm here? Do they know how mad I actually am? Can The Man With The Crab-Like Feet sense me even though I'm not myself?

Tap-te-tap-te-tap.

Dear God, no.

Tap-te-tap-te-tap.

The little boy's fingers drum on the seat impatiently as he stares at us and our flexing, floating, wave. His mother quickly stops him tapping on the bench and draws his attention back to the scaffold.

Thank God for that.

Don't be thanking God just yet, lad.

The monks are dressed like the ones at the harbour; long black cloaks with a deep red trim, the colour of which matches the magenta of angry Incorporeal. Nice to know the Brothers place fashion design at the heart of their religion.

And then I see him.

It really is him. The monk in the centre removes his hood, and at once I feel his eyes, searching. Looking for me. Looking at the people who are afraid to look away.

Tap-te-tap-te-tap.

Tap-te-tap-te-tap.

His robes flow and drape on the wooden stage as he walks, but there's no escaping the sound in my thoughts.

Tap-te-tap-te-tap.

Tap-te-tap-te-tap.

He walks slowly, reverently, to a large podium in front of the gallows. He's taking his time. He wants us to watch, to consider his movements and his message. I want to go. I want to leave now and never come back. I want to fly all the way to Oak Cheating and lock my cellar behind me. Flooded roads and blocked lanes aren't going to stop me in this form.

But I can't move. I can't run away. I'm here to blend in. I have to stay low, especially now he's here. I have to stay hidden.

The Man With The Crab-Like Feet starts to speak. His voice echoes across the amphitheatre, bouncing around and across the people who lean forward to listen as if their lives depended on it. Which I'm fairly sure they do.

'Dearly... dearly beloved,' he begins. His eyes meet those of his congregation one by one, but his smile glances off them. 'What a wonderful day today is. Thank you for coming to worship. Thank you for leaving your homes to join us on this... joyous morning.

'We are taught that man alone is not the best man can be. To reach the true promise God has put within you a man must stand alongside his brother and add his voice to collective... worship.'

The congregation remains silent, with the massed GeoTrolls staring at them with their dark eyes and their roaring chests, as if daring us to disagree.

'This is a time of great change for Dogwood Falls,' Khalid continues. 'This is a time of great... redemption.

'This is a time when men must look to their hearts and question what they find. Many find great sorrow. Many find... deep grief. Many find that the years of war, and battle, and discord have scarred their souls and left them broken.

'Dear, dear friends. Do not despair. Do not weep. Do not be... afraid. We are here to bind your souls to God.

'He will heal you. He will make you... as new. He will treat you as lost children returning home, and will wrap you in His eternal embrace, forevermore.'

There's a shout from the left of the stadium, as a young man pushes off the constraints of his wife – who's obviously trying to stop him doing something stupid.

'KILLER!' he cries. 'Murdering BASTARD!' The roar of the GeoTrolls rises in pitch, and even from this distance I can see a spark in their eyes. 'They'd done no wrong! They'd done NOTHING to you! Nothing! My brother was only young. For fuck's sake, he was getting married next week! He were at the harbour to talk to the fishermen about his wedding feast and you MURDERED him in cold blood! Fuck you, preacher. And fuck the god you believe in!'

There's murmurs from across the crowd as the man stands and stares at Veli Khalid. I don't know how this is going to go. The crowd would back him, I'm sure. Do we back him? Do we all stand and face down the bastards before us? His wife is begging him to sit back down, but he's pushing her away. There's another shout, another cry, and a rock is thrown at the gallows.

'Bastards!'

'Murderers!'

The Axe & Grindstone

The same words carry across the crowd as the volume rises and arms begin to be waved at the monks before us. This is it. It's going to be a full-on proper riot. Maybe this is our chance – maybe this is the distraction we need to break into the Cenobium. C'mon people. Do it for your Landlord – no, *Landlords*. The little boy in front of us starts to get scared, and pushes himself closer to his mother, who looks around at the people either side of her on their feet.

'Please. Please sit down. Please don't make a fuss. My boy's scared, don't you see? Please sit down!'

On the scaffold, Khalid looks around. He doesn't seem bothered. Nothing makes that man bothered! A stone lands a foot away from his robes and the man doesn't flinch. His colleagues in their line-up are looking nervously from one to another, as the missiles get closer and closer, but Khalid doesn't move. Until he nods, slowly, to the GeoTroll in front of him.

The monster dissipates abruptly into a cloud of dark magenta dust, as one by one, so do his fellows to the side of him. The crowd roars with approval. They're leaving.

They're not leaving.

They form a column of smoke and gas, which rises above the crowd in a cigar shaped dart. The shouts and the cries die down, leaving only whispers. The mass of Incorporeal hangs in the air, suspended by anticipation and all around us people are holding their breaths. But not for long. The dart fires down, tunnelling through the air towards the crowd, faster and faster until it punches through the chest of the original protester. It cuts through him and explodes through his back. The man hangs on the ribbon of ghosts, who pull themselves through him, lifting him high up above the crowd to the stunned silence of the people below. As the crimson string completes its journey, the ghosts double back and envelop the man, obscuring him from view. When they flatten out again, descend to the ground, and retake their GeoTroll form, the man is gone.

His wife fills the air around us with screams, and Veli Khalid breathes in, deeply.

He beckons the crowd to sit down, his hands gesturing slowly, and he is obeyed.

No one's going anywhere, and no more stones are being thrown.

'Let us pray,' he commands. 'You will repeat after me. *Deus adoramus te.*'

The crowd sullenly repeat the words. Softly and unsteadily uttering them one by one. *Deus adoramus te.* As one, Nat, Emmett and I stay silent.

'*Deus adoramus te, Fortis es validum. Kyrie adoramus te. Nam invenire est te.*'

The crowd repeat the words after every line, with no idea what they mean. Any semblance of rebellion has been broken. How do you make a stand against a force which can rip through you without even leaving a body to mourn? Khalid looks around, approvingly, and carries on.

God we worship you,

For you are strong and hidden.

Oh Lord, we worship you

For to find you, is to know you.

In nostra nudus... clamoribus. In nostra nudus... dolorem.

Liceat videre... faciem dei.

In our naked... screams. In our naked... pain.

Allow us to see the face of God.

Amen.

'God is smiling upon you. He looks down from beyond the gate and is content. I have seen the face of God, the Re-Creator. I have known Him. Tasted Him. Pleased... Him.

'Many of you think you have known happiness. Many of you think you have known joy. Many of you look into the eyes of your... children and see love, and peace, and delight.

'You are wrong.

'Yesterday was the first day of your re-education. For too long the people of this town have festered in a fake peace, whilst we have watched and prayed for your souls. For too long, those who fought to give you God's paradise on this world were shunned, and hated.

'God does not forgive... hatred.

'God does not forgive... debauchery.

'God does not forgive belief in anyone but Him to show you what is pure.

'For too long, the people of this land have taken for granted His patience. For too long, the... purpose of this land was forgotten. You were put here to glory God.

'The man before you just now was... mistaken. He had placed his faith elsewhere. His faith was a poison, and that poison had to be extracted. He had placed faith in the Council of the Wounded.

'Let there be no mistake now. Let there be no more... blasphemy now. There will be no more communion between races God has put on this land to service Him and Him alone! God created nature for Him and His glory, and through Him we will crack it apart once more! The whole of creation will scream at once and the face of God will be everywhere for all eternity!

'The Council has gone. And once the Landlord of Peacebattle is removed you will know paradise and the paradise will be glorious! From this day forth, you will know true peace. You will know true happiness. You will know true love, and peace, and delight. For God has given me His Scratching: His Spirit and His Messenger to show you how pure you can be.

'The Scratching will remove your pride. The Scratching will remove your deception and your arrogance and your hatred. The Scratching will show you as you are in the arms of the Lord as babes once more, and through your cries you will see the face of God.'

He pauses, his rhetoric languishing in the air as the congregation reflect on what it might mean. I reflect upon Joan's words a lifetime ago, and the life I've left behind.

It's an unnatural silence.

He's waiting for something.

'God is... good,' he says, his voice lower in tone than before, as if he's talking to himself now rather than the crowd. 'God hears our... prayers. When we once asked for paradise, God gave us Eden. Where once we asked for the power to do his work, he gave us the Scratching. He has made me Attuned. And now... now when we ask for a way to spread his word, he gives us another Landlord...'

How...

...the pain shoots through me – us – me as if I've been plunged into boiling water. Every single part of my senses is aflame, and everywhere I turn and struggle it gets stronger. It's building and building and I want to scream and cry but there's no way I can scream and cry because I don't know how to any more. I can hear the shouts of Natasha, I can feel the clawing of Emmett but their voices are getting weaker and further away.

Every atom of my self, every molecule of my being is rotating and being ripped apart from them, torn away from the others and I feel so lonely – lonely and alone and in so much pain. Let me scream. Please let me scream.

I need to let loose the pain, I need to draw in air to make it go away.

Scratching.

I can feel it. I can feel it course through me like never before. The other times were bad. The other times I thought I'd lose it, but it was nothing like this. Nothing at all.

Scratching.

Please...

Scratching then Scratching then Scratching some more.

And I know it's true, and I don't care, but please...

Scratching your Soul and your Self through your core.

I can feel my soul leaching through the gaps in between my cells. The core of my being is ripping apart and please, let me, just once, please let me...

The Landlord will scream and his screaming will call...

Just once...

The Brothers that Bind. Oak and Dogwood will fall.

Please...

The atoms bind themselves once more, they find their rightful places, in their rightful form. As my hands become hands and my lungs become lungs, I thank God, because God is good. He has heard my prayers, and he has answered them. He has heard my prophecy and made it come true.

So with each new and virgin breath that I take, I scream louder than before. And The Man With The Crab-Like Feet looks down upon me, and smiles.

CHAPTER XIX
THE NIGHT OF THE LONG GOOD NIGHT

Well. This is awkward.

It's OK.

No, it'll be fine.

I don't know why I'm worrying.

Relax, Mark.

OK. Mustn't look too relaxed.

Don't make it look like you're an expert or anything.

Shit. How do I look relaxed, without looking like I haven't done this before?

Vodka. Vodka will help. More of the vodka. The nice stuff, not the stuff from downstairs.

But there's no use pretending. She knows you've done this before. Yes, but does it bother her? She takes the piss out of you because you keep on doing it.

Yeah, but this time is different.

This time it's Natasha.

Oh God, I think I need another drink.

Why is that vodka bottle on the other side of the bed? Seems a bit rude. She'll never love you with that sort of bad planning.

Just a little Diet Coke with it. Don't want to drown the drink. Ruins the taste. I'd be a bad barman if I didn't know what ruins vodka, and I've had many things thrown at me before now, but being a bad barman isn't one of them. It tastes a little flat, but I'm not sure I care. The syrup was in danger of running out downstairs but nobody noticed, thank God. I'd rather have almost flat coke from a bottle than drink dirty soda water.

I take a final look around the room to make sure I'm prepared. I've only had ten minutes to clean up. My bedsit – no, my flat – isn't that big, so ten minutes should be OK. Thankfully, the bed arrived last week, so I'm no longer sleeping on a mattress on the floor.

A year of that gets tired quite quickly. I take a moment to shove one lingering pile of clothing under the bed and sit down. To wait.

This was a turn up for the books. This was unexpected. This was not on the cards after I threw the last punter out of the pub and told the team to finish cleaning and grab a drink. They'd worked hard. The boss was away. I can treat the team once in a while so they look forward to working with me.

I've lost track on how many we had, but now I've got my vodka and little bit of diet coke, I'm not sure I care.

Do I look alright? Shit – do I smell of the bar? Quickly, I dash over to the little sink in the corner and splash some water on my face. Damn, it looks like waiting for Nat has given me the stalker sweats. I really don't want her to think I've got the stalker sweats, so dab myself with the frayed pink towel. And quickly throw that under the bed as well.

Down the hall, I hear the loo flush. This is it, Mark. Don't fuck it up. Four months of waiting. Four months of the odd flirt. Four months of making sure the right rotas showed the right names at the right times. Four months to pluck up the courage to tell her you love her.

I'm such an arse.

'I opened a window. Hope you don't mind,' comes her voice from the doorway.

My God, she's beautiful.

'No,' I stutter. 'No, not at all. I meant to open the window but got distracted. Didn't mean to.' This isn't going well. Have to bring it back. 'I poured you another drink. Here you go!' I lean over the bed and offer up the vodka like it's communion wine. She steps forward and takes it, but still stands at the other side of the room, looking at me. Looking at my room. Self-conscious? Me? OK, just a little bit.

'Nice flat,' she says, taking a sip and leaving a faint impression behind on the glass. 'I like your toys.'

'They're not toys. They're limited editions.'

'Yeah.' She picks up an Optimus Prime I bought at a car boot and I wince a little. The tension's gone in his gun-arm, so he's the campest Transformer in my collection and not what I want Nat to be looking at right now.

'Thanks for tonight,' I offer. 'It was a good shift after all that. Need to talk to Barney, though. Fourth time this month he hasn't shown. Think he was down Spicer's last night.'

'Yeah,' she replies with a smile. 'Abi said she saw him. Guy gives me the creeps, I'd sack him if I were you.'

'Alright, then. I'll do it. For you.' I point at her with my glass, spilling some on my sheets. Classy.

'What you really mean is you'll try to convince Richard, who'll give him another chance.' Nat smiles her beautiful, beautiful smile once more and sits on the edge of the bed – narrowly missing the spilt drink seeping into it, thank God.

'Hey,' I smile back, 'I do have some power around here you know.'

'I know you think you do, Mark...'

'Hey, I do! I get to decide when you work and when you have a social life...'

'And you think that's power, do you?'

'More or less.'

'Doesn't seem to work with Barney.'

'I don't need it to work with Barney. I just need it to work with you.'

She edges closer, and suddenly I don't know what to do with my drink. So I take another sip.

'Really?'

'Really.'

And now she's so close and I don't know what to do. She bends down, slowly, ever so slowly without taking her eyes off me. I close mine and feel her hand cup the back of my head bringing my lips to meet hers. The kiss is soft, and gentle, and this is it – this is what I've wanted and needed since I first saw her those few months ago. This is it. This is love. This is different. This is magical and light and everything I dream it would be every time I close my eyes. The touch of her lips on mine, the gentle stroking of the back of my head and the delicate exploration of her tongue. The world is standing still. There is no wider world. Nothing but Nat – and I need to know her more. I shift my weight and move my free hand to her back – anything to bring us closer so we can be one. Anything so I can know her more. Anything. Anything at all. And now she's backing away, so I lean in and try to keep kissing, with my vodka arm flailing awkwardly behind me.

And we break, and she smiles, and her tongue flicks her top lip, and I'm happy.

I take another sip of my vodka, and place it on the floor.

'Hello,' I say, stupidly.

'Hello.' She brushes her dark hair away from her left eye, and I think it a shame because I wanted to do it for her and now I cannot. 'You were saying something about power?'

'Yeah, ignore me on that. I'm an idiot.'

'You're quite a sweet idiot, though.'

'I like to think so.' She smiles again, and I smile again, before she leans in for another kiss which slowly pushes me back onto the bed and lasts for what seems like an age. All I can think of is her. All I want right here, right now, is her. I don't know what to do with my hands – it's stupid, but as they caress her back I don't know what else to do with my hands. This is Nat, not some other girl I barely know and oh, God, all I want is her. She must know that – she has to feel that as she presses against me because I'm just a man, and all I want is her. She breaks her kiss, and sits astride me, one leg either side of my hips. She places her hands on her thighs and looks at me, pressing me down with her weight – and I have to be out of these jeans. But she doesn't move. She's just looking into my eyes, as if she's trying to see my future and her place within it. C'mon, Nat. Don't stop. I shift my hips a little, to try to get some movement going to help things along, but she's still sitting on me, looking at me, and I don't understand. She swings her right leg across, and lies down beside me, propping her head against her hand. I lie on my side and face her, my jeans making me even more self-conscious than before. She places her hand on my cheek and kisses me once again. Soft, but not passionately, no matter how hard I try. I wrap my arm around her, and press myself to her, and we just lie for a moment on our sides – enjoying just the awareness of each other.

Of course this is right. Of course this is what makes us

different. Of course this is what'll make us last where all the others flew away. You have to wait for these things if you're serious.

There'll be other times.

She snuggles into me, and I just lie there for five minutes, stroking her hair.

'This is nice,' I whisper into her ear,

'Yes. Yes, it is. Thank you.'

'Thank me? I don't know what you have to be thanking me for. I should be the one thanking you!'

'No,' she lifts her head to look at me again. 'I know what you wanted. I thought I wanted it too, for one last time. We've had a laugh together, haven't we?'

'You're the best member of staff I've ever had. Knew it the first time I saw you.' I kiss her again on her forehead and cuddle in close. 'I wouldn't say you're the best-looking bar staff we have.... Hey!' She jabs a finger into my ribs where she knows I'm most ticklish and we giggle like school kids holding hands for the first time, before settling back into a comfortable silence.

'Is everything all right, Nat? You seem a little, I don't know, not yourself tonight?'

'Because I'm finally in your flat?'

'No!' I kiss her forehead again, which seems the natural thing to do, and I notice her eyes are closed as she rests her head against my shoulder. 'You seemed a little distracted earlier. You didn't slap the fat guy waving money in your face, for instance.'

'He wasn't worth the effort,' she sighs. 'Made him wait an extra five minutes for his Stella, that's all.'

'And when we closed up? You let those blokes stay five minutes past Time. It was almost as if your heart wasn't in it.'

'My heart's been all over the place lately.'

'That's encouraging.'

Nat opens her eyes. 'Sorry, I didn't mean it like that.' She gets up and collects her glass from the small Formica table at the end of the bed, so I pick up mine from the floor. I'm going to need another one soon. She drains her glass – one of the best drinkers I know – and pours herself another, topping it up only slightly with the flat Diet Coke.

'How long have you been here, Mark?' she asks.

'About four years.'

'You still enjoy it, don't you?'

'Best job there is. Once you get past the drunkards, and the arseholes, and the wankers, those that are left you get to make happy. I like making people happy. You stand behind the bar, and you see people at their best...'

'...apart from the drunkards and the arseholes and the wankers...'

I smile. 'Yes, apart from them. The other forty percent of our customers – you get to see them at their best. You see people relax and be themselves. For one brief moment, you're the most important person in the world to them. You're a part of it. You help people get to know one another – whether they're here on a date, or whether they're plucking up the courage to talk to someone for the first time. You're there, in the middle of it. Everyone's mate. There's never a stranger in my pub. Never someone I get tired of talking to. Even if it's just me on shift, I never feel alone.'

She looks at me again, taking another sip of her drink and flicks her hair, absent-mindedly brushing it away from her eye once more.

'You shouldn't have to feel alone,' she says, slowly.

'I don't, I've got you with me for a start. We have a laugh.' Nat smiles, but looks away. I get up from the bed and walk over, putting my arm around her. She accepts it, and the joy that brings me is absolute. 'We can have more than a laugh, if you want'. We kiss again, before she breaks away and clinks my empty glass with the vodka bottle.

'You need a top up.'

'I do!' I grin. 'I need a top up! Who'da thought? Another vodka, wench!'

Ow – quite a punch on her, I'd forgotten that. Not that I mind. Not that I care. Have I said how beautiful she is? Even now, after a long night, in the early hours of the morning, with her black Fortnights T-Shirt grubby and worn, I know I want to spend the rest of my life with this woman. She passes me the drink.

'Cheers!' I say as I raise it. 'Love ya, girlie.'

Do you think she noticed?

'Cheers, boss.' She raises her glass and gets back on the bed. No, I don't think she did, but now's not the time to distract her.

'You know, Mark,' she says as she takes another large and unladylike swig of the vodka. 'You're one of the only people in this world I feel I can properly talk to about shit.'

'Am I like your gay best friend?'

'You haven't a gay bone in your body. I know cos I can see it from here.'

I sit down again. Awkwardly.

'Do you think I'm cut out for bar work?' She sits, tossing an old stress ball up and down with her hands, in between gulps of the drink. I nod, confused – has she not heard me tell her how good she is? Does she want me to tell her again? Is that it? 'I don't think I'm cut out to be a politics graduate, I know that much. I mean, have you ever known me to take much notice of what other people think, or want?' I shake my head. 'But I get what you say, Mark, about needing to be in the middle of it. I'm not sure Staunton's it though. In the grander scheme of things.'

I swirl my coke around in the glass, trying to get a little whirlwind going whilst keeping the drink from splashing my jeans – which I still have on. This conversation's getting a bit deep for this time in the morning.

'Staunton's all right,' I say. 'It's got everything you need. They're opening a Starbucks next week, so we're moving up in the world.'

'Yes, but Mark there's a much wider world out there. When was the last time you left Porter Street?'

'Last week. I went for a kebab round the corner!'

'Oh, you know what I mean! You stay in this flat, with your toys...'

'...limited editions...'

'Your toys. You go to work in the bar downstairs. You drink with people from the bar, downstairs. You come back up here to sleep before you start all over again. I've seen you polish your car outside, but when was the last time you actually drove it?'

My glass is getting empty again, and I can feel my cheeks

reddening. This wasn't how tonight was supposed to go. I get up and fill it again. That's the last of it. If I want more I'll have to go downstairs – and the alarm system and I aren't the best of friends. Especially when the numbers on the keypad blur into one another.

'I could leave this place if I wanted to, you know,' I hear myself slurring. 'I'm young! The world could be my oyster! Did you know they're aphrodisiacs? I wonder if that's why some people are horny all of the time...'

'Mark,' Nat puts her finger on my lips, and I stumble a sorry whilst still getting a thrill that she's touching me. 'Shush for me, just for a minute.' She stands there with her eyes closed, as if she's searching for the right words, and having to look deep beneath the alcohol she's drunk tonight. Slowly, ever so slowly, she opens them, and draws her finger back. 'Do you mean that?'

I'm confused now. 'About the oysters? That's what they say...'

'Mark!' she sighs, 'I'm being serious. Could you leave if you wanted to? Come away. Start something new with me. Make a real difference. I've been... offered something. An old family thing. Let's do it together. You and me.'

Once again, I sit down on the edge of the bed and this time almost miss it. One hand goes down to steady myself and the glass in the other almost goes for a burton. I down it whilst I think about how to reply. Dear God, I'm drunk. The floor's moving. It never used to move. One of the things I normally like about this flat is the fact that the floors don't move. Or the walls – shit, mustn't look at the walls. Maybe it's time for sleeps. Maybe it's time for sleeps with Natasha – who's still here, brilliantly, still here. I'd do anything for this woman.

'I'd do anything for you,' I say. I mean that. Especially if it means stopping the room spinning. I get another kiss.

'Come away with me? You mean it?' She's smiling. I love it when she smiles. I love it when I'm the one causing her to smile.

'Of course I mean it. Cross my hearts and hopes to fly.'

And then the world stops spinning because Nat has my head in her hands and everything is right with the world. We're lying on the bed and everything is right with the world. She's telling me how grateful she is, and everything is so totally right with the world. She's whispering in my ear, then nibbling my ear, then telling me how she's going to pick me up in the morning.

Hang on.

She's going to do what, now?

She's kissing, and she keeps kissing, and oh, God this is good, but I need to ask.

'Nat... You'll... pick... me...' It's no good – I break off so I can ask properly. 'Nat, I can't go tomorrow. I've got to open up and everything, remember? Stupid split shift. And then Richard is off for a few days, so I have to cover until the delivery on Wednesday.'

She stops, rests her head on her left hand, and looks at me.

'Of course you do.'

'But, if you give me a month – hand in my notice, arrange something for the flat, I could come away with you.'

Nat looks away, and the dark beige woodchip paper has never looked quite as dark and beige as it does right now. I've made a mistake. I know I've made a mistake, but because of the vodka I'm not sure which one it was. Saying I can't just up and leave – which I can't – or saying I'd go away with her without checking what she meant first.

'Besides,' I try to explain, 'It's not like you can just go either – we can't do without you this weekend, for a start. Then there's the whole notice thing, which gets really complicated...' She's not saying anything. Why isn't she saying anything? 'And your landlord would kill you, for a start.'

'Another landlord would get pissed off if I didn't.'

She turns back to me and rubs her eyes. It really is getting late, and I have a nasty split shift tomorrow.

'Never mind,' she whispers. 'It was a stupid idea.' She cuddles with her back to me and as we spoon I can feel my eyes getting heavy. Stupid split shift. Stupid vodka for making me sleepy when I have the girl of my dreams cuddled up with me. Don't snore, Mark. Don't scare her away by snoring.

'Shhh,' I whisper, stroking her tummy gently with my thumb. 'It's OK. I'll make sure it's all right. You don't need to go anywhere, I'll be right here. Right here.' Nat clasps her hand over mine and pulls it close to her chest.

'I know you will be, Mark. I know. Sorry for asking. I just... I just had this funny feeling if I didn't have you along, something bad would happen. I'd regret it. But it's fine. It'll be OK.'

My eyes are closed, and I'm trying to concentrate, but I can feel myself drifting away.

'It's fine. I'll be right... here... You stay there, with me. In my arms. Good night, Natasha.' And I'm drifting further, and I can't help it. 'Good night...'

And as the darkness falls, and our breathing falls into a contented and peaceful rhythm I dream of the many more good nights I know there are to come.

And I'm happy.

Scratching.
Scratching forever.
Scratching eternal.
Scratching then Scratching then Scratching some more,
Scratching your Soul and your Self through your core.
The Landlord will Scream and his Screaming will call.
The Brothers that Bind. Oak and Dogwood will fall.

My eyes feel heavy, and the room feels oppressive. The night is leaching heat, and my skin is clammy and dank. I rub my face with my hands, which come away wet and smelling of salt.

What's wrong?

Something's wrong.

Help me.

I can see myself throwing off the covers to cool down, but once I do it, I see myself echo the action. Two, three times. Someone's taking a very long exposure, and the photo's not quite taken yet.

What's wrong?

Something's wrong.

The sink. My poor, dilapidated porcelain sink in the corner. I turn on the tap and after four, five, seconds the water slowly starts to pull itself through. I push my hands under, expecting the cold to wake me, shock me, cool me. But instead I feel nothing. I splash the water on my face but feel nothing but the oppressive darkness of the room around me.

I need light. I need to get out. I need to breathe in something other than the stale, stagnant, air of my flat. I feel like I'm drowning in thick soup – like I'm fighting to force my way through the air with every step that I take.

Jeans. T-shirt. That's it. One limb at a time.

The mirror, I look at my eyes in the mirror – dear God they're bloodshot. Rub them. Rub them so they're clear. Rub them with salt...

No.

One foot in front of the other. That's it. Open the door – although I see myself do it two, three times before I step through. The front door to my flat is wide open, but that's OK. It's a different colour to the door it usually is. Change. Change is good, and natural and pure. There are metal steps leading from my door to the fire escape of Fortnights and the brave, wider world. Escape. That's it, Mark, escape. I want to run down, two at a time, and crash through the doors with all my strength. I want to get out of this pub as fast as I can before the air chokes and consumes me. It needs to be fast. It needs to be now. I'll throw myself down the middle of the stairwell, cut out the middle-man. Three storeys down. Fast. The bones will heal.

No.

Moving fast isn't an option. One foot in front of the other. One hand holding the handrail, which slowly – far too slowly – guides me down to the ground. I'm forgetting something, I know I'm forgetting something, but memory's fleeting at times like this. These stairs used to be carpeted, I'm sure. There was a picture on that wall yesterday. These stairs go on forever.

There's gravel under my feet, and strangely I'm outside. The fire escape blurs and closes silently behind me. It never does that, but it's fine. Everything's normal. Everything's fine.

There's a faint air of toffee. Toffee apples. Toffees and fairgrounds and summer. With effort, I turn my head to the left to see the bottle bins – as ever – filled to the brim, with bottles dripping with disused lager and spit. You get used to the smell of old ale, mixed with spirits and shots and a night well lived, but tonight it's different. It's drawing me in, and now I'm outside my footsteps can quicken. The side of the bottle bin feels soft, and the contrast with the broken glass, teetering and balancing on top is almost obscene.

Toffee. I like the toffee. Even the burnt, blackened toffee I can smell right now. I'm sure I told Jon to empty these bins. The burnt toffee is distracting, polluting and invading. The smell's inside my nose, it's clinging to my skin. Every pore of my body is seeping with the smell of burnt toffee.

I need to cut it out.

I need to purge it. It's viscous, invasive, and I can feel it flow through my arteries. It'll be fine. It'll feel better. Just think of the relief, Mark. The bottle – the one facing me, it's perfect and'll fit well in my hand. Doesn't that feel good? As I smash it against the wall, the glass flies in slow motion, leaving shards hanging in the air. Unusual.

I drop the bottle neck, and pinch a diamond-shaped extract, suspended just above my left shoulder. It doesn't want to come away, but eventually releases itself into my hand. The edge is sharp, and for the first time since I woke I can feel something. Feel the potential. Feel it leaving a mark as I run it down my forearm.

> *Scratch it.*
> *Scratch it out of you.*
> *Leach out the poison.*
> *Open your soul.*
> *This is going to be glorious.*

There's a scream, and the sound lingers. There's another – a high pitched cry from around the corner. And a third. I palm the shard into my pocket and walk peacefully to the edge of Fortnights and Porter Street. The road is filled with cars – and all of them are burning. There's no more smell of toffee. No more smell of funfairs and sugar and sweet.

Just burning. Petrol, diesel, rubber. Meat.

I'm calm. Far calmer than I thought I would be. I feel the heat again, just as I did upstairs. I look up at my flat and see it aflame. The fire's licking at every window, trying to escape itself. I spend a second, watching it, feeling it, before turning my back and walking away.

'My baby!'

Through an open window above a nearby shop, I hear the screams of a new mother. 'Oh, please no, my baby!'

For a moment, I pause, wonder what happened, and then move on.

There are more people now, wandering, just like me. The windows of the kitchen shop are broken, and the door hangs off its hinges. In the shadow of the doorway a girl sits, holding the handle of a blue tinged butcher's knife, as if considering its place in the world – and then, without a second thought, thrusts it through the bone of her little finger, severing it cleanly. Her scream tears through the street, and for an instant the others in the street turn their heads.

I carry on walking and pass an old man who gently taps my arm.

'Will you tell them that I'm sorry, young man? I need to make room for the new people. They deserve the world more than me.'

I nod, and watch him walk over to a burning car, observe the flames for a second, before plunging his arm into the fire. In a street where all's moving slowly, his panicked waving and desperation is vastly out of place and wrong. When his features are lost, and he stops moving, the world seems calmer again. I walk on.

'Uncle Mark! Over here, Uncle Mark!'

They're in the window of the toy shop, kneeling down and banging on the glass.

Chloe. Ella. My babies.

I press my palms against the glass, and they mirror me, their faces so small, and innocent against the night.

'Have you seen Mummy, Uncle Mark?' asks Ella. I shake my head.

'I think she's gone away,' says Chloe, the elder of the two by just eighteen months. 'She went into the bedroom, and she locked the door, and we couldn't get in. There was this bang, and she hasn't come out yet. Ella started to cry but I've been really brave.'

Be brave, Mark. If Ella can be brave, you can be brave.

I need to get them out of there. I turn to see if there's a brick, or anything else I can use to break the glass. Across the street – there's one.

I move – if this is called moving – across the road and pick up the brick, but as I turn back the explosion lifts me, in slow motion, off my feet and forces me onto my back. The toy shop, and all the shops on that side of Porter Street are now also in flames. I stare and let myself be scorched by the heat.

My nieces.

They were in there.

Dear God, I can hear them. I can feel them. My babies. My babies were in there.

Scratching starts the screaming.
And screaming starts the Night.
And Scratching starts the Scratching,
Starts the Binding Brothers' Light.

And the night needs to come and lift me from this world for this world no longer has anything left for me. I need the release. I need to draw out the infection. I need to feel something again – something other than sorrow and grief and despair. I lift myself onto my knees, and taking the bottle shard from my pocket, take one last look at the sky.

Instead of the stars, there's a familiar purple cloud blocking out the sky.

I don't feel the glass break my skin. I don't feel the blood flow in pulses from my artery.

But I scream anyway because in these, my final moments, I want to see the face of God and tell him I'm sorry.

I'm sorry.

I'm sorry.

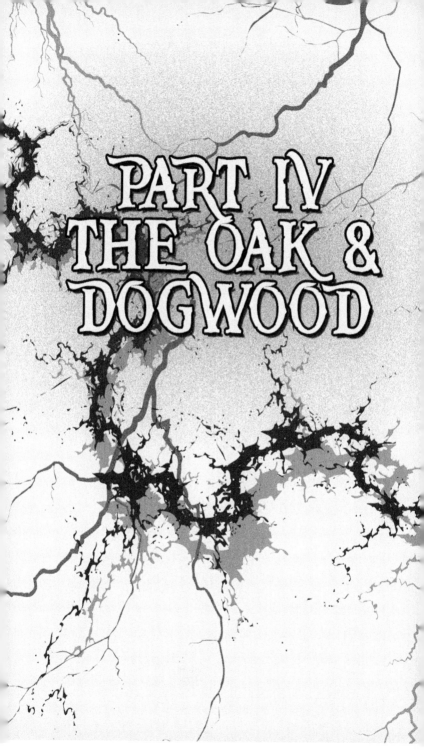

PART IV
THE OAK &
DOGWOOD

CHAPTER XX
THE PRAYERS OF VELI AMASTAD

For the third night in a row, I watch the moon glisten within the bowl of water sitting on the table by the window.

I can't sleep. I know that much now. Whenever I sleep, I travel somewhere deep and dark in my mind – or in the minds of the people around me. I don't understand it, I don't know how it works. I just know that it happens. But it's the lingering aftertaste that bothers me most. The images seared into my head every time I blink. The memories of Nat's last night, and the note I found the next morning telling me she'd gone away. And after... and after...

'You had another nightmare?'

Emmet's voice carries down the hallway from the room next door. I've heard him moving around, banging on the doors and, one time last night, quietly sobbing to himself. The others, I haven't heard.

'I saw it, Emmet. I saw the Scratching and what it would do back home. I saw my babies burn and smelt the air thick with toffee and sulphur. I felt the hope seep out of me, replaced by an urge for release. Any release. The need to be free, the need to leave everything behind. It was horrible. Incorporeal everywhere. Everything on fire, and everyone finding new ways to mutilate, harm and maim themselves. Have you dreamt it?'

'I haven't dreamt of anything since the war, lad. Always thought myself lucky.'

'Yeah, you were lucky last night, I'll tell you that. Any news of Nat?'

'No. If she managed to stay gas, she'd be back at The Grindstone by now, if it's still there.'

'If it's still there?'

'Stands to reason, lad. If you're not there, the protection will fade. Arnold'll have a fight on his hands real soon. Fighting his own kind. I know what that feels like. Wouldn't wish that on anyone...'

We sit in silence for a good half hour, with nothing left to say, and it seems nothing left to do. The room is sparse, but no dungeon in the traditional sense of the word. The bed I'm sitting on is hard, but nevertheless there, and the wooden chair and table in the corner would seem to do their job. I'm a guest – albeit a guest behind a locked wooden door in a locked and foreign world. It's funny, you sit on your backside for years on end, drifting along as you do, watching your heroes defeat evil and save the day, wishing it were you. There's always a moral to be had, always a lesson to be learned.

I think I've learned mine already.

Real heroes don't wish to be heroic. Real heroes don't hang around for years on end because they're comfy in their job. Real heroes don't wait til the girl of their dreams is watching before they agree to step up and save the day. I'm no hero. I'm just a lad from Staunton who gets people drunk and serves them frozen chips. If the world's waiting for me to save it, it's got a long wait coming.

It's funny. If I'm away from the flat for more than ten minutes – unlikely given my previous life – I worry about little things. Did I leave the gas on? Did I lock the door? Did I shut the window that opens onto the scaffolding that's propping up the pub on one side? But now, sitting on this bed, staring at the strange sky, it's all a little bit more dramatic. Is my pub still there? Has Arnold been able to protect the rest of the Council? Has he been able to protect Nat, his wife, and even Gorman – although would it serve that man right if he was thumped over the head with his own stick? Sorry. Mustn't think like that. Did Nat even make it back to The Grindstone at all?

What's that? There's a sound outside. Footsteps. More footsteps. Are they his? Is he coming for me? The echoes bounce up the walls of my room and travel back down the hallway. I crouch back on the bed against the corner and cradle my knees as if they'll protect me. Anything's worth a shot. Is this it? Is this going to be the time they convince me to nick myself one too many times? Use a smashed piece of bedpost to run splinters under my own fingernails? Gouge out my own eyeball using the spoon they'll bring me for soup? Pour the salt they'll provide into the hole that's left?

Maybe.

Maybe it's time.

I've been here long enough.

I wonder what they're waiting for.

I wipe the sweat off my forehead with my arm and freeze as I notice the faint and violent red line running the length of my inner arm. Above my artery. The minute I see it, it starts to sting.

Porter Street. The glass. The arm. The pain. The release. *The Scratching.*

I clasp my other hand to it impotently and hiss, biting my bottom lip. It's OK. It's OK Mark. You woke up. It was just a dream. This isn't upstairs at The Axe. This isn't Becky tying her arm to her oven. It was just a dream. Just a dream. Even if it feels real. Even if it feels like your arm is on fire as hers was. I rush over to the bowl of water and splash some on my arm. It cools for a second, but the stinging's still there. The skin's not been broken, it's just a scratch. Just a long, deep and painful scratch. The echo of the dream pushes through the skin, and there's not enough water in this bowl to dampen it down. I have to get out. I have to leave now. I can't cope with all the shit in my head anymore because I don't know what's real and what's not. The room seems to get smaller and smaller and I'm trapped, and for the first time I miss not having the skill like Nat to split my cells and drift away on the wind. I try to force it. Maybe I stayed too long and made it permanent. No. I can't, and I can hear the footsteps getting closer, and I know he's coming for me and this is it.

This is it.

There's the sound of the key in the lock, and I grip the sides of the bowl. Maybe I can throw it. Maybe if I'm quick enough I can distract him long enough to slip past and get out of here. I can still run. I can take care of myself. I can, I can, I can...

The door opens, just slightly, and I freeze.

'May I come in?'

The voice isn't his. I could tackle whoever's behind the door and make a run for it. It's ajar. I could do this, I could...

'Alright.'

Or maybe I can't. The door swings slowly open, and behind it is a young man, with floppy black hair who keeps one hand on the handle – as if expecting to have to swing it shut to protect himself at any moment. Even from this distance, his eyes make me loosen my grip on the bowl. They're blue – a deep and ingrained cobalt which almost distracts me from the throbbing of my arm. I turn back to the bowl of water in front of me and return to dousing it in an attempt to cool the sensation. It doesn't work. But I'm not going to give the lad in the dodgy frock any more attention than I have to.

'I've brought you some food.'

I don't say anything. Don't look at him. Rub my arm.

'You have to eat. You need your strength.'

That doesn't sound ominous at all. I need my strength, indeed. Fatten the calf before you kill him.

'I have some ointment for that, if you like.'

OK, I'll bite. I look at him.

'That would be a start,' I say, before turning my attention back to the bowl.

'It doesn't look too bad.' Although he's still tentative, there's a confidence in his voice now I've replied. 'I've seen worse.'

'I'm sure you have.'

'I didn't mean it like that.'

'I'm sure you didn't.' I turn my back on him and reach for a rag which hangs from a hook on the wall. I pat my arm dry, holding the rag against my skin in the belief it'll make a difference. 'So are you going to come in, or not?'

'Yes. Sorry. There must be a draught.'

'I hadn't noticed. But then I'm not wearing a dress.' Even without turning round I can tell he's self-conscious about his clothing, but I don't really care. I hear him walk into the room, place a tray on the floor, and lock the door behind him. I can smell mushrooms, and my stomach clenches a little. I can't remember the last time I ate. I just got caught up with the marathon of my new life. Once I started running, I guess there was no time for anything else. He places the tray on the table behind me, which I suppose ought to be the cue for my attention. I turn round.

'It's not much, I'm afraid,' he says with an annoyingly humble smile. 'We have no meat, and the mushrooms are foraged from where we can find them. We don't have the selection we used to have.'

'It must be very hard for you. I run a pub, you know. I haven't checked, but there's probably some chips in the freezer. There normally is. I've got a microwave and everything. I could rustle you up a pie. We could be there in an hour if we start off now.'

The lad looks down at the dust on the floor. I don't need to look at it. I know it's there. I've stared at it myself.

'I... I don't think the Elders will be happy with me if we do that.'

'You think?' I sit down. Might as well take the boy's food from him. 'Are the Elders generally happy people?'

'They find joy in all God's creation.'

'You surprise me.'

'Do I? I didn't mean to. I'm normally not a very surprising person.'

'You surprise me.' I put the bowl of water on the floor and move the tray closer. I'm almost ashamed at how good this smells. 'Did you cook this?' I ask.

'Yes... yes, but it's nothing really.' He flicks his hair, which could do with a wash, away from his eyes. I take a sip of the soup. I'm assuming it's not poisoned. I could resist eating it, but then I'd still be hungry. And I'll need my strength. Or so I'm told.

Caution be damned.

'It's not bad,' I tell him in between sips.

'Thank you.'

'If you get bored of torturing people, I could do with a good chef. Between you and me, microwaved pies aren't all that.'

'I don't torture people.'

'That's not what I hear... sorry, what's your name?'

'Thomas. I mean Amastad. My name is Veli Amastad, primary level Initiate of the Binding Brothers.'

'Well, Thomas, cheers for the food, mate. Was there anything else? I'm sure you have things to do. All that non-torturing, and all.'

'I mean it.' I glance over at Amastad, as he goes to sit on the bed. Great, I have a friend. Whoop-de-do. 'I've never tortured anyone. I only initiated a few weeks ago.' He rubs his chest. 'It still hurts sometimes when I breathe.'

'Poor you.'

'Thanks for your concern.' He doesn't get the sarcasm, but I'm too tired to explain it to him. 'Sorry. Did you mind if I sat down?'

'Would it make a difference? What have you done with my friend?'

'I haven't done anything with your friend!' Amastad's brow creases, putting another couple of years on him. 'He was giving me an earful earlier when I got in his way. Got a bit of a mouth on him.'

'That sounds like Emmet.' The soup's good. My willpower's terrible. It's not going to last that long, and neither is my animosity towards this young lad looking nervously at me on the edge of my bed.

Dammit. Landlord of Peacebattle. Friend to all. Even if you're a torturing bastard, it seems.

'So I suppose I should thank you for the soup. It's not bad.' I toast him with the spoon. 'Tell me, Veli Amastad. What's your story? Why are you sitting on the edge of my bed, talking to me? You can have the room if you want it. Pretty sure I'm up for a swap.' His hands twist and turn in his lap, betraying his nervousness at being in the same room as me. I'm fairly certain he's not supposed to be here.

'That's all right,' he mutters, 'bed's a bit hard.'

'Is it? Hadn't noticed.' There's an uncomfortable silence between us as I continue eating my soup, and he continues sitting there looking awkward. I don't look at him as I finish eating. I'm not sure when I'll eat again. Need my strength. 'So what can I do for you?'

'I'm not sure I know what you mean.'

'I'm not sure I believe you.'

'I don't know what you're looking for.'

The Axe & Grindstone

'Well I don't know why you're here. I don't know why I'm here. I don't know why I didn't throw that bowl at you and make a run for it the moment you opened the door. I don't know where my friends are, I don't know why you've left me in this room for three days, and I don't know why the fucking Binding Brothers seem to be in my head every time I close my eyes. I'll ask you again, Veli Amastad. What can I do for you?'

'I want to know what it's like.'

'What what's like?'

'Being you. In your world. I've heard the stories.'

'This place seems to run on stories,' I snort. 'And rhymes. There's nearly always a rhyme. Far too many rhymes. What do you mean being me?'

'You are the Landlord of Peacebattle, aren't you? The man from Oak Cheating? One of the five Embodiments of The Union.' Amastad's eyes are wide and he edges forward on the bed, like a teen reaching for his autograph book.

'So they tell me.' I put down the spoon and turn my chair to face him, although I'm not sure what this Five Embodiments shit is all about. 'Although I hear you've got Landlords coming out of your arse.' Amastad flinches. 'Oh, come on, Thomas. You don't find the word "arse" offensive, do you? Not after the shits and the fucks and the tortures.'

'I told you,' he raises his voice, 'I've never tortured anyone. Not yet. I haven't attended my Enlightenment yet.' He stops, as if he's choosing how to phrase his next few words. 'Besides, the other one doesn't talk that much. I think they were waiting for you.'

'Waiting for me?' I rub my arm again. 'Where's this ointment you promised me?'

'Yes, sorry...' He rummages around in a deep pocket at the front of his robe and brings out a small tube, which he quickly places on the table and sits back down. 'Don't tell anyone though. I'll get into trouble.'

I take the tube, unscrew the end and sniff its contents. 'Don't worry,' I tell him. 'I won't.' I squeeze, and a thick blue paste is piped onto my finger. It smells of burnt peanuts. I'll never open a bag of dry roasted again. Nothing to lose, Mark. Nothing to lose. I rub it into my arm. Immediately, a cool wave spreads up my limb like a burst of spearmint and the pain dulls. I nod to Amastad.

'Pretty decent,' I admit. 'You could make a fortune with this stuff.'

'It's Extract of Hallweed,' the lad explains. 'Keep it. We get given it after our initiation. To help heal the scars. It doesn't always work, but it stops some of the longer lasting pain, so we can spend more time in prayer, preparing to see the face of God.'

'Preparing to make men scream, you mean. I do know what you do. I have seen it with my own eyes.' I slip the tube into my pocket. Amastad pauses, then nods and breaks eye contact with me.

'It's not like that,' he tells his shoes.

'I'm fairly sure that it is. Were you at the harbour?' He shifts his attention to his thumbs, which weave in and out of each other in his lap and doesn't answer. 'I asked you a question, mate!' With one smooth motion I sweep the soup bowl off the table and it smashes onto the ground into three large pieces and half a dozen tiny ones. The remains of the soup leak in between the stones and the straw which litters the floor. Amastad jumps to his feet. 'I asked you whether you were at the fucking harbour!'

'I have to go,' he murmurs quickly, 'I shouldn't be here.' He makes for the door, but before he can get there I've beaten him to it, scooping up a broken shard of china as I slam my back into the door. I wave the remains of the porcelain at the startled monk, and I'm not sure which of us is the most afraid as I wonder what the hell I'm doing. I wasn't expecting this.

'No,' I tell him. 'Were you at the harbour or not? Did you murder those people? Did you look into their eyes as they screamed, and enjoy it? Did you burn them, and cut them yourself, or did you force them to amputate their own hands so yours wouldn't get dirty?' He shakes his head quickly. 'I don't know how you can't stop screaming at the thought.'

'Please don't hurt me, Landlord, I'll tell you anything you want to know.' His eyes are staring at me, pools of water which descend for ever, his arms outstretched. My hands are shaking, as I grip the piece of broken pottery. Do I believe him, this boy in front of me who protests his innocence? Do I take him at his word, even though he's a scared piece of shit who trusts in a god who demands pain as an entry ticket to his world? Can I use this weapon and push it against his skin until he opens the door? Oh, sod it. This isn't me.

'No, of course I'm not going to bloody hurt you. At the moment, anyway.' I drop my hands to my sides and he does the same. 'But you need to start telling me stuff, and then you've got to get me, and my friends, out of here.' I quickly walk over to the chair, pull it in front of the door, and sit down. 'When you're ready, mate.' God, I hate that phrase.

'They'll punish me.'

'I'll punish you sooner. Why were they waiting for me, and why haven't they touched me since I've been here?'

'It isn't the right time.'

'Time for what?'

'The Rise of the Waning Crux.'

'That's helpful. What the hell's that, and what's it got to do with me?' Amastad reaches into his pocket and pulls out a small leather-bound book, the pages of which are lined with gold trim. My Nana used to have something like it in her handbag every Sunday.

'My Enlightenment Ceremony's in a couple of days,' he says. 'When you turned up at the Gate, Veli Khalid could sense you.'

'He has a knack of doing that,' I reply, but as I speak a chill runs down my spine. I wonder if he can sense me now. I wonder whether he can hear me now. I wonder whether I can run away as fast as I can before he gets here.

'He's one of the Attuned,' Amastad continues, 'and one of our highest Elders. He has this connection to the Embodiments – I can't understand it, but I wish I had it too. I sometimes think it would make life simpler, and less confusing if I could touch the faith – feel the faith like he does.'

'You don't want to be like him, Thomas. Once you're inside his head, all you can feel is – I don't know how to explain it – contamination. Your mind's best when it's lonely, believe me.' He looks down at his feet again, and amongst the fear, adrenaline and sadness I start to pity him. I don't know why, and I don't know whether it's for the best, but I stand, place the broken pottery in my pocket, and go to sit next to him.

'Where's Fox, Thomas?'

'Fox?'

'The Previous. The other Landlord of Peacebattle.'

'I'm not sure. I think I heard him screaming once, but the screaming stopped a few nights ago. Or maybe they got mixed with the others. It's hard to tell, sometimes.' This is not a good sign. The plan is to get Fox and somehow combine our Licences. If something's happened to him...

Amastad's found the page he was looking for, and keeps it marked with his thumb. 'I've been looking for a chance to meet you,' he says. 'They say you're the friend to all. You listen.'

'You could have just bought me a pint. But I guess that's what I do. In a roundabout sort of way. You were explaining about the ceremony.'

'Yes, yes, sorry. It's where I get to see the face of God for the first time.' He breaks eye contact. 'Between you and me, it's not something I'm looking forward to.'

'No, neither am I.' I look at the lad, who seems to diminish in size with every passing minute. He couldn't even bring himself to force me out of his way when I was blocking the door. How's he supposed to make a man scream?

'I've been praying – praying so hard that He would show himself to me in some other way. A man's soul is so hidden, so complex and guarded, that it's impossible to see through. It's all we're taught. My prayers haven't been answered.

'When you showed up at the Gate, the final texts started to fall into place. Veli Khalid hasn't touched you, or seen you, or allowed anyone near you because he's waiting for the Rise of the Waning Crux.'

'Yes, as I said, he's waiting for what, now?' I don't like the sound of that. From what I know of the man – from what I've felt of the man, he's the sort of creature that acts on impulse. He didn't wait for Fox. He couldn't resist having a Landlord in his needle-like fingers. I felt the craving, the need to inhale another man's pain. Fox was the whisky to Khalid's drink problem – once in his hand, the temptation was far too great to resist.

'The Rise of the Waning Crux. At least, that's what we other Initiates think. They said I could find a way in here to meet you but...' He opens the book and starts to read.

> *Scratching and Scratching and Scratching some more,*
> *Scratching your Self through your Soul and your core,*
> *The Landlord will Scream and his Screaming will call*
> *The Brothers that Bind. Oak and Dogwood will fall.*
>
> *At the edge of mankind, all nature will weep,*
> *For the blood of the Landlord will flow thick and deep*
> *Three hands he will have, and two voices to cry*
> *At the sight of the cross hanging low in the sky.*
>
> *Only there in the presence of those who believed,*
> *Will the true face of God be truly received.*
> *And the Scratching will grow, tearing nature and law,*
> *Til the oak seeds forgiveness and peace reigns once more.*

Well, some of that certainly sounds familiar, although most of it's news. I found it difficult to read my own bible when I went to church, let alone get to grips with the religious texts of the Binding Brothers.

'So where's that from then? What's the book? Doctor Seuss has got a bit dark.'

'It's *The Book of Blackwood*, Exiunt XVI, verses forty-one to forty-three.'

'I don't think we covered that one at Sunday school.'

'I don't understand...'

'Never mind. He's waiting because...'

'Because he thinks the prophecy will come true. The Waning Crux is a constellation to the west of the second moon. The Founder saw it as a sign that the pilgrims were led to Dogwood Falls – or Blackwood Falls as it was back then – as a gift from God. It rises into view once every twenty-five years. That's tonight.'

Of course it's tonight. He thinks the prophecy will come true.

Prophecy, prophecy, prophecy. Back home people are waiting for the Second Coming of Christ because of a prophecy they've read in Revelations but they don't count down the dates on an advent calendar. Well, most of them don't.

Shit.

Shit, bollocks, shit.

The blood of the Landlord will run thick and deep.

'You've got to help me get out of here, Tom.'

'My name is not Tom any more, it's...'

'Tom – you've got to help me get out of here. Please! I know what it means, I've seen what it means, and I know that it's true. It's all falling into place. I'm not one for superstition, but you guys really are. He's going to sacrifice me and my friend, and he's going to make you watch.' He turns his face away. Hang on.

'No, your Enlightenment – it's tonight, isn't it? He's going to make you do it, isn't he?' Amastad looks again at his feet and suddenly sprints for the door. I leap up and take his hand – he pulls his head back at me as he tries to break free. 'Look at me, Thomas, look at me! You came in here for a reason, didn't you? You came in here to see if you could do it! You wanted to look into my eyes to see what they're like without fear – because the next time you see them you'll be wielding a knife!'

'You don't understand what it's like!' he cries at me, his eyes now red and strained. 'I had to see, I had to know! I prayed – dear God I prayed – to be able to look into your eyes, as a true and proper Embodiment, and see reflected the face of the Lord. Your soul – I prayed for your soul – so you'd be the one to show the Brothers they're bound to a different path. Can't you hear it, Landlord? Can't you hear the screaming? In the walls, in the food, in the earth that glues the bricks of this room together. I'm scared I'll see it the way they do. I'm scared that it is like you say – that it's true. I'm scared once I make you bleed I'll see the face of God in your soul and he'll bind me forever to his truth.'

He's pulling away and reaching for the key in his robe.

'Thomas – wait!' I shout, but he pushes me away – to the end of the room, far stronger than he looks – and I crash into the table behind me. Before I can get up, he's slammed the door behind him, and I hear him turn the lock tight from the other side.

I bang on the door. 'Thomas, listen to me! Please! "At the edge of mankind, all nature will weep" – don't you see, that's everything! Oak Cheating, Dogwood Falls, everything. Thomas, I've seen the sky burn, I've seen people live for the moment of dying. I've seen the sound of Screaming and it's eternal. "The Scratching will grow" and it won't stop growing. Your people split nature apart once – don't let them do it again! You have to get me out of here, please, Thomas, please!'

I can hear his breathing from behind the door – he hasn't moved away, he can still do this. There's still hope, there's still time for him.

'Get me to Fox. Take me to him! You can still do this. You don't have to go through with it. You don't have to become a murderer like the others, you never have to make a man scream for the rest of your life! This is your choice to make – real, proper enlightenment! Just let me out of here. Listen to me,' I press my face to the rough, splintered side of the door. 'I once had a faith, too. I still have it, deep down. I've heard about the face of God. I've seen the good it can do, and how good it can make you feel. My priest – my vicar – told us back then that God was reflected in all of us. The last time I saw her, she told us it was the remembrance of all the joy we find in each other. She said it was forgiving someone for making a choice we wouldn't make. I didn't believe her, Thomas, but I do now. I know you can't find him through what's planned. It's a trick. They're brainwashing you. You always have choices – no matter how dark they seem there's always a way out. Never think that just because the choices are hard, there's always an easy way out. Get me to my friends. Get me back to my pub. Thomas. You can do it. Show leadership. Make the right choices. Take charge.'

There's silence from the other side of the door. He's walked – I've lost it. He's gone to prepare for the end of the world.

The sound of the key scrapes the inside of the iron lock. With an old time slow motion, the handle turns, and I step back. Thank God. Thank you, God. You've answered my prayers, he's letting me...

The Axe & Grindstone

The door swings open, and the tap-te-tap-te-tap is all I can hear, and the eyes like tar and fingers like needles are all I can see.

'His name is... Veli Amastad,' states Khalid as he walks through the door, and what's left of my time feels now lost forever.

CHAPTER XXI
THE DARK PRICE OF FRIENDSHIP

I jump back. I've got to get away, please God don't let him get me.

He follows me, tap-te-tap-te-tap, and matches me step for step, as he enters the room. I keep scrambling backwards, until my thighs hit the hard wood of the bed and I fall onto it. Keep moving. Got to keep moving. I back on to the bed, but all too suddenly there's the wall. This room is too small, why is this room so small, there's nowhere else to go and he's by me, rising himself up until his thin black hair is touching the roof and he's close – oh so close – and I can feel his needles start to press themselves into my chest.

'Did you think I'd forgotten you?'

I turn my head away and clasp my eyes shut. This isn't happening. If I can't see it, then I can't see it happening.

'Please...' is all I can get out, as his oiled and peppery breath becomes the only thing I can taste.

'Please? You respect your Elder. In itself, this is... pleasing.' He tightens his grip on my chest and the knives of his fingertips are going to break the skin. I bite my bottom lip, hoping beyond hope it'll dull the pain – but it seems among my many, many follies is the vain and stupid belief that'll work. I cry out and feel Khalid inch even closer to my face.

'Open your eyes, Landlord. Let me see who you are.' He tightens again and it's like five fires in my heart, all fighting each other to burn brightest. I can't help it, I try and be brave, I try and be strong, but I can't help the second cry as it escapes, bringing him even closer – but I keep my eyes screwed shut. Please stop, please...

'I've been waiting for you. I've seen you in your sleep. I've known your dreams and your desires. You've seen my paradise and you've tasted my joy. Tell me, Landlord. Tell me of your...

excitement. Do you still not know of your place in the re...creation?' He clenches his hand a little more, and this time I scream. 'Yes... Landlord. Yes... You've heard my hymn. You know the words. Sing it for me.' He pushes his face closer, and I can hear his pleasure. He finally, finally releases his fingers from my chest and I collapse onto the bed and open my eyes, gasping for breath and clutching the five sodden red patches on my T-shirt. Khalid walks away, and turns to Amastad, who's standing in the doorway, ashen.

'Veli Amastad. I am disappointed in you.' Amastad stares at the floor.

'I'm sorry, Elder.'

'Look at me, Brother. I instructed you to look me in the eyes when you address me, did I not?' The younger man slowly raises his head, as if acting against years of enforced ingrained habit.

'I'm sorry, Elder.'

'You apologise well.'

'You have taught us humility, Veli Khalid.'

'Obviously.' Khalid turns to look at me. 'Tell me, Veli Amastad. What do you see when you look at what's on the bed before you?' Amastad steps forward. He leans on the open door, almost hiding behind it as he glances towards me.

'I see a man, Elder.' Khalid takes a step forward and I curl into the corner. He crouches down, his left hand resting on the cold, stone floor.

'You are wrong. This is becoming a habit. The Landlord of Peacebattle is not a man. He is a gift from God. And what do we do with gifts from God?'

'We accept them, Elder.'

'And?'

'We accept the gift and use it for the glory of God.'

'We do indeed.' Khalid smiles and bares teeth as sharp as his nails. 'God has indeed been... gracious. He gave us the Previous. Have you heard the Previous scream, Amastad? He screams well. He screams as if he knows they are worthy for the altar of the holy of holies.'

The pain in my chest is still there, but it's fading away. Don't let him beat you, Mark.

The Axe & Grindstone

'I know my place, Khalid.' I spit at the Man With the Crab-Like Feet. 'And it's nowhere near your re-creation. What have you done with Fox?'

'The Previous is resting. He is preparing for the coming Enlightenment. I have been helping him prepare. He has been grateful. He can teach you much, Landlord.' He glances over his shoulder. 'Veli Amastad. Do you need further instruction before your ceremony?'

'No, Elder. Your instruction has been thorough.'

'Are you... sure? You over-passed your authority this hour. A Veli of the Binding Brothers does not serve our guests their food. A Veli should be in service to his Brothers and to God. Did you think you could look down upon this gift and see the face of God before your time?' Once again the younger man casts his eyes down to the dust at his feet. 'Perhaps you are not ready.' He leans forward on his haunches, towards me. 'Perhaps I should take the Enlightenment from you and unfurl the screaming myself.'

This is my chance. This is the only one I'll get. I spring from my crouched position on the bed and slash at Khalid with the broken shard from my pocket. He shouts as the sharp pottery opens his cheek – he tries to grab my ankle as I leap from the corner and run towards the open door.

'Amastad! Grab him!'

It's no use as I barge the boy out of the way with my shoulders and run through the open door slamming it behind me. The key's still in the lock! I twist it shut and see the handle turning uselessly from the other side as I do. Shit, now what do I do, where do I go? Left or right? Left – probably. I start to run down the corridor to the sound of Amastad thumping the door I left behind.

'Emmet!' I cry, 'Emmet, where are you?' There are doors all around and we were talking just half an hour ago. He can't be far. He must be around here somewhere! 'Emmet!' A door opens to my left and he's standing at the door, slumped in the frame with a black eye and a large cut above his cheek. 'Emmet, thank God.'

'What? What's happened? What's goin' on?'

'We're getting out of here, c'mon.' I grab his hand and pull him away. 'Which way out? Can you remember?'

'No, no I can't remember.' He staggers behind me as we move down the corridor. Hurry up, man! 'Wait a second, lad...'

'We haven't got a second Emmet. We have to get out. I know what's coming.' Hang on. Shit. I turn to look at Emmet. Just like back at The Grindstone, his downy hair is upright and prepared for a fight. 'Fox. We can't go without Fox.'

'I know, lad.'

He's just standing there.

'Well?' I'm imploring him now. 'Which way?'

'I didn't want to come.'

'Neither the fuck did I, but we're here and we haven't got the time!'

'Mark, you don't understand...'

'Emmet, come on!'

SCRATCHING.

And the fire's in my head, forcing me down to my knees.

'For the love of God, I said *Fuck off with your Scratching!*' But it's everywhere, and like every migraine I've ever had, crammed into my head all at once. Wave upon wave of pain shoots through my brain, and I can't see for the thumping, thumping lights. I reach out, one hand holding my head, the other pleading out in front.

'Emmet!' I shout.

Scratching and scratching and scratching some more.

'Emmet, please! Make it stop!'

SCRATCHING YOUR SELF AND YOUR SOUL THROUGH YOUR CORE.

'You stopped it before! Help me!' But he's just standing there. Why is he standing there?

He walks past me, slowly, edging against the wall.

'I'm sorry lad,' he says. 'I've had no other choice.'

I don't understand. What's he mean? Where's he going? Why isn't he helping me?!

'I can't... Stop... It!' I shout at his back, as I curl up on the floor. 'Emmet!'

But no. He's... He's turning the key. He can't be. He's opening the door to the room I was in, and they're there, the two crab-like feet tap-te-tap-te-tapping slowly and patiently towards me.

And the pain subsides, leaving me sobbing, curled up on the floor like a scalded child. A child scalded by a bloke he thought was his friend.

A bloke I'd freed from an unlocked room.

Veli Khalid crouches down beside me, hunched and dangerous.

'That was... unfortunate,' he mutters, pausing to choose every word before he says it. He wipes a small spot of blood from his cheek and rubs it inbetween his thumb and forefinger. 'Almost... blasphemic.' I pull myself over to the wall and prop myself against it, the flashing in front of my eyes slowly subsiding.

'Emmet. Why?' I gasp. He looks at me with the eyes of the soldier I know he once was.

'Because the world's a cruel place sometimes, lad. Because bad things happen to good people. Because when we needed the Council most, they became corrupt and introvert and did more harm than good. And because this is the only way to save her.'

I remember. It starts to make sense. *'Sometimes the Council drives a man to make hard choices. Sometimes... sometimes they're not the ones you want to make... I've made some tough decisions lately; had to look hard at my life and the life of those I love. You have to know your place in the world, Mark Adams. Could you kill people to keep it?'*

The air is thin, as his words sink in. This is why he was so confident he'd survive. Amastad shuffles up beside me and lifts me to my feet. As I lean on him for support, he lifts my arm and a look of concern passes across his face. Five minutes too late mate.

'Your arm,' he whispers quietly. 'I don't understand...'

'The barman and I,' states Khalid as he stands, 'have an arrangement.' He walks over to Emmet and, one by one, his pale fingers wrap themselves around his chin. 'It takes a certain... something to make a bargain with God. He will be allowed to remain here once we are gone. I'm not sure why he wants to, mind.' He keeps his eyes locked onto the orange skinned traitor. 'Veli Amastad!' The boy drops my arm and addresses his master.

'Yes, Elder?'

'What does history record of those who remained in Eden once Adam and Eve had left?' Amastad pauses and looks at me.

'Nothing, Veli Khalid. History forgets the first gift.'

'Indeed. They were forgotten, as was Eden itself. Once this land was given to us, to prepare ourselves, to nurture ourselves.' He turns back to me and lets go of Emmet's face. 'Now, Landlord, it is time for you and the Previous to open nature once more, as nature intended, and unlock the Heaven we found here back into the world from which we came.'

'You're crazy,' I spit, and turn to look at Emmet. 'And you! You fucking bastard. I was learning to trust you. You made me start to think I could do this. We drank together – I thought we were gonna be mates. Tell me why. Why did you lie to me?'

My barman looks me straight in the eyes for the first time. 'You weren't there, Mark. You didn't understand, you've only just arrived. You've no idea of the politics, or the cost of standing up for what you think is right. I'm the Last of the Gifted. I'm not going to be alone no more.'

My legs collapse under me, and I have to rely on Amastad to keep me from falling at his feet. Khalid steps towards me, and grips my face, one needle at a time, just as he did Emmet.

'When your colleague there enabled me to enter your... establishment and "befriend" the Previous, I knew the time long promised had come. When I heard of your arrival in Dogwood Falls, I was sure. The Rise of the Waning Crux is tonight, Landlord, and now you are here, delivered to my gate. God is good. He has delivered what was written. And what was written will come true.'

He turns abruptly and walks away, the hem of his over-cloak hiding his heels from view. He reaches a dark brick arch, at the end of the corridor and turns back to face us. His thin lips curl at the edges, as if he's discovering how to smile for the very first time.

'Glory, Landlord. The greatest glory. A glory I've prayed for all of my life. A glory the Previous failed to bring on his own. It is time for you to see for the first time the true face of God.' He turns and walks – *tap-te-tap-te-tap* – out of sight.

I throw off Amastad and stand on my own two feet. I could try and make a run for it again, but I'm still too damn shaky. 'What does he mean?' The younger Veli looks at me.

'It's time for the ceremony.'

'You don't have to do this.' There's no reply. I turn to Emmet. 'Emmet. Mate, C'mon.'

'Leave it,' he snaps, and jabs me in the chest with his finger. 'Just do what yer have to do. I said yer needed to come and I meant it. If you were telling me the truth back at the pub, about loving Natasha, you'll go through with this. For her sake.'

'Don't talk to me, arsehole.' I grab his wrist as it heads towards my breastplate once again. The hairs on his skin spring up and I drop it straight away before they bite too deep into me.

'I'm not jokin', lad.' He pokes me once more. 'You do yer duty. You get these bastards out of my town. You get 'em to leave us alone. You get 'em to fix Natasha.'

And with that, he follows Khalid.

'Wait, what?' I go to follow him, but before I take more than three steps, the floor vibrates under my feet, and the sound of fire and roaring sweeps down the corridor. I know that sound.

'Quick,' mutters Amastad. 'Before they get here. Let me look at your arm.'

'Will it help me get away?'

'This is a place where miracles happen every day, Landlord. God may smile on you yet.' The vibration gets more and more pronounced, and I guess I have nothing to lose so – what the hell – I offer him my forearm, clenching my fist pointedly as I do so.

'Fine,' I snap. 'Hurry up.' He takes it gingerly, and then looks me in the eyes once more.

'I don't believe it. It's a true miracle. I never thought I'd see it. Your scratches, they're gone...'

I pull my arm away. I don't have time for this. I have to get away, but I glance down at my arm, and he's right. The marks that were there five minutes ago have now disappeared. What the... Instinctively I put my hand over the pocket of my jeans where the tube of Hallweed is sitting. But the roaring's getting louder. I look back at Amastad, who's smiling – whatever's happened it's not normal.

'How did you get here? Quickly. Tell me how you got here.' But before I can answer, four GeoTrolls turn around the corner, their eyes bright with the furnace within. Shit. They march over to us with feet which continue to make the ground shake.

Boom.

Boom.

Boom.

Boom.

The sound which drew me to the cellar in the first place. The sound which started the nightmare.

They take up position, two behind me, two in front. They tower over me, staring straight ahead, and I feel as if I'm cocooned in a mass of living rock. I'm shaking. Oh God I'm shaking. Where are they going to take me? How long do I have?

Leadership. Choices. Charge, Mark.

Even now, show leadership. Make the choice to do this with dignity. Take charge of your own response.

'Right then,' I mutter, making myself sound so much more confident than I feel. 'Cheers for the soup and gloop, Thomas. If it is you later on, try not to enjoy it too much, will you.'

Deep breath, Mark. Deep breath.

'C'mon then, fellas. Mustn't keep God waiting.'

Every step I take feels as if I'm walking through treacle.

I want to slow down. I want to stop and put this off. I want to run as fast as I can in the opposite direction, but I know this is it. I never thought it would end like this.

One by one the GeoTrolls start to move and I have no choice but to move with them. I look back and glance at Amastad, his deep blue eyes staring back at me. I hold the gaze for as long as I can, and then look straight ahead to wherever my destiny will take me.

Chapter XXII
The Face of God

Every time I try to engage them, the roaring in their chests get a little louder.

I can't be doing with the silence, though. They've got to give me a little something.

'I could kill for a cigarette, you know.'

Nothing.

'So, any of you guys know a chap called Arnold? Doesn't say much. Likes the cherry brandy. Good with his hands.'

No.

The walls of the Cenobium are thick and brown and drip with condensation. The whole place smells like musty bedsheets, as if it's been shut to the world for generations. We've been walking for what seems like hours which, to be fair, is perfectly fine with me. I don't want to get where we're going. We turn left, and right, and left again until we run out of corridor and a heavy wooden door blocks our path. It reminds me of the door to The Grindstone, with its iron plating and muscular bolts. I miss it. I want to go through that door, not this.

The GeoTrolls stop, and the one at the front approaches the door and thumps it with one boulder-like fist three times. He declares us in a voice which half burns, and half chills to the bone.

'We bring the anointed, the chosen, the pre-prepared. We bring the gateway to paradise. We bring the doorway to Heaven. We demand entry to the Enlightenment of All Mankind.'

The door creaks open, and a gasp of wind streaks silently through my hair. The air carries with it the briefest sense of the taste of toffee. I take a step backwards, and another, and another before my back makes contact with the beast of the thing behind me, the roar of it increasing in pitch as a result. I turn to look into its eyes, and it stares back into mine.

The Axe & Grindstone

'This is your time,' it growls. 'This is the reason for your birth and our re-creation. This is the place where eternity begins. Move forward and enter the light.'

He pushes me, and we walk through the door. I'm still only wearing a T-shirt, and the breeze pricks at my skin, raising the goosebumps one by one. The courtyard is circular and cloistered – wooden beams above the walkway support drooping plants long dead and display the moonlit sky. There's not a cloud in sight, and the hundreds of stars in the sky are shining down. It's beautiful – or it would be if they weren't shining on the sunken stage in the middle of the courtyard, where a hundred Binding Brothers sit, looking up at me in their circle. They're sitting around a large cone which is covered in carvings and inscriptions. Each of the Brothers is hooded, and once or twice I see a flash of their eyes, as one of Dogwood Falls' two moons reflect across them. The passageway opens into a flight of stone stairs, and we descend to join them. As we reach the stairs, the Brothers start to murmur an incessant, droning chant.

Two of the GeoTrolls turn and take my arms, and their stone hands clamp down on my wrists. That's it. I have to struggle, I have to get away, but they're too strong, and I can't break free. I'm not going to make this easy for them, though, and I kick and I kick and I lash out with everything I've got. It just takes one small movement, one tiny reflex from the thing on my right arm, and I'm on the floor begging for it to stop. I'll stop fighting, I'll stop struggling, just release my fucking hand! That's it, I'm sorry. I didn't mean to struggle, didn't mean to put up a fight. Dear God, that hurts. He releases me, and the chanting increases. The four GeoTrolls push their hands to their chests in salute to the conical altar, and as one they dissipate. Rubbing my bruised wrist, I look up, and follow them as they burst up to the sky and join the Incorporeal now circling overhead. Within a moment the sky is a dark purple, and the world looks as though it's within the eye of a storm. There's just one spot of black sky left, in the centre of the circle, above the cone before me. Without another protest, I allow my hands to be tied behind me to a ring on the floor.

'It's good that you're kneeling. They don't like it if you don't kneel. They find it offensive. You end up kneeling in the end anyway.'

I turn to look at the bloke kneeling and chained to my right. Although forty-something, he looks in his sixties, his face weathered, tired, and freshly scarred. His shirt was once white, but now looks mottled and bloody spots – in groups of five – give it a grim pattern. Where his left arm used to be, there's now just a bloody stump.

'Fox. You're Fox, aren't you?'

'I am.' He speaks with a faint lilt which I'm sure is Welsh. He looks around at the spectacle around us. 'I take it you're my replacement. How did that work out for you?'

'I've had better jobs.'

'Know the feeling. Natasha fill you in on all this?'

'No. She kinda let me figure it out all by myself.'

'Oh, that's a shame.' He looks at the darkening sky above us, where Incorporeal continue to add themselves to the gathering storm. As they do so, the distant roars of the GeoTrolls within gets louder, and the monks try to match them beat for beat. 'She had a bit on her mind lately.'

I don't have time for this.

'I guessed as much. Listen. My name's Mark. Mark Adams. I came here to find you. There's a way to end it. We can banish them forever. I've got a Licence for The Grindstone. You had yours ripped away from you,' I have to start shouting the words, as the noise from the crowd is getting louder and louder as the seconds roll by. 'The Council, when we knew you were still alive came up with a plan. They said we can combine the two! A Licence in Perpetuity, they called it! We need to link arms, or something, and perform the ceremony – we can bar the Binding Brothers from Dogwood Falls forever!'

Fox looks at me and smiles, weakly.

'Mark, my boy, it's nice to meet you and everything, mate, but look around you. We're far past Licences now. You shouldn't have come here. Have they read you the prophecy?'

'They read me something. The Scratching keeps forcing itself into my head. Have had no choice in the matter!' Fox shakes his head.

'Before you turned up, Khalid was playing with me,' he shouts. 'He thought I was the last – it was the first time they'd broken a Licence! But he knew – someone told them – you'd been recruited...'

'It was Emmet!' I cry. 'He's just told me! I couldn't believe it but...' Fox slumps back on his heels.

'Makes sense. After Nat was killed, he lost the passion. Dammit.' A gong rings out and carries itself from person to person. There's another, and seconds later a third. 'But after they knew about you, he left me untouched. You've made scripture come true, Mark. You did this to me!' He motions to his stump and I retch at the thought of Khalid's fingers breaking the bone and tearing the flesh from the muscle. I shiver as another cold breeze races through my hair. 'He made me memorise it, Mark! The bastard made me recite it to him, as he cut my fucking arm off!' I look away – I don't want to hear it. I want the singing and the roaring to cut out the sound of his words. You wanker. You utterly stupid wanker, Mark. As he recites the lines I heard half an hour before, I can see them written as plain as day in my mind.

'At the edge of mankind, all nature will weep, for the blood of the Landlord will flow thick and deep. Three hands he will have and two voices to cry at the sight of the cross hanging deep in the sky!' He keeps shouting the words so I have no choice but to hear them. 'Only there in the presence of those who believed, will the face of God be truly received! Three hands, Mark! Three hands! A Landlord of Peacebattle with three hands at the Rise of the Waning Crux!'

The crowd goes silent, and the roar of the Incorporeal sounds deadly and all-pervasive in the sky.

Oh fuck. Oh fuck. Oh fuck.

Another gong echoes through the courtyard. And another. And another.

And now even the Incorporeal go quiet.

All around us the Brothers look on and look up. I follow their gaze as, *en masse*, they too fall to their knees. In the circular hole in the middle of the Incorporeal a solitary star slowly drifts into view.

'The Waning Crux,' mutters Fox. 'They don't understand the science of it, the religious fools. Once every couple of hundred years that particular constellation of four stars crosses a nebula and disappears from view. When it comes out, people go crazy. That's it, there. Always wondered what it would look like...'

Another gong cuts Fox off. I shuffle my hands, trying to get them out of the chains.

'Fox, shuffle over towards me,' I whisper. 'We can extend the Licence. C'mon!'

'And how are you going to do that, Mark, eh? Can you remember how you got your Licence? The exact words which were used? I'm guessing you came here with other people who were gonna do that for you, right?'

Damn. Of course. I assumed it would be simple. I assumed it would just be a case of us holding hands, or skipping down the road, or something as equally simple. I've no idea how to create a Licence in Perpetuity. Why would I have? This plan was doomed from the moment I collapsed at the Gate of Fourteen Fellow Men.

I let Fox's question hang in the air, as Veli Khalid, Veli Amastad, and Emmettaman Savage walk solemnly up to the base of the cone, their steps enhancing every drop of silence in the courtyard. Emmet turns and looks at us both, then glances up at the sky.

'I warned you about falling in love with her,' calls Fox. Emmet stares straight ahead, no longer looking at anything in particular. 'I warned you about becoming too involved...'

Khalid raises his hand – and Fox stops short and gazes back at the floor, a defeated man. I take my cue.

'You're all crazy, do you know that?' The Cenobium is silent and all I can hear is my voice. 'You have no idea. You think you know God? You think this is what He wants? You think good people look into the eyes of each other and seek glory through pain? You're crazy! Thomas. One last time. Don't do this mate. Remember what I said earlier? I was told the face of God is forgiving someone who's made a choice you wouldn't make. Emmet – for the love of God you know this isn't right. What have they promised you? What did they lie in order to get you to help them do this?' Emmet just stares blankly away.

'They would have promised to make Natasha corporeal again,' mutters Fox, quietly.

That's impossible.

That's got to be impossible, right?

I don't know.

Jesus.

I stare up at Khalid, who raises his hand once again.

'This is a lie,' I state plainly, so everyone can hear. 'There's no holiness in screaming. There's no Heaven in a lifetime of pain. This man is lying to you. If there is a God, he'd despise every single last one of you.'

'ENOUGH!' Khalid's voice forces its way across my speech and, like Fox, manages to shut me down. 'There will be no more desecration! You dare to speak of God as if you know him, Landlord. You deign to believe in your own right of way!' He addresses the crowd. 'Brothers. Many generations ago the Founder believed this place was a gift from God. He was... wrong!' The Incorporeal roar. The Brothers chant again.

'*In nostra nudus... clamoribus. In nostra nudus... dolorem*!' the Veli repeats. 'In our naked screams and in our naked pain we came upon light. We understood the essential spirit of the universe. The power to hold back death in perpetual service!' The Incorporeal roar in approval and, above us, spin in their cloud faster and faster. 'The Landlords speak of the God the Founder worshipped! The one he believed sent him here!' Within the eye of the storm we can see three stars, in a lopsided triangle. I know what's coming. I know what'll happen when the fourth star appears and there it is.

The Waning Crux. In the sky at last.

And the Brothers cheer.

Khalid turns to the two Brothers by the altar. He takes a thin paring knife from his robes and hands it to Amastad. 'It is time for Enlightenment, Veli Amastad. And today we shall all truly be... saved.' They step up in front of us.

'*Faciem dei. Faciem Dei. Faciem Dei*,' come the chants.

Oh please. Don't let this hurt.

'*Faciem dei. Faciem Dei. Faciem Dei*.'

The Axe & Grindstone

'Emmet, please!' I try one last time. Fox has his eyes closed.

'Don't scream Mark. It might not work if you don't scream...'

Kahlid brings his face close to his, so only the two of us can hear.

'Oh, Landlords. You think you know. You have no idea. We don't worship the God the Founder believed in. We don't worship the fake God of your world. The Founder himself became God. And tonight you bring his return.'

Khalid drives the knife into Fox's chest and the two of us scream at once. He twists, and grins, and twists again. Fox turns to me, his eyes wide open and I see nothing inside them at all but fear. With one swift action, Khalid removes the knife and Fox falls flat on his front, his blood flowing into the carvings of the cone before us. He's dead.

'Please, God, no,' I plead. I plead and I plead and I plead in the hope I can change what's going to happen.

'Amastad,' Khalid warns the shaking boy in front. 'It is your time.'

'Thomas, no...'

The pain of the knife in my shoulder blocks out everything, as the boy drives it through the skin.

'NO!' I scream, and there's nothing else but the pain, I clench my eyes shut, but feel Khalid's fingers prise them open. He takes the knife and rips it from my arm. The pain is immense and there's nothing I can do but bite my tongue and hope not to scream again.

'Press it in,' mutters Khalid. 'Use your fingers Amastad. Make him scream for longer...'

But the ground beneath me starts to shake and the two men stagger back away from me. I blink back the tears and stare at the altar. The top of the cone explodes, shooting a bright red fire up towards the stars and through the heart of the Incorporeal. Khalid and Amastad fall to their knees, the younger of the two scrambling backwards towards me.

'BEHOLD!' shouts Khalid, his arms outstretched. 'Behold the face of God himself. Behold the Founder of all civilization. Behold the Enlightened and Golden and Everlasting Ichabod Blackwood, Father to All. Behold the Scratching made form, to make every form the Scratching. May your Glory be everywhere, for ever more!'

The world shakes under my feet, and the sound of screaming bursts from the cone into the sky above.

Perpetual Screaming from Perpetual Scratching.

Ichabod Blackwood. The Founder of the Binding Brothers, and the cause of the Hundred Holy Wars, has returned and is Scratching immortal.

CHAPTER XXIII
THE HOLINESS OF SCREAMING

There's chaos, as all around me the Binding Brothers either flee or fall prostate on the ground.

A few of the younger ones scream in terror and, as they do, shards of dark red light erupt from the column of fire and strike them through the heart, lifting them above the ground.

They hang there, screaming and screaming and screaming.

Even though I can see from their eyes they are dead.

'My BRETHREN,' thunders a voice which punches through my body. 'My BROTHERS. I am the RESSURECTION of PARADISE, and faith REBORN. I am INCARNATE INCORPOREAL. I am the everlasting FATHER of RE-CREATION. Kneel Brothers. Kneel before your GOD and take JOY in the HOLINESS of SCREAMING.'

One by one, the Brothers fall back to their knees. Emmet's stumbled onto his backside and is scrambling towards me. Amastad looks up at the light, stunned.

'Dear God,' he whispers, his face frozen in terror. 'I never thought... I never knew... I wouldn't have... I didn't think it was real. The whole "Face of God", thing. It was symbolism. All of it symbolism! The others – when they made men scream, it wasn't like this. Dear God, what have I done?' He turns to me.

'Quickly. In your pocket. Let me get the Hallweed.' The pain floods through my shoulder and I gasp every breath as if it's my last.

'Get away from me, you sick bastard,' I hiss back at him.

'I'm sorry,' he whispers, as the monks start to crowd around the base of the cone, pressing themselves against it and, for the moment, obscuring me from view. 'I had to, you know I had to.' He reaches into my pocket and pulls out the small tube, squeezing some onto his fingers. 'I went to your shoulder because I knew you would live.'

The Axe & Grindstone

'Look at this, Thomas. Look at it!' Ichabod's column of barbed red fire pulses and flows upwards and upwards towards the cross of four stars which moves across the hole in the cloud. The sound. Can't you hear the sound of it? The scratching and clawing and screaming of generations to come, distilled into one moment in time.

'That's your God! That's not glory, or truth, or enlightenment! Agh!' He tears my T-shirt away and exposes my wound. I feel sick. It hurts to breathe, it hurts to move – it hurts just to sit here and feel the blood flow down my chest. Flow thick and deep. Just like he said.

'Get your filthy hands off me,' I gasp. 'You killed Fox. He was our only chance to prevent this.' He doesn't listen, and I'm getting so tired. I can't stop him from doing it – can't stop him from rubbing the blue ointment on the ripped muscle. I bite my bottom lip so hard... don't scream, Mark, now of all moments, don't scream. After two seconds the pain starts to ebb and the shoulder begins to cool. He tears a strip of robe and sticks it to the wound.

'I know,' he says quickly. 'I couldn't have prevented it.

It's better than what would have happened otherwise. Khalid was fond of saying The Previous screamed too well.' All of a sudden I feel the rope slacken behind me.

'Emmet., what the hell do you think you're doing?' I shout over the clamouring voices of the Brothers who still crowd forward around me. 'Do you know what you've done?'

'Shut it, lad. I've done worse than this in my time, and all for good reason. This ain't the time and it certainly ain't the place to start yappin' about it. I'll give yer my apology when we're far away from here.'

He pulls the ropes away – I want to punch him, right here, right now, but we've been lucky enough not to get noticed this far. Don't push your luck.

'Getting away may be a bit tricky,' says Amastad, quickly pointing at the sky. The cloud of Incorporeal are breaking off, and falling to the ground.

'Come to me, CHILDREN OF HOLY WARFARE, who have longed to see the FACE OF GOD for themselves. Come, all you FALLEN, of

The Axe & Grindstone

TEMPORARY FORM and find PERMANENCE in my BEING.' The voice of Ichabod Blackwood rumbles through the sky, and is answered by the roar of the ghosts above. Shoots of Incorporeal land on the ground and converge into their solid forms amongst the crowd. One by one they dissipate once more, and flow into the fire, which grows more barbed, and a deeper red with every one it absorbs. With every single Incorporeal it feeds upon, it grows larger and thicker, spreading itself further down the cone, like lava flows down a mountain.

And the Scratching will grow, tearing nature and law...

We have to leave, and leave now. Emmet and I – and Amastad, it seems – start to edge back towards the stairs, but freeze when Khalid lifts himself up, and onto a platform at the top of the cone. The light of Blackwood's fire reflects the shadows on his face. I hate him. I've never known anything like it in my life. I've prided myself in seeing the best of everyone but not now. Not today. I hate him. As his voice calls out to the gathered, all others fall silent. Only the roar of the ghostly and the godly remain.

'My God and my Lord, I... submit myself to you.' The Man With The Crab-Like Feet lowers himself onto his knees and pulls out his knife. The light of the fire glints across it, and even from this distance I can see its reflection in his dark and empty eyes.

'I offer myself as... Descendant. Your High Veli of the Binding Brothers, grown and nurtured in service of your name. Let me... bind to you, Father of Re-Creation, so we can be one. Father, Descendant and Scratching.' He lifts the knife high, gripping the handle with both of his spindly fingers. The force of Ichabod's voice blows the man's hair back, and as the tube of fire gets larger, everyone in the courtyard is finding it more difficult to look directly at it.

'HIGH VELI. Is your BLOOD of my BLOOD? Have you kept my NAME immortal and my WORK intact?'

'I have, my lord. Your blood has made me... Attuned. I have made many men scream and through their screaming conversed with you. I have heard your calling and I have heard your passion. I have...' he grins, '...collected Embodiments of the Union. I have spilled the blood of the Landlords of Peacebattle and broken the

Protection of Dogwood Falls. I have harnessed your Holy Scratching and pushed it out into the world. I request your... sanctity and coronation as Descendant to make your glory complete. The oak shall now fall, and all worlds shall be yours to gift as you please! Here, at the edge of mankind, let nature weep!'

He throws open his robe to reveal his scarred and deformed chest – hundreds of cuts and bruises streak across it, perverting his skin with his history of worship. He takes the knife and plunges it into the barbed red fire. It glows red in his hand and the stress on his face betrays his pain. Slowly, he pulls it out. The knife glistens and crackles with abhorrent unholy energy, violent and red.

'Very WELL. Brothers of BLACKWOOD RISING, behold your DESCENDANT. Spread my SCRATCHING throughout the world. Break the OAK and make my Glory COMPLETE!'

Khalid draws the knife across his chest and in one deep and vicious move, slices himself open. The Man With The Crab-Like Feet screams a guttural cry, as blood pours out of his chest and out of his mouth. At the sound of his screaming, a bolt of fire erupts from the column and bursts into the open wound. The fire lifts him, as it did the others who still hang suspended on spikes of flame, and still scream as they do. Unlike them, however, the spike's not bursting out the other side. Instead of being impaled on the sharp barbs of fire, the man is absorbing it. He's feeding on it.

'Now's our chance,' I suggest, nodding at the stone stairs. 'I'm leaving. It's up to you two whether you want to come with me.' I push back, wincing at the memory of my shoulder pain, and wade through the men pushing each other out of the way to get to the altar, and those already on their knees. None of them try to grab me. None of them want to make themselves stand out. That's fine with me. Keep it low key. Whatever's happening is screwing Khalid. The bastard's not going anywhere now.

We reach the stairs, and there's a roar from the altar, followed by an intense flash of light. I blink and blink again to try and get the flash from my eyes – and the shapes refocus into... no. The stairs. The bastard's blown up the bottom three stairs.

'You promised you'd keep me alive!' shouts Emmet as all three of us turn with the same sense of horror and dread. 'We had a deal! You'd keep me and her safe!'

'The promises of GODS must be EARNED, foreigner, and you have not yet paid the PRICE.' The voice is Blackwood's, but the sound comes from Veli Khalid, who's hanging like a puppet from a barbed tendril of fire which keeps erupting from the column. Khalid's eyes, once black and cold, now dance with a horrific golden light – as does his abhorrent open wound, which pulses with energy and a dark passion I can feel from here. Incorporeal continue to rain down around us, forming and dissipating as the column of fire absorbs them and grows. The tendril holding Kahlid snakes down and through the crowd of Brothers who move out of its way in respect and fear.

'I am now the Father of Re-Creation. I am now the Descendant!' roars Khalid's body, 'I am now the Scratching and the start of the holy night! Scratching will start the Scratching, and my Binding Brothers' light will begin in truth. Another Hundred Holy Wars begun and ended in the blink of an eye. Thanks to you, Landlord of Peacebattle. Thanks to you, the barman whose heart bled his friends,' he turns to Amastad and points, 'and thanks to you, the fakest Veli of all, who's Enlightenment failed as I knew it would. The death of the Previous brought back my presence. The death of the Landlord will now bring the re-creation.'

Amastad looks at me in panic and I shake my head quickly, as clueless as he. I quickly look up at the rubble of the stairs and wonder whether we can somehow clamber to the top – but a hundred Binding Brothers, and their mad god, are now staring at us. We wouldn't make the first stone.

'Do not think of running, Landlord.' Khalid's feet touch the floor, and the tendril of flame retreats into the ever expanding column behind him, leaving him standing alone, a glowing religious zombie. Great. Shit. OK. Nowhere to run. The monks look from one to another, unable to fathom their god now walking among them. He steps forward and, without looking, stretches his arm behind him, and points a needled finger at a kneeling man. 'Veli Cardosa. Scream for me.'

A man in his twenties with short blond hair gasps and looks at the Brothers to his left and right, who slowly edge away from him.

'Now... if you please.'

The man slowly, and with shaking hands, produces a thin paring knife from his robes. He looks again to his friends, and again to his god, looking for confirmation. He can't. Surely he can't? The monk to his left nods to him, and with one last pleading look at the back of the thing that that told him to, he thrusts the knife into his arm, deep to the bone, and drives it forward to his wrist. His screams bring a tight smile to Khalid's face, and immediately the man's impaled on a spike of holy fire from the cone and lifted into the air. The Brothers beneath him swiftly break left and right, to avoid the torrent of blood raining down on them. Veli Cardosa's screams do not die as he does.

'Veli Amrata, Veli Marlon, Veli Calvason. Scream for your master.' Khalid's eyes stay locked on mine, as three more of his followers viciously murder themselves adding their cries to this hellish noise. We're surrounded – although at this rate we'll last longer than those surrounding us.

'You'll run out of monks soon, Khalid,' I shout at him. 'Was this in the prospectus before you joined up, Thomas?'

'Not quite!' the lad shouts back, 'Those were my friends!'

'You always think small, Veli Amastad. And Landlord, you may call me Blackwood. You can be the first of millions to proclaim my name as it should have been proclaimed so many years ago.' He takes a step forward, and we take a step back. Four more Incorporeal drop from the thinning sky, reform into GeoTrolls and disperse again into the column, the base of which has spilled over the edge of the stage.

SCRATCHING.

SCRATCHING, THEN SCRATCHING.

THEN SCRATCHING SOME MORE.

'Fuck off with that shit!' I shout back, clasping my hands over my ears, as Emmet places his round my shoulders.

'Hang in, lad. With me by your side you can beat that bollocks.' The thumping in my head subsides – he's right. He's what stopped it before.

'Don't you realise, Blackwood,' he shouts, 'I work at The Grindstone fer a reason, y'know. The Protection of Dogwood Falls is mine to control. I've helped him beat the Scratching ever since he stepped foot in my town! I protect the Landlord. I hold the Council's greatest weapon, and it's my job to teach him what that means. I failed the last one 'cos I let you get in my head – and I'll scream on the inside for the rest of my life 'cos of that. But I'll never, ever let one breath of it escape my lips and give your bastards the pleasure of hearing it. I knew she'd find us a new Landlord, and I'll protect this one to my final dying day.'

I look at Emmet and he nods a small and silent nod at me. So he was there as my protector, this small, spiky orange man with a bad taste in biker jackets. It does make sense – when the Scratching really started to hit me, he was by my side snapping me out of it. When I first entered The Axe, he was behind the door I thought I saw moving. A few hours ago, when it hit me trying to escape, he waited just as long as he needed before stopping it again. He's still a treacherous bastard, though, and I'm damned if I'm going to be his padawan.

'Your Scratching doesn't scare me, Blackwood,' I shout over to him pretending I believe it. The wound in his chest glows brighter, and he closes his eyes as he takes a deep, contented, breath.

'Veli Anaske, Veli Blacker, Veli Haverast!'

Three more bodies lifted into the air. Three more screams added to the mix.

'For it is written: Scratching starts the screaming, and screaming starts the night. And Scratching starts the Scratching starts the Binding Brothers' Light. You may hold the Protection of Dogwood Falls, traitor,' he points at Emmet who takes another step back, his hand still on my shoulder. 'But that Protection is loose and broken. My Scratching is already in the Landlord's world, but the screams are weak and fleeting. They last for seconds. When I, as Father of Re-Creation and Descendant, step foot on that earth, the screaming will be eternal and my glory complete! Behold my Light!' He raises a hand and gestures behind him.

The tree.

The column of red, barbed, fire has become a tree.

Branches of fire, flowering men who'll scream forever.

'Do you like it, Landlord of Peacebattle? Do you like my tree?

Dogwood Falls, indeed. An insult to my work, but prophetic none the less. The Dogwood rises again. It grows. It shall seed itself in your world. For it is written, Oak and Dogwood shall fall. My dogwood fell before, when I was hung at the Gate of Fourteen Fellow Men. Now it's the turn of your oak, and through that your entire world.'

Four more Incorporeal fall to the ground and enter the tree. The sky is black again, as the final three begin to fall. One large cloud of angry purple gas is heading straight for us. Blackwood looks up.

'My followers are dedicated. They will dissipate your bodies, dispersing them throughout my soul, throughout my Dogwood, and your screams will please me for eternity. You three, you glorious three, will break the Protection of Dogwood Falls for the final time. The final death of the final Landlord will unlock the gate, and Heaven shall be mine.'

The cloud is almost upon us. There's nowhere I can run to, there's nowhere I can hide. The last three GeoTrolls stand at Blackwood's shoulders, as the last Incorporeal falls down. I look to the two men either side of me – neither innocent, but neither deserving what's about to happen.

'I'm sorry lads,' I say quietly, as the Incorporeal smothers us and I feel the unnatural tear as my body is ripped apart once again, atom by atom, thought by thought and my soul is laid bare to all around me.

I know how this feels, I know how this tastes. There is no air in my lungs but Them. I try to reach out to Emmet, or Amastad, but I cannot for They are blocking the signals to my arms, and my eyes. I cannot run away for yet again They are now my legs and one by one They start to dissolve my toes. The Hell around me starts to dissipate and I thank God I can't feel the fire any more, nor the pain in my shoulder. I can't see anything anymore and – again – although I've lost feeling I have sensation. New and abhorrent...

No.

Not new.

Not abhorrent.

Warm.

Warm and relieved.

I know that.

I feel that.

I... love that.

Natasha! But...

Don't but me no buts. All of a sudden the Incorporeal were allowed into Eden. We came as soon as we could. There was quite a show from where we were sitting, but couldn't get to you until all the others had gone. We saw everything.

Fox...

We saw everything. I don't want to talk about him right now.

Nat, I'm sorry. I thought I could make a difference.

Emmet.

Emmet, I think it's best if you stay quiet for a bit.

Will someone tell me what's going on? Am I dead?

Everyone, this is Thomas. He's technically one of the bad guys, but one with a conscience.

I face – if face is still the right word – back to see the Gate of Fourteen Fellow Men pass swiftly beneath us and the Cenobium recede into the horizon. From this distance I can see the true horror of the Dogwood, as it juts high in to the sky. I can still hear it, even now, as it collects more branches of screaming men. Give it another ten minutes, it'll cover the Cenobium. Give it an hour, it'll cover the island.

OK. What are our options?

We hold the breach. We protect the pub.

Fair enough. I'm in the mood for a fight. A barbed, red and gold bullet shoots out of the Cenobium's central courtyard and heads towards us.

Nat, can we fly faster?

We're lucky we can manage this speed. This is only the second time I've done this, and the first carrying three of you, with one a complete stranger. No offence, Thomas.

If I will it, we can go faster, I know it. C'mon, Mark, fly faster, like a pro. Fly home.

The streets below us are empty, save for a few villagers still trying to drag their belongings to what remains of the harbour. A few boats have managed to leave but not many and not enough. We weave in and out of the shuttered and blocked houses, the front of our wave breaking against the air which pushes against us as we fly. The sky is now black and clear, with the only clouds being us, and the thing that's pursuing us.

Faster and faster, Mark. Push it. Push it, man.

Down into the valley we go, past the second circus of memorials and into Peacebattle Lane. Down, close to the cobbles, we lap at the moisture on the ground as we turn the last corner and finally see The Grindstone...

...burning.

The atoms of my being reshape and reform and the memory of their natural form takes over. I can feel arms become arms once more, and my legs become legs as they run towards my pub and the people dousing it with water.

'My pub!' I shout over to Arnold, as the only friendly GeoTroll I know crashes a barrel of water over the left wall, extinguishing the last few flames. The smell of burnt wood and singed hair drifts up into the sky in a black trail of smoke. 'What happened, is everyone all right? We need to get the Council up into The Axe where it's safe.'

'I defended. Fought my brothers again,' the rock-man growls, the roar in his chest increasing in volume at the memory. 'Kept the breach. Did my job. Pub still stands. Lots of villagers safely through.'

'Good man, I owe you a pint. Hope the weather in Devon keeps nice for them.' I turn to look at the sky and the golden dart in the distance. 'But not just yet. We need to defend it one more time.' Nat, Emmet and Thomas stride towards me. Nat's got one hand firmly on Emmet's shoulders.

Leadership. Choices. Charge, Mark.

I raise my hand.

'Thomas, I need you to take the Council up to The Axe. Explain what's going on. Leave Emmet here – I don't want him inside.'

'You need me, lad – or the Scratchin'll get inside your head.'

'I need you where I can see you, Savage.' Arnold looks at me and raises one rough eyebrow.

'What's the score?'

'Yes, Mr Adams, what is the score? Where's Mr Fox?' Gorman bangs the base of his stick on the cobbles of the front porch. I point at the sky.

'Fox is dead. Killed by Veli Khalid. Because of that, your old friend Ichabod Blackwood is back from the grave and is the god they all worship. Most of them are now dead too, I reckon. If you scream, you scream forever, and he's growing. That,' I gesture at the growing ball of flame, 'is Blackwood in Khalid's body attempting to get to Oak Cheating. He,' I point at Emmet, 'helped them in last time and wrecked our plan, and he,' I finish by pointing at Thomas, 'is seriously questioning his faith.'

I turn to look at the old man. 'And before I hear another word from you, Gorman, you get your Council upstairs into Oak Cheating where you have at least a handful more options than you do at the minute.' I turn back around. 'And you,' I walk over to Nat and wrap my arms around her tight and whisper in her ear, 'don't leave me again.'

'I won't,' she whispers back. 'Although this time, it was technically you who left me without saying goodbye.'

'Well, I promise not to do that again either.'

'Good.' She pecks me on the cheek. 'Not in front of the punters, Mark.' She unlocks my hands from her, walks over to Emmet, and punches him firmly in the jaw. He stumbles onto the ground. 'That's just for starters,' she shouts, leaning over him. 'Fox was my friend, and what happened to me was not his fault, nor that of the Council you stupid, idiotic fool of a man. You have no right to "claim" my safety for you, no right at all.'

'I'm sorry, I really am,' the barman mumbles.

'I'm glad,' she states plainly, her hands across her chest.

'Now pick yourself up and do your job. If we live for the next ten minutes we'll talk about this again.'

I nod at Gorman.

'Go.'

'You know,' she mutters, 'That's what Fox said, the last time I saw him alive.'

The Axe & Grindstone

'Well,' I say, as the ball of fire reaches the ground at the top of the hill, 'he survived for weeks after that. I'm happy with those odds.' I nod back at the old man. 'Go. You know your way up. Lock the cellar door behind you – there's a lot of scared people in Oak Cheating right now. We'll keep the Protection going as long as we can. Head to a place called Long Barrow Ridge. You'll be able to hold up there for a while. I'm guessing that's the reason you employ that scary Jen woman.'

'Miss Jennifer Peynton is our lifeboat and sanctuary. Our retreat if retreat is needed. Good luck, Mister Adams.' Gorman gestures towards me. 'You didn't turn out quite as badly as I thought.'

And with that, he leaves. It's just the four of us, standing outside my strange little pub, on this strange little street under strange little stars. I look for the Waning Crux, but it's gone once again. Maybe I'll live long enough to have children who'll see it again...

'Well,' I say to Nat, Arnold and Emmet, as we line up across the street. 'It was nice meeting you all. On the plus side, I don't care about your bar bills too much right now.'

'Don't listen to him,' says Nat, arms on her hips as she stares at the top of the hill. 'I care about your bar bills. He's new. He was a nightmare at balancing the books at his last job.'

'Bloody management,' I growl back. 'My pub, my rules.'

'Have you always wanted to say that?'

'Could you tell?'

'Just a little.'

'Oi,' Emmet pipes, pointing at the top of the street. 'You may want to save that fer later.' There's a red and golden glow coming from a shadow standing at the top of the street. Blackwood. He slowly walks down towards us, and with every step his scars burn brighter.

Tap-te-tap-te-tap.

Tap-te-tap-te-tap.

'I need a drink,' says Arnold, and the fire in his eyes also grows brighter. 'Want to do the honours? One last time?'

'Guess I should,' I sigh. I can do this. I can do this. 'Where once was war...'

The ground shakes beneath my feet.

'There will be WAR again, LANDLORD.' His voice. Punching through the air.

'...where all shed blood...'

'And the SECOND HUNDRED HOLY WARS will be DECIDED in an INSTANT!'

'...through me communion, the Oak and Dogwood! For discord and schism...'

'Keep going! He's gettin' closer!' shouts Emmet.

'...for those you have scarred, Ichabod Blackwood, the Landlord has barred!'

His laughter sweeps over the buildings as he keeps on walking.

Tap-te-tap-te-tap.

Tap-te-tap-te-tap.

'This is MY TOWN, Landlord. I BUILT IT! The Protection of DOGWOOD FALLS does not extend to the HOLY!'

He's close enough to see, and as a line we step back.

'I could take him,' mutters Arnold to me.

'No. Protect the others. Stand your ground.'

Blackwood smiles as he looks up at the sky. 'My Brothers have done their DUTY!' He roars, as streaks of barbed fire race across the sky from the Cenobium towards the pub. They wait, just above our heads. 'All of my Followers are now part of their GOD. Soon, so shall you, and my holy fire shall enter your world.' He steps forward and again we step back. We're losing ground, not holding it. A couple more steps and we stand at the threshold of The Grindstone, with nowhere else to go.

'Your protection is failing you.' He presses one hand against the air, which shivers for a second, and then releases its tension.

'Mark, it's failed! He's broken your Licence!'

I turn to the others. 'Get into the pub. All of you. Up to The Axe. Now. Arnold – take Natasha! Go!' With a roar, Arnold tries to throw Natasha across his shoulders but she's having none of it. Emmet stays by my side.

'I meant you as well, Emmet.'

'No chance. We stick together, so the Scratchin' can't hurt

you. Plus, I need to make it up to yer.'

'Sod off, Emmet. Remember what I said at the cloisters. Even though I disagree with your actions, you're forgiven already. All right?'

Blackwood smiles once more. 'You misunderstand your God. I am the Father of Re-Creation and the Descendant as one. My fire,' he looks up at the flames across the sky, 'is Scratching made physical. Mine to control, direct and destroy. Watch what your forgiveness means.'

His scar crackles with energy, and he raises his hand towards Emmet. Sparks of power leap from finger to finger, and time seems to stand still.

It's funny. You never think of this happening to you. You never think there'd be time for all the things to flash in front of your eyes, like they said it would. In the split second it takes for me to decide, the acorn sings in my palm.

I hear the words of the woman who really brought me up, on the fateful day I accepted this job – *I see death, but I also see compassion, and peace; forgiveness, and love* – and I finally understand. I see my life in Staunton, the interview at Fortnights, the first and last moments with Natasha, and the times when I should have moved on, but didn't. I see the faces of everyone I've ever loved, but the faces just keep merging into her. She's there at my school, she's there at my birth, and everyone I've ever known wears the face of the girl I'll love forever. I hope she'll be OK without me. I hope she'll be happy. I hope that by saving Emmet he'll use his powers to protect her instead of me. I hope, I hope, I hope...

The fire leaves the hand of Ichabod Blackwood, and I feel myself move without feeling and without thought. I push Emmet out of its path and it hits me square in the chest instead. It burns but I don't scream. I can't scream. I won't let myself scream.

You're alright Mark. It's over now. You've done that stupid oak tree and its dumb little acorn proud. You've believed in what you can see, and feel, and touch. You've shown leadership, you've made the right choice and you've taken char.....

....

The Axe & Grindstone

...
..
.

250

Alternate

'They're coming!'

The little boy runs down the potholed lane which leads to the pub at the edge of the village. He keeps brushing his wet, blond hair from his eyes, but it's far too long and keeps getting in the way. He's run this fast just once before, when the monster carried him away from the bad man under the bad red sky. It seems like a lifetime ago. Life never used to be like this. The olden days are long gone now.

James runs to his mother. The rain has stopped – they say it always rains in Oak Cheating – and as she takes him in her arms, he whispers his message in her ear once more. 'They're coming.'

'Shhh, James. We know.' She brushes his hair from his eyes.

'You need to be a big boy today, all right? Promise me that?' The little boy nods and, with his left hand, touches the great oak tree under which his old town has gathered.

'I thought this was pretend, too!' he tells her, in awe. His mother looks up at the intertwining branches, and the strange sky beyond. She places her spare hand on his.

'No, honey. It turns out this is real too. Lots of things are real now.' She turns her head back towards The Axe Public House. 'Although sometimes,' she whispers, 'I wish some of it were make-believe.'

'Uncle Thomas!' She sees her brother at the same time as her son shouts his name, emerging from The Axe with the leader of the Council of the Wounded. 'Mummy, look – it's Uncle Thomas!'

'Yes, James. Yes, it is! Maybe he listened to me after all. Maybe he...' She puts James down, and he runs over to his uncle.

Thomas's face breaks into a wide smile, as James jumps into his arms. The boy points at his mother, and the smile falters a little as he walks over to the tree.

'You left them then,' she tells him as he puts James down by her feet.

'I couldn't go through with it, Emma. You should have seen it. They're coming. I told James last time to warn the Landlord so he could get away, but it made no difference in the end. This time they're breaking through. He's risen, Emma. He's going to start the Hundred Holy Wars all over again, and there's no one to stop him this time.'

Emma takes her brother's hand and sighs. She places it on the cold, wet bark of the oak tree and places her hand over his, just as she did with her son.

'The Council say the oak will protect us, Tom. It's the only thing left to have faith in.' He looks up at it and he, too, sighs.

'Have to transfer my faith into something, I suppose.'

'Mark! No!' Natasha's shouts are lost amongst the roar of the GeoTroll standing beside her. The body of Mark Adams hangs in the air, punctured front and back by the sharp spear of fire which continues to erupt from the fingers of Ichabod Blackwood. As Arnold strikes down a fist upon him, Blackwood lifts his forearm and casually tosses him aside. He lies still, fifty feet from the front door where he falls.

'You bastard!' shouts Natasha. She takes a step forward but is blocked by Emmet who pushes her back.

'Don't, Nat – he'll go after you, next.' She tries to force herself forward, but he keeps blocking him.

'I'll tear out every single one of your fingers – and slice you so small your fucking followers won't know which direction to pray to!' she shouts again.

Blackwood chuckles a deep, throaty laugh. 'I think NOT woman. I think, perhaps, I'll make you tear out your OWN fingers, one by one.' He takes one step forward, and Emmet backs Natasha inside The Grindstone. 'Perhaps, when YOU scream and cannot stop, I'll place your head near my altar, so I can enjoy the look in your eyes for ETERNITY.' Emmet takes up a chair and throws it at the god as he steps over the threshold, but one flash from his free hand and the chair is burnt with an angry red fire. He brings Mark's body into the pub with him, suspending it just out of reach. The smell of the fire which lights her dead friend's face reminds Natasha, with a sickening thought, of toffee.

'Were you ever gonna keep yer promise?' Emmet has another chair in his hands, the four legs pointing uselessly at Blackwood. It won't work, but it's the only barrier he has, and the small protection it offers might be enough. The guilt is overwhelming, and it offers him something to hold onto, if nothing else.

'You were useful,' Blackwood replies, as he raises his free hand. 'But leaving you alive would be... blasphemic. Why would I deprive myself of two worshippers? The Incorporeal woman will add to my essence, and the screams of the Gifted would feed me for centuries.' Red sparks begin to cross his fingers again. 'You scream so well. I remember from the last Hundred Holy Wars. The route of your people at Ket. The number of dead counting thousands. The medical tents where the sound of screaming was the sweetest song I heard.'

Natasha stops and raises her own finger. *Hang on. Just one second. Something's wrong. Something's supposed to...*

'And how's that screaming working out for you, your holiness? It doesn't sound as loud as it used to.' She points at Mark's body, and Blackwood follows her gaze. A flicker of concern passes across his face and the flames that light the scars on his chest dim slightly, as if he is drawing power to solve a mystery. Gods are not used to problems. Gods are not used to unforeseen circumstances.

'What... what Council sorcery is this?' He reduces the length of the flaming spike impaling Mark and brings his face level with his. His free hand stops crackling, and with one finger pushes Mark's chin upwards. 'Scream for me,' he commands quietly. 'Scream for your God.' He releases Mark's chin, and the man's head falls forward once more.

Silently.

'I SAID... SCREAM FOR ME!' He throws the Landlord into the ceiling, against the wall, then down on the floor. Natasha takes Emmet's hand, and slowly makes for the door to The Axe. 'DO NOT

DEFY ME, LANDLORD!' His scars burn brighter now, and his free hand crackles with fire. 'I COMMAND IT! SCREAM FOR ME OR YOUR WORLD BURNS!' He fires a column of red flame over the top of Emmet and Natasha's head, and the wall beyond them explodes. Stone, wood and glass rain down upon the two, as they hide from the blast under the door. 'SCREAM!'

'This is it,' Emmet cries. 'This is our chance.' They make a run for the door, clamber over the rubble and into the hallway beyond. Another blast lifts them off their feet, and they land with a cry in the cellar of The Axe.

'Go!' shouts Natasha. 'It's given us a couple of minutes at the most.' They run up the stairs and into the bar but are knocked to their feet again as the ground shifts beneath them. 'Oh, you've got to be kidding...'

The floorboards explode and the column of red fire shoots through the roof and into the sky above. Wood, brick and plaster fall down, and narrowly miss them both. In the hole in the floor, Natasha looks down to see Blackwood dragging Mark's body – no longer impaled, and no longer connected to the God – through the crack in nature and into the cellar of The Axe.

'I WARNED YOU!' the God roars. 'OAK AND DOGWOOD WILL FALL!' He lifts both hands to the sky, and another burst of energy flows from him and into the world.

Scratching.

Emmet and Natasha clasp their hands to their ears as they fall to their knees. Emmet's eyes are drawn to a fallen ceiling joint, lying on the ground, broken and dirty before him. It's sharp. It's inviting. It can bring relief, and worship.

Scratching.

Natasha feels the call in her soul. She feels the space between her cells want to twist and turn and become one with the Re-Creator. The pressure of not being locked to one form would be relieving. So relieving. There would be nothing to stop the worship for ever.

Scratching.

Outside, by the Life of Oak Cheating, the villagers of Dogwood Falls gasp as they see the light pass by the single solitary moon.

Gorman's knuckles whiten as he grips his cane. He wonders if he can break it in two. The splinters would satisfy the Re-Creator. It would bring blessed relief, and worship.

Scratching.

James buries his head in his mother's shoulders, as his Uncle Thomas looks at his broken robe. The rope around his waist could suspend him, and make the blood run faster as he makes the first cut with his paring knife. He saw his Brothers do it. He saw the relief, and the worship with his own eyes.

Scratching.

A few miles away, in the park at Long Barrow Ridge, Jennifer Peynton stands on a bridge. The villagers don't need her sanctuary now. It wouldn't be too hard to step over the guard rail. All it would take would be to let go. The fall, the wind in her hair, the echoes of the scream bouncing around the Ridge for ever. The relief at the end of it all.

Scratching.

In Staunton, on Porter Street, at the end of a night which saw more arrests than most, the crowds at kick-out time rejoice in their new freedom. Jon Butler sees a man lock himself in his car and set it alight. All down the street, people throw themselves into shop windows, and use the glass to open their veins. Jon falls to his knees and waits to embrace the Dogwood. Across the town the police embrace the screaming, as one by one the screamers are lifted into the air on shards of red fire, and the unending sound that follows is the sound of the holy of holies.

Blackwood steps over the crouched figures of Emmet and Natasha, as they writhe under his crab-like feet. He kicks the ceiling joist over to the barman, and smiles as Natasha's body begins to dissipate, losing distinction and form as the urge to become Incorporeal and one with him becomes too much to ignore.

'There...' he says, softly, as he bends close to Emmet's face. 'I knew you would scream for me. You were always going to scream for me.' He looks over to the villagers falling to the ground by the oak outside. 'I think I'm going to wait here until you do. I want to see your soul. I want to see... my Self reflected in your eyes.'

'It's not much to look at, to be fair.'

Blackwood bolts upright as a voice calls out from behind the bar. 'I've seen your screaming. I've seen your scratching, I've seen your Dogwood fall. You should read your own scripture once in a while.' The man throws the small copy of the *Book of Blackwood* at Ichabod's feet, and the energy crackles around him once again.

'You DARE defy me again? Who are YOU to lecture me on scripture? Who are YOU to lecture me on MY holy work?'

Mark Adams steps forward into the moonlight streaming through the roof of the pub. His T-shirt, torn and shredded after the night's events, now bears a burnt hole through its centre. In his hand, being passed from finger to finger, is the small, misshapen acorn.

'I'm the Landlord of Peacebattle, mate. Now get out of my pub.'

CHAPTER XXIV
THE LANDLORD OF PEACEBATTLE

He stares at me, but I'm not scared. He raises his hand towards me and I'm not scared.

He's standing over the one girl I let slip through my fingers and I'm not letting her go. I'll come back from the fucking dead if I have to, but I'm not letting her get away again. What I've just seen, where I've just travelled, this bastard has nothing left to scare me with.

The small acorn, the one hidden in the ground beneath the oak, is itching in my fingers. It's sung me its final song. It knows where it wants to go. It's told me where it wants to be.

As Blackwood raises his hand to unleash another column of fire, I throw the acorn directly at the open glowing wound which still splits his chest in two. Bullseye – the fire inside him burns brighter and turns from its angry mix of red and gold, to a dark and vivid green. Blackwood stumbles back, and claws at his chest, the cocky, smug smile finally gone from the remains of Veli Khalid's face. He looks at me, and pleads with his eyes...

'But how...'

'Strength, security and steadfastness. The oak's been here for centuries, mate. It knows you. It's been waiting for you. It's been waiting for me.'

'But I am immortal! I am holiness incarnate! I am your GOD!'

'You're just a bloke who struck lucky. So am I, it seems.' A loud booming roar rips itself from Blackwood's chest and he sinks to his knees, next to where Nat is lying. Slowly, she brings herself back together and into the form I know so well. Emmet clambers to his feet, stares, and pulls her away as soon as she has a hand to grab hold.

'Mark?' Nat blinks at me, concerned, then turns back to Blackwood on his knees.

'Scripture says the oak will fall! Agh!' He throws his head back as green sparks pass between his fingertips.

'The oak *did* fall, Blackwood. I am the oak. I am the Landlord. You're forgetting one line.' It comes as easily to me as the end of a fairy tale, and as I recite the words, I can see them forming in my head. *'And the Scratching will grow, tearing nature and law, Til the oak seeds forgiveness and peace reigns once more.* What's coursing through you right now, is the seed of the oak nurtured through me forgiving my mate over there.' I nod to Emmet, who helps Nat to her feet. 'That's the true face of God, buddy. You see – and you can shut your ears now the pair of you – I'd do anything for that woman as well, so it's not that hard to understand why someone else wouldn't feel the same. Bit misguided mind you, but never mind.'

The sparks in Blackwood's fingers begin to ignite – he's trying to contain it, I can tell, and it's taking all of his concentration, but it's not going to work. It's just a matter of time. I walk around the bar, avoiding the various holes in my establishment, and crouch down in front of him, just as Khalid did to me.

'It seems, Ichabod Blackwood, that when you're Incorporeal – even for ten minutes or so – the bits of your body take a little time to snap back into place. It freaked Thomas out earlier, as his Hallweed was a bit more effective than normal.' I look him in the eyes. I wonder if I can see his soul.

'By rescuing me, and flying me back here, my friends saved my life. I was told that when you're Incorporeal, you're pretty much hard to kill. I wasn't quite my old self yet. Your holy fire didn't work. I didn't scream for eternity – the oak in that seed became part of you, just as the Incorporeal at your place became part of you. When you let me go, and I wasn't impaled on your fire and connected, the bits of me snapped back into place. Bad timing on your part – give it another five minutes next time, til I'm properly a fully formed bloke again. But you see, the best part is you never understood, did you? You never realised the true meaning of the scripture you wrote yourself. When the line in that book over there says *Oak and Dogwood will fall* it doesn't mean the people of Dogwood Falls. It meant you, and your Scratching. You can remove my Licence, Ichabod, but I still know my place. It's with my people. It's the Oak *and* Dogwood. The Axe *and* Grindstone.'

'NO!'

He loses it – he loses control and erupts into a column of green fire which shoots upwards, through the roof and into the night sky. We clamber back, as more pieces of my ceiling come crashing down.

I can hear the screaming of a god in pain. I can hear the screaming of a being who's learning to scream for the very first time. I never want to hear a scream ever again.

Slowly, the column recedes, and the fire goes out.

The Man With The Crab-Like Feet lies on the floor of my pub, unburnt and unmoving, apart from a small shallow rasping breath making his chest rise and fall. One sharpened finger beckons me towards him. Fine, I'll give him his last moment.

I kneel down and take his head in my hands. The fire is gone, the god is no more, and Veli Khalid is left alone before me.

'He's... left...' Khalid whispers, and I nod. The air is still, and the only sound apart from his rasping breath is a small child crying in the distance. 'Did you... see it, Landlord?' His voice is faint and sharp, and seeking approval. 'When I screamed... just now... did you see the face of... God?'

I look at him, lying in front of me with his crab-like feet, eyes like tar and fingers like needles. What kind of a creature he is I think I'll never know. His already thin face seems sallow and grey, and his chin still darkened from the blood of his sacrifice. I could lie to him. I could tell him his beliefs were sound and give him the peace he was searching for. I look up at Natasha and Emmet and find no answers in their eyes. I look back into Khalid's. There's been too much deception today.

'No,' I tell him, with the authority of one who's seen the face of death himself. A tear rolls down Khalid's cheek as his eyelids start to droop. 'You'll have to keep looking for that.'

His head goes light in my hands, and his eyelids close gently. The knuckles on his exposed feet curl up on themselves, and he finally lies still. Wherever he's going, I think it unlikely he'll ever find the face he's searching for.

The Axe & Grindstone

A hand rests on my shoulder and I stand to bury mine in the shoulders of Natasha Bennett. We hug each other like that for a good couple of minutes before the thick wooden door to the Axe opens with a creak, and the sound of Gorman's cane bounces off what's left of the wooden floor.

'You alright?' she asks, pushing the hair from my eye again. 'I was worried about you for a minute there.'

'Oh were you?' I smile, my hands staying around her waist.

'Too right! Do you know how hard it is to get someone to run this place? Couldn't be arsed going through all that again!'

'Swine...' I gently tickle her like I used to, and we stop, and we kiss a gentle kiss which feels exactly as it did all those years ago, and so many lifetimes away.

We cover Khalid's body with an old tarpaulin that's lying in the beer garden, and even though I saw his dying breath, I still keep an eye on it just in case.

I know from experience that sometimes death doesn't always mean death.

One by one, the villagers from Dogwood Falls come back into The Axe. Being the good Landlord that I am, there's drinks waiting for every single one of them. The little boy – James, his name is – has never tasted lemonade before, and I see a market opening up that's ripe for expansion.

Natasha's told Gorman everything about Emmet, of course. There'll be a lot of explaining to do, and the man will have to stand trial for what he's done. The two of them have left for the Council to come to some sort of agreement. From what I can gather, using the radio in my car, the effects of the Scratching were felt far and wide and people will be looking for ages into the cause. Radio Five Live is having a field day. It lasted for only a few minutes, but a fair few people still died, and the usual suspects will be wheeled out to explain that there was an anomaly with the moon. Or something. There won't be too many people looking in the right place, however.

A large brass bell hangs by the door behind the bar. It rings out across the crowded bar and off into the Devon moor beyond.

'Right, you lot, that's Time,' I call out, the rope of the bell feeling natural in my hand. 'Haven't you got homes to go to? Line up, single file, and you can go back through the cellar. Mind the hole in the floor as you do.' Nat, standing beside me polishing a glass, puts it down.

'I did wonder why you went through the cellar,' she smiles. 'There are easier ways, you know?'

'I'm sorry?' I rest one hand on the pump and face her.

'Emmet went and ripped out the manual, didn't he, the git?'

'There was a manual?'

Nat rolls her eyes. 'I should have checked.' She walks round the bar towards the skittles table by the west wall. After all the banging, and the mess, and the end of the world, the skittles are still standing. 'You don't think every bloke from Oak Cheating who wants a pint goes to The Grindstone through the cellar do you? It's hardly a secret round here. People from all nations, mixing as one? Including people from, say, Long Barrow Ridge?'

She knocks over the back three skittles, which are fixed to the green with a thin central hinge in the centre of each one, and a section of the back wall swings open. Instead of the beer garden, there's a small carpeted corridor leading to the back of a dart board. The Grindstone.

One by one, the villagers leave the pub through the new side entrance and make their way home. As the last one goes through, I stand up the three fallen skittles, and close the door.

I pass a drink to Nat. 'So,' I turn to Nat. 'Where do we go from here?'

'Well, after an impressive start, you still have your six-week trial run. Then we'll see where we go from there. Although,' she adds with a flick of her hair, 'between you and me, I think you're going to be all right.'

I look at her and tuck her hair behind her ear. 'Are you talking about the job or us?'

She flicks my nose, gently. 'Both.'

'Because if I do stay, if I don't just get in my car and go away, you have to be honest with me.' I'm being serious now. 'What happened to you, Nat? How did you... you know? Why did Emmet say that when he needed the Council most they became corrupt and introvert, doing more harm than good?'

She takes my hand and looks me straight in the eye, as if she's deciding where to start. She opens her mouth, closes it again, and then gently brushes her lips against mine.

'Six-week trial run, Landlord,' she whispers, 'Then we see where we go from there.' She pulls away, the taste of her lips still lingering on mine. 'You coming?' She smiles at me, the smile I held in my head for so long and heads through to The Grindstone. Of course I won't leave. Until I said the words I didn't know they'd be true. Of course I know my place.

The Axe and Grindstone.

'In a second,' I call after her. 'I'll be there in a moment.'

I close the door behind her and take from my pocket the Waiter's Friend, given to me by my friends in Staunton before I left. I flick the corkscrew in and out and feel the weight secure in my hand. For the first time, the inscription seems less than ironic.

The dark Devon sky is clear, for a change, and the Life of Oak Cheating still stands there, watching me, as it's watched generations of Previous before me. I cross the lane and sit for a second in the oval moss-covered seat.

'Hello again,' I say to the tree, not feeling as self-conscious as

The Axe & Grindstone

I might have done. 'Me again. I'm still here.' I pause. 'So are you, I guess.' A breeze rustles through the branches, and I notice, for the first time, the various sounds of the Devon countryside at night. 'I suppose...' I tell the tree, 'I suppose I could stay for a while. The locals seem alright. And, to be fair, I've had worse. You're lucky you were planted out here in flood country. You should have seen what people did to the trees in Porter Street after a pint or two.' I pause again. 'What do you think?'

Another brief gust of wind.

'Hmm.' I sit for a second. No new epiphany. No new sudden relationship with nature. But, deep down, I can honestly feel a connection.

The longest in a long line of keepers of the peace.

An Embodiment of the Union, sitting in the arms of another Embodiment of the Union.

'And I still don't know what that's all about,' I sigh. 'But I guess you don't learn everything in the first couple of days of a job.'

Still nothing.

'Well then. Best get going. Cheers for listening and all that. See you around.' Another gust of wind, and something falls into my lap as I start to get up.

An acorn.

A small misshapen acorn. In December.

A Christmas gift, to keep the connection strong.

I smile and place my hand on the old Oak tree's bark and say nothing. I *think* my 'thank you', because I know it will understand me for the rest of my life.

The Axe Public House, they say, gives you a warm welcome, a world away. And as I step through the door to The Grindstone, three cheers ring out as the locals welcome me home. Nat stands behind the bar, and as I join her, I get the feeling this will be a lock-in long remembered. The locals crowd in three-deep, wedged into two free spots either side of a large, rock-shaped regular, sitting on his favourite stool and unwilling to move for anyone but his wife standing beside him. He has an empty tankard in his hand.

'The usual, Arnold?' I ask with the bottle of cherry brandy

The Axe & Grindstone

already in my hand. This is my world. These are my locals.
'The usual,' comes the gruff reply. 'And one for yourself.'

TIME

The Axe & Grindstone

Paul Phipps-Williams trained as a film producer, wandering around student films shouting 'Time is Money' at people before stealing their cake. Having figured out that wasn't the most successful way to get hired, he went on to sell pencils and pints for a living because people always seem to need one or the other.

For the last eighteen years, Paul has told people he works for the government in the hope they will think him a super spy. He isn't, but that's what you'd expect a super spy to say. He's passed a couple of new laws, convinced one government minister to quote the Spice Girls in the House of Commons, and spent London 2012 in an underground bunker. On at least one occasion he's had tens of thousands of people march through central London protesting against what he's doing with his life. Whether this was work related or not, we'll leave to your imagination.

When he's not Making The World A Better Place/Contributing To The Fall of Society (delete according to your political affiliations) Paul is also a photographer and can be regularly found at cult TV events telling people to smile as they stand nervously next to their childhood heroes. His motto is 'What happens in Paul's photo studio, stays in Paul's photo studio.' At least, that's what Paul's been told by his lawyers. His photographs have been published in an eclectic range of magazines, from *The Amorist* to *Scottish Field* and *Doctor Who Magazine*.

Paul writes audio books for Big Finish Productions' gothic horror series *Dark Shadows*. 2020 sees the release of *Windcliff*, a terrifying thirteen-part full-cast audio horror serial set in an asylum and performed in real time. Other audio books for Big Finish include *Doctor Who: A Small Semblance of Home*. He was a contributor to *A Thousand And One TV Series You Must Watch Before You Die* where, amongst other things he was paid to watch *The Real Housewives of Orange County* and a programme about a cowboy cop in New York City. He's not quite got over it yet.

The *Axe & Grindstone* is Paul's first novel, and he's had to convince his mother that its main character isn't really based on him. She's not entirely convinced. He lives on a roundabout in Lewisham with his husband, Gareth, and their two cats, Billy and Hartnell. His favourite pizza is an abomination of hot and spicy things with BBQ sauce and his favourite colour is TARDIS Blue (1987-1989).

BAD
PRESS
INK

BAD PRESS INK PRESENTS THE AXE & GRINDSTONE WRITTEN BY PAUL PHIPPS-WILLIAMS
WORST BOY IAIN PARKE MANUSCRIPT TAMER PAT BLAYNEY TROLL WRANGLER VIKKI SPIT MR INAPPROPRIATE LORD ZION
BOOK COVER DAVE HOWARTH (HMDESIGNERS.COM) - NO AUTHORS WERE HARMED IN THE MAKING OF THIS BOOK

Printed in Great
Britain
by Amazon

31791878R00159